Free To Go

a novel by
Wanda Ryder

Note for Librarians: a cataloguing record for this book that
includes Dewey Decimal Classification and US Library of
Congress numbers is available from the National Library of
Canada. The complete cataloguing record can be obtained from
the National Library's online database at:
www.nlc-bnc.ca/amicus/index-e.html
ISBN 1-4120-3628-3

Printed in Victoria, BC, Canada.

TRAFFORD

Offices in Canada, USA, Ireland, UK and Spain
This book was published *on-demand* in cooperation with
Trafford Publishing. On-demand publishing is a unique process
and service of making a book available for retail sale to the
public taking advantage of on-demand manufacturing and
Internet marketing. On-demand publishing includes promotions,
retail sales, manufacturing, order fulfilment, accounting and
collecting royalties on behalf of the author.
Book sales for North America and international:
Trafford Publishing, 6E–2333 Government St.,
Victoria, BC V8T 4P4 CANADA
phone 250 383 6864 (toll-free 1 888 232 4444)
fax 250 383 6804; email to orders@trafford.com
Book sales in Europe:
Trafford Publishing (UK) Ltd., Enterprise House, Wistaston Road
Business Centre, Wistaston Road, Crewe, Cheshire CW2 7RP
UNITED KINGDOM
phone 01270 251 396 (local rate 0845 230 9601)
facsimile 01270 254 983; orders.uk@trafford.com

www.trafford.com/robots/04-1456.html

10 9 8 7 6 5 4 3

For my daughters,
Deborah and Krista

ACKNOWLEDGEMENTS

I am grateful for the support, encouragement and friendship shown me by members of Prarie Pens writing group—especially Donna Gamache and Helen Mulligan for their editorial assistance. I am also indebted to Suzy Laevens for her cover design.

SUMMER 2000

TEN DAYS AFTER HER DAUGHTER'S WEDDING, NORA COULDN'T shake the feeling that something was amiss or that she had forgotten an important detail. She felt it as a real presence tugging at her coattails, nipping at her heels. It was hanging in the air when she got out of bed in the morning, and now lingering unidentified, mingled with odors of burnt toast and stale coffee.

There were still clean-up jobs waiting to be done. Lots of them. But that wasn't it. She'd get around to them sooner or later. There was no hurry. Nora's head thrummed with the effort of trying to name the thing that was missing. Perhaps she had committed some unforgivable sin. Lately, it seemed her life had been made up of transgressions. At least, she assumed that to be the case since her husband had become somewhat remote and certainly self-absorbed.

"Maybe Walter's just depressed," her friend, Maggie, had suggested one day. "And maybe you are, too."

Nora thought about what Maggie had said and decided that she was more puzzled than depressed.

Then she re-tied the bow on her old cotton house-coat, sighed and surveyed the chaos of her living room. Sandra's wedding dress still hung precariously on the back of the door leading to the kitchen as it had ever since the wedding. Although the gown was safely ensconced on a sturdy padded hanger, the beautiful satin and lace creation deserved better, for it represented hours of Maggie's patient and loving stitches. Two hundred self-covered buttons marched down the back onto the train and, just the thought of their fabrication and attachment, caused Nora to sigh again. This time, in remembrance of the dogged endurance shown by the seamstress.

Nora shuffled over and re-folded the yards of glistening satin so none of the precious material would be in contact with the floor. She would pack it away in tissue as she'd promised. Dark blue tissue to keep the whiteness from yellowing. If she could locate some. Maybe even later today. She hadn't forgotten about that. The cake top, too. A proper sized box would be required to house the silly little Barbie and Ken-type bride and groom. She smiled at the memory of the tiny stick figures riding the crest of her creation where she'd rammed them deep into the hardened icing to give them secure footing. Still, she'd had lots of compliments on the cake and no one, except Sandra, mentioned that the happy doll couple was visible only from the knees up.

Nora plopped down on a chair at the dining room table which was still laden with wedding gifts too large or too fragile to fit into the happy couple's van. She fingered a pair of silver candlesticks, laid them aside and examined a crystal bowl, wondering where old Aunt Minnie had found the money for such a gift. Perhaps she had stolen it—Aunt Minnie was known to do such things. Twelve crystal goblets nestling in tissue also waited to be properly packed.

Twelve! Who needs twelve? Sandra and Nick were young teachers, not business tycoons—a fact of life Trevor had mentioned with some cynicism in regard to the wedding preparations. Nora sighed.

Perhaps if Trevor hadn't come home for Sandra's wedding things might have turned out differently. How her own son and daughter had come to such a bitter parting of the ways was beyond Nora's comprehension. True, they'd had plenty of childhood spats, some even when they were almost grown, but nothing like this had ever happened between them before. She had no idea how to intervene or make things better. Walter's advice was simply to ignore the rift and say nothing about it to either child. But fathers didn't seem to have the same kind of emotional involvement with their children as mothers had. At least not in Nora's experience. And, lately, Walter wasn't interested in discussion of any kind.

She tried to give Sandra and Trevor equal time in her excuse department. A week before the wedding, Trevor had come home from his summer job in Vancouver acting as though he was making some sort of concession to a sister's whim. He seemed to take no interest in the preparations and spent most of his time either in bed, or lying in the hammock strung between two ageing Manitoba maple trees in the back yard.

Nora had watched him through the kitchen window, gazing off to the newly-green crops in the adjacent field. The pallor of his skin she attributed to a life now spent almost entirely indoors and thought, perhaps, his time at home under the trees would be of benefit. But she worried about his stillness. For some reason, Trevor's hands—long-fingered and thin—seemed young and vulnerable and made Nora feel unaccountably sad. Questions about his health went nowhere, however. "Have you been feeling sick?" Nora had asked when he turned down the breakfast omelette she'd made him.

"No, I'm fine. Just not very energetic. I think it must be this damned allergy."

"But you always loved omelettes. Come on, it'll give you some energy."

"Mother, please. I'm just not hungry."

"Have you seen a doctor?"

"No, just taking antihistamines. That's all they'd prescribe, anyway."

"Are you in some kind of trouble? You can tell me, you know."

"No. No trouble. The pills are making me sleepy, I guess." Then he yawned and went out to the hammock.

Nora accepted the allergy theory but Sandra wouldn't buy it. She was disgusted with her brother's behavior at first and then furious when Trevor refused to attend the stag party for Nick.

"It's because Nick is Russian, isn't it?" Sandra shouted at him.

"Don't be such an ass! I have nothing against Nick. Or his ancestors. I'm not even biased against Ivan The Terrible. Just tired, is all. Give me a break."

"How can you be tired when you haven't done a lick of work around here? How can filling out dumb reports in a cop shop deplete your energies to such an extent that you've turned into a slug? All hundred and seventy-five pounds of you!"

"One-sixty-five at the most. And I've been giving Mother a hand now and then."

"That's a crock—on both counts."

Nora had intervened at that point but Sandra was not to be mollified and Trevor was adamant in his refusal to attend the party in honor of the groom. He gave no further hints about his problem (if there was one) and Nora could only guess that he'd had a love affair that didn't work out—was dumped, or some such thing and, perhaps, some day, he would tell her. Trevor was a big boy—he'd have to sort things out for himself if he didn't choose to confide in anyone. Still, there was no doubt he wasn't being very helpful or considerate of Sandra's feelings.

Nora could understand Sandra's disappointment in her brother but thought she might have been a bit more diplomatic. Nora looked at her tall, intense daughter and asked, "How do you treat your pupils when they object to doing something you've asked them to do? Do you yell and scream and call them lazy nincompoops—or worse?"

"Don't be so silly. Of course not! But then, I give the orders in the classroom and, so far, I haven't had any complaints. And I *do* have the reputation of being a good teacher."

"I'm sure you are, dear. It's just that... Well, maybe Trevor doesn't want to be treated like one of your pupils."

"I'd like to treat him to a black eye."

Nora tried a more confidential tone. "I have reason to suspect he's not feeling very well right now. Or something. Something's wrong, I can tell."

"In a pig's eye, he's not well. A little pale from being inside all summer. All he needs is to get out in the sun and do a little work. He just wants to embarrass me, that's all. And you figure you have to stick up for him all the time. Oh well, I guess it's too much to expect that things would ever change around here. Trevor always came first."

Nora had bitten her tongue and didn't remind her daughter that both her father and grandmother had always seemed to put her first and, as far as the wedding was concerned, she was also putting Sandra's wishes first. She might also have reminded her that she was not being very much help in the preparations. Instead, she'd tied on her apron and said, "Time to cut that big fruit cake and wrap it for the guests. How about a hand?"

"Didn't I tell you? I have to go to Lori's this afternoon. She wants me to decide what jewelry to wear with her bridesmaid's dress. Why don't you ask Maggie? Or that big hulk lying out in the hammock." Then she was off.

Nora rolled her eyes in exasperation and said nothing more on the subject. In any case, she was far too busy to spend much time worrying about the fragile egos of her children when there were so many other things left to do. "You are both spoiled little brats," she'd said to the empty space where Sandra had stood before she left, slamming the door behind her.

While Nora worried over it, she assumed the sibling row would blow over. Like the fights they used to have about whose turn it was to use the family car. But it didn't blow over. Perhaps if she'd taken some action all those weeks ago, things might have been straightened out between her children. A direct confrontation with Walter might have cleared the air with him as well, but she wasn't keen on confrontations.

Although Nora sensed for some time that something was weighing heavily on Walter's mind, she didn't believe it had anything to do with Sandra and Trevor. She wondered if he was having an affair and, if so, who might qualify as the 'other woman'. She reviewed possibilities from the recent past. Several came to mind. The most obvious would be Inga, the neighbor with the long blond braid, turquoise jewelry and white Samoyed dogs. Inga had moved, alone, into the small cottage about a half-mile north and sometimes called upon Walter when she needed advice or assistance with her septic system which never seemed to be in top working order. Inga revealed little of her background except that she was divorced and had once been a bookkeeper for a large company in Toronto. Nora distrusted Inga. For one thing, she didn't believe for one minute that the blond hair was a natural color or that her name was really Inga.

Then there were Ruby and Fran. Both had husbands and families and couldn't really qualify as neighbors since they lived two and three miles south. For some reason, though, in the weeks prior to Sandra's wedding, the two women had taken to going for long walks together. And, almost every morning, after parking their vehicle in the old churchyard just up the road, had passed Walter and Nora's front gate. They were actually headed for Inga's house, but if either Walter or Nora was in view, the women stopped to chat. Walter called their walks 'Fact Finding Forays' and, indeed Ruby and Fran were noted for exactly that. Gossips, both of them. Nothing escaped their attention and subsequent redistribution, and Nora thought that they included Inga in their walks in order to satisfy their own curiosity about the blond newcomer to the district.

Although Walter had made fun of the women, Nora often watched through the window as she washed the breakfast dishes and observed him laughing and joking with them. She joined only in when it couldn't be avoided. The two varied their walk times and Nora couldn't always predict when Fran and Ruby might pass by (or if they had already passed by) so she was sometimes caught in the yard watering the hanging pots or just admiring her roses. On those occasions, her stomach lurched and she felt a wave of nausea as though she were a child about to be called up on the carpet by an irate principal. She knew the women—Fran in particular—would have some questions ready. Nora never knew how to answer and always seemed to be caught off guard. Like most trusting people, she put gossip in the same category as home invasions and was always surprised by the slyness of these meddlers. She had no ready answers. All the clever retorts came to her long after the interview was over and the women had gone on their way with whatever fresh news they'd managed to extract. And they usually managed to extract some item—however small.

"Is your friend from the library still away on her trip?" Fran asked slyly one morning. Nora knew the question was put to determine if Lucy had stayed in New Brunswick or come back to her husband, and she didn't know how to avoid answering. Whatever she said, it would be used to denigrate her friend. Nora doubted if Fran even knew Lucy, except by sight, but that didn't matter, apparently. Nora feigned ignorance on the subject.

Usually the questions were more personal, though. Such as the day Nora was asked, "Do you go with Walter when he does all that work for Inga?" All she could think of to reply was, "No, I don't know a thing about septic systems." But they got what they were after—Walter went alone! So!

Later, it had been: "Doesn't it ever worry you that your husband has taken to driving around alone at night all the time?" As usual, it was Fran who did the interrogating while Ruby stood, stalk-still, with her head cocked to one side like a robin listening closely for a tasty morsel. Nora had to wonder how the women knew of her husband's nightly habit, but she didn't intend to dignify the question with an answer. Instead, she turned on her heel and walked into the house. In fact, her actions probably constituted an answer, of sorts.

Most evenings, Walter did go for a drive 'to look at the crops' he said. Nora wondered if Walter's diligent surveillance of the grain achieved greater yields, or if he was like an artist admiring his work or a mother admiring her baby. But, until lately, she'd never considered that he might be seeing someone and said nothing, even when he took a much longer time than ordinary crop-watching should account for. It seemed part of his new, distracted and rather anxious demeanor. After the gossips raised the question, however, vague suspicions insinuated themselves into her mind. Inga? Ruby? Fran?

Nora also disliked Ruby and Fran for reasons that had nothing to do with their gossiping ways. Early in the summer, when Nora was out in the front yard, the two paused to make a magnanimous offer. They extended her an invitation to join them on the daily walks. Nora, caught by surprise as usual, was confused as to their motives, for she felt there had to be motives.

For no reason that she could think of at the time, Nora asked, "And would Inga be coming along as well?"

"Of course," Fran said.

"How about Maggie Kroeger, then? Could she come? I mean, she could use some social outings."

The women exchanged glances. Meaningful glances, Nora thought. Then Ruby replied, "Oh, we think not. She's not as educa..."

"Doesn't fit in as well," Fran put in quickly. "She's a bit... You know, a bit..."

"A bit different," Ruby supplied.

Nora was used to Maggie's somewhat eccentric ways, but was genuinely puzzled that anyone would consider her differences to be a social liability. "Different in what way?"

"You know. Not like us," Fran explained.

And thank God for that, Nora thought, but said only, "That's not a crime, is it?"

Fran smiled patronisingly. "Of course not, but we've tried to limit our morning walks to intellectual discussion. Women who have more in common..."

Nora was quiet, but remained in control. "I think I may not have that much in common, either."

Neither woman responded to the remark, but Ruby had risen smoothly to the occasion with a change of subject. "Anyway, we gather she's pretty busy making Sandra's wedding gown and all. You must be busy, too, with all the plans that go into a wedding."

Nora had wondered how in the world they knew about the dressmaking arrangements. But then, these women seemed to glean information from the very air.

"You're likely up to your ears in housecleaning, too. We hear the groom is from around Kamsack. Russian origin? Quite a poor family, I suppose? Wouldn't be used to hotels. I imagine you'll have to put up some of his relatives?" Fran managed to make the inquiry insulting and racist in one easy speech—a record, even for her.

Nora had known why she'd been asked to join the walkers. They needed fresh grist for their mill and she was being invited to supply it. Their rare, brief encounters with Nora weren't bringing in enough good material, but an hour or two of constant mining might yield a mother lode. In her outrage at the presumption, and at the slur against Nick's family, Nora said something she later regretted, "Oh no. We're just going to throw some fresh straw in the mangers," then turned and went into the house.

On top of this, the insinuation that Maggie wouldn't be fit company for their high-minded talks! When Nora finally got over the worst of her rage, she'd had to admit that she, herself, sometimes grew weary of Maggie's flighty ways and the fractured English that Nora couldn't always resist correcting. But, even though she knew it was useless to keep dwelling on their past boorish behavior, the memory of the manner in which Fran and Ruby had dismissed the idea of including Maggie on their walkathons renewed Nora's feelings of disgust.

Ever since the Kroeger parents had been killed in a freak car/train collision fifteen years before—leaving Maggie to keep house for her brother, Martin—Nora and Walter had acted as surrogate parents. Maggie had been seventeen then and Martin three years older. Nora and Walter had done what they could to help the young people carry on the farming operation and Maggie became an 'almost daughter'.

Maggie was also a good friend in many ways. She would lend a hand to any difficult or dirty job—usually without complaint. Often, without invitation. And she wasn't gossipy or malicious or jealous. Once in a while, some of her homespun advice even made sense—especially if it applied to sewing skills. Still, she did expect to have favors returned from time to time. Today turned out to be one of those times.

THE FAVOR

As Nora gazed out the east window wondering what action she might have taken regarding her feuding children and what, if anything, was ailing Walter, she spied Maggie dashing across the small field that separated their farms. It was early in the day for a visit—even for Maggie—but on she raced. Nora watched as her neighbor sprinted across the road, disappeared into the ditch and rose from the tall grass on the near side with each individual red hair seeming to stand at attention.

Despite her talents as a seamstress, Maggie usually looked as though she'd bought her own clothing from the Sally Ann—which she often did. But this morning, Nora thought she spotted some new blue garment before Maggie was lost from view behind the caragana hedge. She reappeared at the side door and walked right in.

"Oh my," she panted, "you're still in your housecoat. And we're already late!"

"Late? Late for what?"

"For what!? For my appointment with the eye-doctor, that's what. You know—the new optimist in town."

So that accounted for the new blue skirt. For the new 'optimist'!

"You said you'd drive me. Oh dear!"

"I did? Oh Lord, I forgot."

"It was only yesterday I come and told you my truck had broken down. Martin says he can't fix it. Says if it was a horse, he'd have to shoot it. Not funny."

"I know. Brothers are sometimes quite unsympathetic."

"Not only that, he doesn't seem to understand...."

"What should I do? I mean, I haven't showered or brushed my teeth. I'm not even dressed."

"I can see that."

"And my hair! Look at my hair!"

But Maggie wasn't looking at Nora's hair. She was rummaging in the hall closet. "Here," she said, holding out a long black cape that Sandra had worn during her 'lady of mystery' phase. "It'll go on right over your housecoat. Nobody'll know the difference." Then she snatched an orange wool toque from the top shelf. "This'll cover your hair."

Before Nora could object, Maggie had flung the garments on her and located Nora's purse which was a mate for her own. They'd bought them just last month at Wal-Mart. Quickly she located Nora's car keys and they were racing across the lawn to the garage.

Nora stumbled. "Oh blast! My slipper came off."

"Never mind, I'm already five minutes late."

"But it's my left one. I use my left foot to brake."

"You won't need to brake. Anyway, you can use your bare foot if you do."

"Maggie, I can't drive barefoot."

"Today you can. Come on. Nobody's gonna see you. You can sit and wait for me in the car. Here, I'll lend you my sunglasses, then if anybody sees you they won't recognize you."

The drive to town took only ten minutes, but by then of course, Maggie was fifteen minutes late. They had driven in total silence, an unusual state of affairs for which Nora was grateful since driving one hundred kilometres per hour over the gravel roads took all the skills at her disposal. And the cape was a bit of a hindrance.

They screeched to a stop at a parking meter in front of the doctor's building. As she leaped out of the car, Maggie advised, "You might want to scrunch down a bit. Maybe you shouldn't get out of the car." As if Nora would want to get out of the car!

Then Maggie was off to see the new 'optimist' in town.

It was July, the morning was beginning to heat up and Nora sweltered in her 'disguise', as she had begun to think of her bizarre outfit. Her head was hot as well. And itchy. She finally took off the toque, tipped the rear-view mirror down and gazed at her face in despair. Lipstick and a comb would help, but when she opened the purse on the seat beside her, she discovered to her dismay that it belonged to Maggie and contained no comb or cosmetics of any kind. "This is what I get for forgetting. This is my punishment for having a non-functioning brain," Nora thought, and wondered again about Alzheimer's disease.

Luckily, the street was quiet, but as Nora was about to toss Maggie's purse into the back seat, she saw, to her horror, that a young meter man was approaching from behind. The meter was on violation waiting to be fed. Another scrabble through Maggie's purse turned up no dimes, nickels or quarters. The meter man tapped on the windshield and mimed the question, "You gonna put money in this thing, or what?"

Nora rammed the toque back on her wild hair, shrugged elaborately and shook her head.

The young man regarded her curiously and while he was writing up the ticket, Nora rearranged her body to a near-reclining position in an effort to reduce her visibility to any casual passer-by, and wished she could disappear entirely. She heard the ticket being slipped under the windshield wiper blade and, breathing a sigh of relief, stared nonchalantly, she hoped, at the roof of the car.

In a few moments, and with some effort, Nora attained a more prone position on the seat with her knees bent under the steering wheel and her head resting on the passenger door. Again she removed the orange toque, then unfolded a road map and placed it over her face. She was uncomfortable, but unless someone came along and peered directly in, Nora imagined the car would appear to be unoccupied.

Forgetting her promise to drive Maggie to the eye doctor's appointment could be classed as a sin of omission but could not, in any way, account for the dark thing that shadowed all her waking hours. In her sweaty cocoon, Nora thought of the estrangement of her children from one another. Sad, but time would surely heal the rift and there was nothing she could think of to do at the moment to facilitate a reconciliation. But, what was to be done about Walter? Or, at least, what was to be done about his new and unexplainable disposition? And what in blazes was keeping Maggie?

Nora shifted uncomfortably, thinking of all the times she and Walter had shared a laugh regarding some of Maggie's exploits or twisted expressions. All behind her back, of course; she wouldn't hurt Maggie for the world. Except, that right now she wanted to kill her.

21

In that frame of mind, Nora dozed off. Presently, there was a tapping on the driver's window and she jerked herself to a sitting position under the steering wheel to find that she was almost nose to nose with an RCMP officer. Just under seven feet tall, she calculated, judging from the way he had to hunch over to peer in at her. Nora sat up and wound down the window.

"You own this car?" the officer asked.

"Yes."

"Kind of hot in there, isn't it?"

"Stifling," Nora agreed.

"Dressed a bit warm for the time of year, eh?"

"It was chilly when I left home."

"May I see your driver's license, please?"

Without a moment's hesitation, and without thinking, Nora opened the purse, extracted a wallet, removed the license and handed it over.

He looked at the document closely and then studied Nora's face. "You Maggie Kroeger?"

Nora suddenly knew what she'd done but was too embarrassed to admit it. She decided to bluff her way through.

The officer still held the license. "This picture doesn't look like you."

"I've lost a lot of weight."

"Take off the sunglasses, please." She removed them. "This says Maggie Kroeger's eyes are brown. Yours are blue." Nora shrugged. "Take the map off your head, please." She did as he asked. "Why were you wearing a road map, anyway?"

"The toque got too hot."

The policeman sighed. "You look kind of familiar. This isn't your driver's license, is it?" Nora shook her head. "Do you have a license?" She nodded. "Where might it be?"

"I believe it's in the doctor's office."

"Why would it be in the doctor's office?"

"It went in with Maggie Kroeger. My friend. She took my purse instead of hers. By mistake."

"Good God! I mean, excuse me, Ma'am, but why didn't you say so in the first place?"

Nora really had no idea why she let the charade go on once she knew what was happening. Obviously the officer was suspicious. Why wouldn't he be, under the circumstances? She couldn't think of anything to say that would sound sane.

"Have you been drinking?"

Some memory of drinking was trying to get through—something that had nothing to do with the present situation, but might have some bearing on the black phantom that seemed to have taken over her life. She spoke as though reminiscing with a friend. "I had a glass of wine at Martin Kroeger's birthday party."

Nora's reply to the officer set her thinking and served to fine-tune her mind until she got a clear signal—Walter, at the party, going home because he said he had to make a phone call when there was a perfectly good phone at the Kroegers. And he didn't return to the birthday celebration at all. Later, when she questioned him about it, he simply said he didn't feel like going back. Period. No reason, no excuse. It was not like Walter to walk out on a party and Nora now assumed there must be another woman behind his rude behavior. That was the cause of her misery! Or one of the causes.

The policeman, interrupting Nora's thoughts, cleared his throat. "I asked when you had that glass of wine. How long ago?"

"Last Sunday," she replied absently. "About six-thirty in the evening."

"Three days ago?! Look, Ma'am, it would be better if you didn't get smart with me."

"Me? Smart? I'm not a bit smart. Otherwise... Otherwise..." Nora could feel herself near tears. The heat, the humidity, the stupidity...

"Otherwise, what?"

She felt that the man was sympathetic, or at least, curious. "Otherwise, I'd have figured it out before now."

"Explain yourself, please." He was clearly exasperated.

"I think my husband is having an affair." Nora sobbed and slumped over the steering wheel.

The policeman cleared his throat and said, helplessly—probably the first thing that came into his head. "Well, that's not against the law." Nora sobbed harder. "What I mean is, that's not my department. Not illegal, so to speak. Look, is your friend, Maggie inside the doctor's office now?" Nora simply nodded and looked, helplessly, for a Kleenex.

"Very well, then, I think I'll just go in and have a word with her. You can put the map back on your head if you like. My God, what am I saying!?" he babbled before leaving Nora to her birthday party recollections.

It seemed like hours but was probably only ten minutes or so before Maggie returned, opened the driver's side door and said, "Scoot over. The cop said I gotta drive." Nora did as she was told. There didn't seem to be anything she could say at the moment, so she blew her nose on a crumpled tissue she'd located in the cape pocket and put the toque and sunglasses back on. Her friend didn't notice anything amiss.

Maggie was used to driving her old Chevy truck with the stiff accelerator and Nora's Plymouth sprinted forward like a scared rabbit when she pushed the pedal to the floor. "Whee!" she said, "this is a gutsy one!" And then she began to whistle one of her tuneless ditties.

"I darn near roasted," was all Nora could think of to say.

"Take off that silly cape and toque, then. We're almost out of town."

"You thought they were perfectly all right when we left home."

Maggie looked at her thoughtfully. "We could have maybe made a better choice. Anyway, I had to wait about twenty minutes. You could of changed before we left."

Nora was almost speechless with anger. "I could have stayed home entirely and Martin could have driven you."

"Martin and Walter went away somewhere this morning. Early. That thing there a parking ticket?"

"Lucky guess. What do you think? There wasn't the right change in your purse. You had mine you know."

"I know. Good thing, too."

"A good thing!?"

"Yeah. There wouldn't have been enough money in mine. To pay for the eye exam."

"You used my money?"

"Don't get snarky. I'll pay you back."

Nora knew the money would be returned. That wasn't the point. Maggie hadn't even asked permission.

"Didn't think you'd mind. This once."

"It's not a question of minding. I just like to be notified about these things."

"Well, I'm notifyin' you now."

"My comb and lipstick were in that purse."

"I know. I used them both. When I knew I had to wait, I used their washroom and fixed myself up a tad. Lipstick's brighter than I'm used to, though."

"But you hardly ever use lipstick."

"I run out last winter and never can remember to buy more. Gonna get me a new tube soon, though. Maybe I can get one of them short, curly perms, too. Hair's gone all to hell. As you well know. And I'm not crazy about these black roots."

Apparently the new 'optimist' in town was the reason behind Maggie's proposed make-over. "Well, what's he like? This eye-doctor friend of yours?"

"He's not married."

They were about a mile from home—creating a major dust storm in their wake as the car hurtled north and Maggie's attention was pretty much concentrated on keeping the Plymouth in the center of the road. When they came to the last turn-off, she looked at Nora. "He was some amazed when the cop called me right out of the examinin' room. And you could have knocked me over with a fender when he asked me if you were on drugs or anything. But I just laughed and said maybe a Tylenol once in awhile, although I personally believe you should be on Prozac. Then he wanted to know if you had any mental problems. I said you were as sane as anybody and he said it sure didn't look like it to him and maybe I better drive home."

"Watch the road, then! Jesus Murphy!"

"You don't usually swear, Nora."

"I'm not usually regarded as an idiot, either. Particularly by the constabulary."

"The what?"

"Never mind. I wonder if I'll get demerits for the disguise."

"I'll pay for the parking ticket if that's what's worryin' you."

"That's the least of my worries. The very least."

Maggie was amazed. "You got worries, Nora?"

It really wasn't Maggie's fault that she was incapable of imagining that Nora might have some very real worries. In spite of Nora's remarks about Walter's remoteness, Maggie had blithely suggested that it might just be a touch of depression—temporary and not serious in any case. She seemed to assume that the Fields' marriage itself was rock solid, could withstand anything, and Nora had passed on no real details to make her think otherwise. Maggie would be terribly upset if she thought there were serious marital problems in the household.

Nora just sighed and said, "It's OK, Maggie, nothing important. You just run along home now." Then she went into the house, threw the offending cape and toque in the corner and collapsed on the sofa to review her life.

THE LEAHYS

Usually, whenever Nora started to feel sorry for herself, she would conscientiously try to count her blessings. Sometimes it worked, and sometimes it didn't. Attempting to compare her present life with the one she'd once had living with her own family, was a risky business. For one thing, the security she'd always had since marrying Walter was a far cry from the past when neither she, her sister, Audrey, nor her mother ever knew when Robert Leahy might decide to move on to another town—another province. Memories of these sudden uprootings still had the power to produce a small pit of anxiety in her stomach.

"Don't worry, dears, your father knows what he's doing. Business here hasn't been very good at all. You'll like the new place. You always do." But her mother's reassurances comforted no one. Not even herself, as far as Nora could see, for the older woman's red-rimmed eyes were evidence of lost sleep or lost arguments. Never were angry words heard, though.

If there were disagreements between their parents, angry protests, the girls never heard them, or heard about them.

But Audrey knew how to protest—loud and long. She had just made new friends, she'd been elected class treasurer and what would the kids think when she ran out on them? She had a solo in the upcoming spring variety concert, a job delivering papers, the odd baby-sitting engagement and so on. Nora had many of the same reasons for wanting to remain where they were, although not so many friends as Audrey, since she was the eldest and expected to help out in the house while her mother worked in the family's shoe store. She never voiced her disappointment at another move, letting Audrey do the complaining for both of them. A cowardly attitude, to be sure. She knew that.

"I could just wring your stupid neck," Audrey raged just before their second last move. "You just stand there like a wooden Indian while I tell the old bugger why we need to stay here, in one place. For once. Do you like being drug away from a place just when we're getting settled in? Do you like being a gypsy? For that matter, do you like the old-maid clothes Da makes you wear?"

The latter question having nothing to do with the family's relocation, but a lot to do with the overly-modest clothing he insisted that his daughters wear. Not that it affected Audrey to any extent, since she simply rolled the waistband on her skirts until the hem was a more fashionable distance from the ground. Nora, meanwhile, dragged around in calf-length outfits, wary of setting off her father's cold anger.

Nora's answers to all of Audrey's questions would have been a whole-hearted 'no', but she knew that anything she might add to the arguments would be ignored just as her sister's were. All she was able to contribute was a hopeless shrug, and the advice, "Don't call him an old bugger, he might hear you. It's just the way he is. There's nothing we can do."

"You make me so sick! You're just like Mam! Well, I'm not going. To hell with him."

"Where would you stay?"

"I've got friends who'd take me in."

But, of course, Audrey didn't stay. Robert Leahy either sold or gave up his business and they all moved on without any regard for the complications the girls faced by changing schools in mid-term. It was grossly unfair. Their mother should have known that, must have known it. Obviously, there was nothing she could do about the situation and Nora often wondered, bitterly, if she ever tried. Although she undoubtedly loved her daughters and provided them with the only warmth and encouragement they had in their lives, Mary Leahy was unable to do much else for them and was completely incapable of standing up to her husband. The most she ever said by way of complaint was, "I don't care much for these moves, either, girls, but your father is the bread winner and we have to follow him. Have to make the best of it."

These platitudes only enraged Audrey. "I wonder what kind of a hold the old bugger has on her. What's he holding over her head?"

"I can't imagine there could be anything. Mam is a really good person."

"I know that! But there's gotta be something. I'd sure like to know what it is."

Although she rejected the idea at the time, in later years, Nora had to agree with her sister, although she never admitted it. A 'hold' of some kind would have accounted for Mary Leahy's almost constant depression. For that's what it must have been—this tired sadness that hung about her like a veil. Later, her inability to concentrate might have explained the accident that took her life. Otherwise, why would Mary Leahy absentmindedly step in front of a fast moving truck? Why, indeed?

Still, life before Walter did have some lighter moments. The girls were allowed to go skating, to attend any fairs or circuses that came to whatever town they happened to be living in, and to go to the local library. Robert Leahy, apparently had some respect for learning and didn't discourage Nora's reading habits. Nor did he try to monitor the subject matter of the books she carted home. Books were where Nora discovered the little she knew about life and she mostly lived in them and through them. Friends weren't as important to her as they were to Audrey who, although quite clever in school, was anything but a bookworm.

"Your eyes will fall out of your head before you're seventeen if you don't get them out of all those damn books," Audrey scolded.

But all Nora could think to say was, "Don't say damn, Da might hear you."

"So what? I don't see him going to any church at all. Or taking us, or letting Mam go." And it was true, none of them ever darkened a church door. The girls didn't know why since it might have provided them with, at least, some social life. But social life was not a factor in Robert Leahy's existence and he didn't see any reason for his family to feel the need of any. As to spiritual life, that was never discussed.

The one time Nora had joined anything, it was through a school friend. Adrienne was well on the way to becoming a 'best' friend and Nora treasured their relationship—it made her feel almost normal. Nora was flattered when Adrienne invited her to come to C.G.I.T.—Canadian Girls In Training—a group connected with the Protestant Churches. She managed three meetings before her father discovered that she wasn't studying with Adrienne on Tuesday evenings, and he quickly put an end to her association with the girls' group. Nora was heart broken and, because she had no real idea why she was being forbidden that innocent activity, she also had no idea what to tell Adrienne. At first, she made excuses for not attending meetings and then, ashamed, avoided Adrienne altogether. Nora yearned for the lost friendship.

"We're a weird family," Audrey complained to her parents. "Just plain weird."

Robert Leahy looked up from his dinner plate and stared at his youngest daughter. "In what way do you consider us weird?"

"Every way I can think of. We don't *do* things, don't *go* to things. We can't have friends over. You and mother don't have friends over. You don't even *have* any friends, as far as I can see. We don't *do* anything!"

"We do what's right for this family to do. And *you* will do exactly as I say. Right now, you can go to your room, young lady. I don't want to see your face around here until breakfast time." All this was said without emotion as their father stirred his tea.

Audrey got up from her chair, walked to the doorway, turned and looked straight at her father. "You're mean and ugly and I hate you!"

Robert Leahy's face turned white and he half-rose from his chair as though to give chase, thought better of it and only snarled, "Get out of my sight, you... you Jezebel!"

Audrey scooted to her room. No more words were spoken during that meal and, as usual, Nora's stomach ached for hours. Robert never struck his daughters, only abused them with his words and hard looks. Nora often thought a beating would be easier to take.

Later, when Nora had finished the dishes and gone up to bed, Audrey asked her if Jezebel was a relative. Maybe an aunt or a cousin back in Ireland. Nora didn't think so since her father had implied that Audrey *was* a Jezebel, not *like* a Jezebel. When Nora looked the word up in the dictionary, she found that Jezebel was the wife of Ahab, notorious for her evil actions. 'A bold, vicious woman'.

Audrey's bottom lip trembled at the news. "I'm not bold and vicious."

Nora put an arm around her sister. "Of course, you're not. Da's the mean and vicious one." Then, after giving her sister a kiss on the cheek, she said, "Now then, let's look up Ahab." Although, at that particular time and place, the girls had separate bedrooms, they slept curled up together in Nora's bed that night.

Nora was eighteen and Audrey sixteen when their mother was killed. There had been no funeral. Robert Leahy and his daughters were the only ones present at the graveside for the interment. There might have been a few others turn up had Robert not ended the short announcement of her death in the local paper with the terse information, 'Private service'.

But, of course, there was no real service. Just the three of them, huddled together in a cold April rain. The girls each carried a red rose (Nora's idea) and they dropped them on the casket before the funeral home operators lowered it into the ground. When they turned to leave the cemetery, Nora saw two men, standing at a respectful distance waiting for them to leave. They would, she knew, fill in the grave as soon as the family left.

Audrey was inconsolable and turned to Nora for comfort. Or, rather, they turned to one another.

33

Robert turned to no one.

Without her mother to help with the clerking, Nora was pressed into service to fill the gap while Audrey, was supposed to do the housework and cooking. As Nora was in the last year of high school, she also had a good deal of homework. Audrey did, as well, yet she seemed able to breeze through school without much time spent with her books. Nora was amazed and pathetically grateful that her father actually consented to her finishing Grade Twelve.

Less than a month later, the girls discovered that they were to be on the move again. Robert had made a deal to sell the store back in March. The girls were stricken. "Again?" Audrey asked. "We like it here. We go to school here, for God's sake!"

"Hasn't it ever occurred to you," their father asked coldly, "that I am the one who provides the money to run this household and that I make the decisions?"

"And we provide the free labor, "Audrey put in, cheeks flaming.

"Enough! No more out of you."

"Did Mam know you were planning to move us again?" Nora asked.

"Of course, she knew. I told her my decision in February, found a buyer in March. Why would you ask that?"

"I don't know. I just wondered is all."

Robert seemed to soften ever so slightly. "In any case, you'll be able to finish your school year here. The place in McClung won't be ready until June. I'll go on ahead then and you girls can look after the moving as soon as school is out."

"Where in hell is McClung?" Audrey asked Nora when they were alone.

Nora was tired and every part of her seemed to be aching. She plopped onto a kitchen chair. "I have no earthly idea. And what's more, I don't bloody care."

Then she put her head on the table and wept for a long time, knowing in her bones why their mother was no longer with them.

Later that evening, while piling laundry helter-skelter into the old wringer washer, Audrey sighed, "How are we going to do it, Nora? I mean, how are we going to get us moved, along with all the other things we have to do? And don't tell me 'one day at a time' the way Mam would have. Da won't lift a finger, we both know that."

"Quite a bit of stuff is still in boxes. Never unpacked from before. Some of it hasn't been unpacked in years."

"Maybe we should throw it out then."

"Sort it first, if we ever get time," Nora said.

✐

But the 'stuff' never got sorted before the frantic move to McClung. Since Robert Leahy was too busy getting the new shoe store set up to help the girls with the household goods, it was their task to organize that part of the venture. Months later, many of the necessary house-keeping utensils were still in boxes. Somewhere.

"Where do you suppose we stashed the egg beater?" Audrey asked on a day when she was supposed to be making a cake for their supper.

"You should know, for heaven's sake. I can't spend all day working in the store and do all the kitchen stuff, too."

"Well I can't go to school and do everything here, too. It's too much. It's just too damned much!"

"Don't complain. At least you're going to school. At least you get to see some people now and again."

"You see people!"

"I see their feet. Mostly I see just their stupid big,

35

flat feet. And if an interesting looking guy does happen to come in, Da makes sure I don't get to wait on him. He sends me back to the stock room to count boxes or something."

"Maybe he's afraid you'll run off and get married. Or pregnant, or something."

"Fat chance of either. Anyway, the store's closed for the day. I'll beat your icing with a spoon while you set the table."

"Good. I've got a date later."

"Does Da know?"

"Are you kidding??"

"What are you going to tell him?"

"Oh, I'll think of something. A baby-sitting job, maybe. That's it. A baby-sitting job."

Audrey managed to get around their father one way or another most of the time and had a much more active social life than he ever suspected. Meanwhile, Nora's social life was in the doldrums, had never gotten off the ground. At one point, just as she had made up her mind to join a church with a view to meeting some young people, her father delivered one of his familiar anti-religion rants. It ended with, "And Ireland wouldn't be in the mess it's in today if not for the Papists on one side and the Bible Thumpers on the other."

Nora didn't know a great deal about Ireland, but she was ever after convinced that her father was a mind reader. Audrey tried to set her straight on that assumption. "A lucky shot. That's all. We've heard it all before. You know that. Forget it. Anyway, there's other things you can do to meet people."

"Like what?"

"Well, for one thing, he's always let us skate. There's fowl suppers, concerts, dances..."

"Dances! That'd be the day!"

"I suppose. Da approves of walking. Walk down to

the Coke-And-Choke once in a while for heaven's sake. A lot of the young people meet there."

"By myself?"

"You know what? You're eighteen years old. You don't need somebody to hold your hand. You could go off and do something on your own. Walk around town, go into the other stores, talk to people, for crying out loud!"

And so Nora vowed to try to make some inroads into McClung 'society'. She went out of her way to chat with the young women who came into the store and, eventually, became quite friendly with several of them. Occasionally, one or two invited her to join them in a movie, which she eagerly accepted. Sometimes she was even asked into their homes for coffee after skating at the local outdoor rink.

Lucy, the one who worked in the library, became a good friend and the two often walked at night after their workdays were finished. Lucy was engaged to be married, though, and most of her energies were directed toward her coming nuptials. She even asked Nora to be her bridesmaid. "You'll look wonderful in the sky blue taffeta I chose. It'll match your eyes exactly. With that curly black hair and petite figure, you'll be a knock-out. Boy! I wish I could look like you!"

Nora treasured that compliment. Until then, she'd only thought of her diminutive stature as a liability—particularly when compared with Audrey's long-legged build. And it certainly hadn't occurred to her that she might be considered pretty. The best man, however, also noticed Nora's good looks and made a date with her for the Saturday night following the wedding. They were to go to the movies and he stopped at the store to pick her up. Unfortunately, Nora's father spoiled the evening by subjecting the young man to such an inquisition before allowing her to go out with him, that he never came around for seconds. No one else ever tried. Word got around, she assumed.

At Audrey's suggestion, Nora became a volunteer. She made herself available for every door-to-door collection for charity. In this way, she met most of the townspeople at one time or another. It wasn't the best way, because some householders resented being asked for money and often gave grudgingly. She never got over the feeling that the job turned her into a kind of beggar, even though she knew better. It didn't cure her shyness, either.

But her shyness wasn't the only problem. In the way of many very settled, very old, small towns, people seemed a bit suspicious and standoffish and not in any hurry to accept a new family into the community. The Leahys, apparently, had to prove themselves in some way. This wasn't a new problem—it had been the same every time they'd moved to a new place, but somehow, their mother's warm smile had a softening effect on anyone she met, which always made the family's transitions easier. People liked her. Not so, Robert Leahy. But he could adjust, ignore any chilliness he might encounter and usually responded in kind. Since his was the only outlet for footwear in town, though, business prospered about as well as could be expected even if his personal reputation did not.

Audrey was sympathetic when Nora described their father's treatment of her one date. "The old bugger"

"Probably you shouldn't call Da an old bugger."

"Well, he is and you know it. Why don't you just pack up and get out of here? He's only using you as a work horse."

Nora knew that was true, yet she couldn't imagine being on her own, leaving her sister. "I think I'd better hang on until you're finished school."

"Well, you can be damn sure that when I'm finished school—whether I'm eighteen or not—I'm getting as far away from McClung as I can." And Nora knew she would.

🖋

It was another two years, though, before Audrey made her escape. "On a scholarship," Robert Leahy told a customer, in an unaccustomed burst of conviviality. "To Ryerson. She's going to be a journalist. Now, just what sort of a dress shoe were you interested in?"

Nora, in the stock room, as usual, overheard and thought, "He's proud of Audrey!" and wondered what she could ever do to gain the same respect. Certainly, her father didn't seem pleased by her recent association with Walter Fields, although he hadn't gone so far as to ban it. She and Walter had been dating, rather casually, for almost a year and Nora felt their relationship was deepening to the point where he would soon ask her to marry him. She was more than ready to accept.

Walter wasn't the dashing, romantic hero of novels, but he was good looking and very kind. He made her feel special and loved—treated her as though she might break—and there was no doubt in her mind that he was the man she wanted for a husband. Not that she had anyone to compare him with, but she knew in her heart that he was a good man.

So, when Walter did ask her to marry him, she didn't hesitate to accept without a thought of what her father might say. Robert Leahy, however, was accustomed to being the one in charge, the one giving orders so, of course, he did what he could to discourage the marriage. He'd always resisted anything that wasn't to his particular benefit. But

Walter's no-nonsense attitude apparently persuaded Robert Leahy that there was no use in opposing the union and he eventually ceded ownership of his daughter to the tall, determined farmer. Much to Nora's surprise and gratitude.

Through the years, Nora took Walter's steadfast devotion to his family and his farm for granted. He was a good provider and had always been there when she needed him. Therefore, it mystified her when he began to change, become restless, remote—and, perhaps, not entirely honest. At first she suspected depression, as her friend Maggie had suggested, but as time wore on, she had the gut feeling that it was more than that.

Nora desperately needed someone to talk to, to confide in. But Walter had always been her only confidante and he was no longer willing or able to discuss whatever it was that ailed him. She hadn't many women friends and, in any case, wouldn't have dreamed of joining any husband-bashing conversation. There was really only Maggie with whom she felt any real closeness.

Sometimes Nora thought that having Maggie for a best friend showed some serious deficiency on her part. Most women probably had level headed, likeminded people for bosom buddies. Nora had Maggie Kroeger.

THE KROEGERS

Although their backgrounds were miles apart, Maggie and Nora both loved the same man—Walter. Maggie's love was as that of a daughter's affection for her father, though, and to be truthful, Maggie loved everyone in the Fields' household. Her visits were numerous and often coincided with differences of opinion she had with her brother, Martin, since it was the one place she could go with her problems— and be welcomed into the bargain.

If her parents had lived, things would have been different. Maggie and Martin had often discussed possible reasons why the elder Kroegers hadn't seen the train coming and had come to the conclusion that they were involved in some disagreement or other. Of course, neither could guess what their parents' last words might have been, but Maggie could imagine them. Her father was probably saying, "What do you intend to do about that harum-scarum daughter of yours?" (She belonged only to her mother whenever she was in trouble.) Her mother's reply

41

would have been typical. "I have no idea. What do *you* intend to do about *yours*?"

Even if the two had survived, they wouldn't have been able to alter Maggie's harum scarumness to any extent. After all, they'd had seventeen years to work on it—without success. During the years since their demise, Maggie continued to be set on doing the things she wanted to do in her own way and in her own time. Take for example, the tree house she built in the old elm tree outside her bedroom window. It had taken a lot of planning and effort, but she managed it even though it had taken all her spare time throughout one entire summer. Martin only objected once and, when she threatened to throw the claw hammer at him from her perch on the highest limb, he'd retreated. No doubt, he considered the plan to be weird—even for Maggie—but he knew her aim was good. She'd been twenty-two at the time.

Now, ten years later, she still used the tree house. It was accessible from her bedroom window and was where she took afternoon naps when the weather was good, or added to her legendary collection of afghans. (She'd given up making them for her own hope chest but there was always somebody she knew getting married and requiring a gift.) Her lofty perch was also handy for doing a bit of spying now and then. With a good pair of binoculars, she could see for miles and knew the routines of her closest neighbors.

There had been an eight-month period when she'd been banished from her refuge, but she didn't often think about that dark time. Maggie didn't like to dwell on dark times. Her banishment followed on the heels of Martin's marriage to Dorinda, or 'the pit bull with lipstick', as Maggie called her. Martin had been twenty-seven when he rushed into the marriage—three years older than Maggie and ten years younger than his bride.

Up until then, he had been a good brother to Maggie and, with Walter's help, had managed the farm so expertly that it was now equipped with good machinery and they had a cash surplus. Martin had put Maggie on a modest salary and, as her needs weren't great, she managed to buy herself a used pick-up truck and put a little money by, as well. Her stash, as she explained it to Nora. But Martin's marriage altered that.

It was the fall of the year when Martin had succumbed to the lure of Dorinda. What the lure was, Maggie couldn't imagine, although she knew Martin was surely as unskilled in the ways of women as she was in the ways of men. Still, he should have been able to figure that one out. And he hadn't even objected too strenuously when Dorinda insisted that it was time Maggie was out on her own.

Her savings weren't much by current standards and, when Maggie was unceremoniously expelled from the Kroeger household by her new sister-in-law, and obliged to try life in the city, they barely covered five months' rent on the seedy apartment she took on Furby Street. Maggie did have her vehicle, as Dorinda pointed out, and she was able to get a job using her only saleable commodity. Sewing. It was a legacy from her mother and enabled her to get work doing alterations at Eaton's Department Store.

The only actual advice Maggie remembered hearing from her mother was, "Don't ever learn to milk because you might marry a farmer. God forbid!" So she hadn't and the deficiency bothered her not at all. (Not that the option had ever presented itself.)

But, Lord, she hated the city and dreamed, not of a handsome farmer, (although a handsome man of any persuasion would have been quite acceptable), but of her tree house back home. She still thought of the farm as her home but never felt inclined to visit— mainly because she wasn't invited to do so. She kept tabs on the proceedings at the Kroeger residence, however, by almost-weekly visits to Nora and Walter Fields' house just across the road. They made her welcome and gave her their daughter's room to use. Sandra, clever girl, was off to university in another province and seldom came home. Trevor was in his last year of high school then, but he was a quiet kind of a guy and got along well with Maggie. Better than with Sandra, or so Nora claimed.

Apparently, Martin again failed to raise objections when Dorinda moved her mother in with them a month or two after their marriage. 'The Old Battle Axe' as Maggie called her, was there by Christmas and was in residence when Maggie got her one and only invitation to visit the threesome. For Christmas dinner.

She stayed only until they'd finished eating; the women were dozing and Martin was busy putting dishes in the spanking new dishwasher. Thinking of all the dishes she'd done by hand, leaning over the old kitchen sink, was too much. She said her thanks to Martin and left the house.

Outside, in the crisp clean air with snow sparkling like diamonds in the moon light, Maggie almost believed that the stories of Jesus might be true. She paused a few moments, drinking it all in before dashing across the road to the Fields' residence.

"The old girl can cook—a person has to admit that," she told Nora later. "And she was dressed to the nines. A long blue evening gown no less. I think she musta bought it at one of them specialty shops. It certainly didn't come from Eaton's. Had a neckline down to her belly-button. And some of them darts over her ass shoulda been let out. I figured they might bust

out on their own after all the turkey she ate. And
lipstick! At least an inch thick. Got smeared around
a lot by the gravy. And drink! She put away more
wine than Martin and I would drink in a year. They
all drink a lot. Scotch and soda before dinner. I tasted
it. Like horse 'you-know-what', if you don't mind me
saying. Coulda knocked me over with a fender to see
an old lady swill down all that stuff. Get pissed at a
fancy dinner. You ever seen her?"

"Only from a distance. Martin and Dorinda have
never invited us over, even though he and Walter work
together all the time. And Martin never comes in our
house anymore. Of course," Nora added, "We've never
invited them over here, either. And it'll be a cold day
in hell before we do. I'm glad they asked you to dinner, though. At least it was something. How did the
Duchess behave toward you?"

"The Duchess? Oh, you mean Dorinda. Like always.
As though I was just a cow turd in the pasture of life.
And she was got up in a long black skirt and a white
angora sweater with a fancy necklace. Diamonds, she
told me. Earrings to match. She's sure got old Martin where she wants him. All new dishes, too. I didn't
see any of Mom's Old Country Roses that we usta
always use for good. Do you think she might have
thrown them out?"

Nora sighed. "I'm sure I don't know. I hope not.
They should be for you. Yours. If anybody deserves
those dishes, it's you."

"Well I don't have any use for them right now. I
bought a set of Corel which do me fine. Someday
maybe I can use the Royal Albert. All new rugs, she's
got. I couldn't even get Martin to get me some new
linoleum for the kitchen. New furniture, too. White
leather. Like sitting on an iceberg." She giggled.
"Makes a farting noise when you sit. on it. Real classy.
By the way, I noticed a new Lincoln Town car in the

garage. Whose is that, do you think?"

"I don't know that, either. It showed about the time the old girl moved in. I don't see Dorinda driving the Chevy now. I guess they traded it in on the Lincoln. Did you give them a Christmas present?"

"Yeah, but I wisht I hadn't. I'd boughten one of them black velvet pictures with the little girl with the big eyes. You know. Sorta sad eyes. But I don't think they'll ever hang it up. The Duchess and the Battle Axe sorta exchanged funny glances. Martin said, thanks, though."

"Did they give you anything?"

"A Timex watch and some leather gloves. Gloves have already been worn a bit. You can tell, you know, kinda bent at the knuckles. Here, you can have them. I only wear mitts anyway. I guess I can use the watch sometime."

"Thanks, but I don't have any use for the Duchess's used gloves. Never mind, dear. We have something nice for you."

For the first time in almost a year, Maggie cried. When Nora and Walter presented her with a red satin housecoat and slippers to match, she was overcome. "Oh, you shouldn't! It's way too nice for me. Where would I wear them?"

"Nonsense, they look perfect for you. They look smashing. Wear them while you're watching TV, or whatever, in the evenings. You deserve nice things." With that, Nora wept, too, and suspicious moisture gathered in Walter's eyes.

"You might get invited somewhere, or have a boy-friend over," Trevor offered, helpfully. "That's when you could wear them." Then, as his gift, he handed her an envelope with a pair of tickets to the Manitoba Theatre Centre.

Maggie said a faint 'thank you' but was quite taken aback. She bit her bottom lip. "I've never been there.

I wouldn't understand the play. Probably wouldn't even understand the scenery." Her lip trembled. "Anyways, who'd go with me?"

"Me. I will, if you'll have me." Trevor said. "Notice, they're for the end of the month, I'll still be on holidays and Dad says I can have the car." With that, he hugged her, an unusual gesture for him, and they burst out laughing—for no reason at all, it seemed to Maggie.

Then Maggie remembered her present to them and ran up to 'her' room, bringing back a large, rather awkwardly wrapped gift—a huge Christmas cake. "Here, I thought you might, could use this."

"Oh my!" Nora gasped at the sight of Eaton's finest. "How did you ever guess I didn't bake a Christmas cake this year?"

"Just figured, with Sandra visiting her boyfriend's folks in Kamsack this Christmas.... You know.... You might not bother with a lot of baking."

Nora and Walter assured Maggie that she was the most thoughtful girl in the world and they all ate fruit cake and drank sherry until they were almost too full to move. Maggie proclaimed it to be a wonderful, good Christmas. "Especially when I didn't know what I'd do or what to expect."

"You can always count on us," Nora said. "Now, off to bed with you."

✐

That was Christmas. By Easter, when Maggie was again visiting the Fields, she asked Nora when the screened-in dining tent had appeared in the Kroeger's front yard.

"Just a couple of days ago. You know, when the weather turned warm so suddenly." Nora laughed. "We'll see how it fares during the next snowfall.

There'll be one. You can bet your boots on that."

"It's just the kind of one I always asked Martin to buy for us. Only I'd of put it at the back—nearer the kitchen. Make more sense. The Old Battle Axe still there?"

"As far as I know. I could see the three of them sitting in the tent drinking beer, the day they put it up."

It was a warm spring, Nora's predicted snowfall didn't materialize and the tent was still in good shape when Maggie visited in early May. Walter was busy getting seeding equipment ready and, in fact, had already sowed some barley. Arrangements had been changed, though, and Walter was now working with another neighbor. Martin, apparently, had hired a young man to help him and no longer needed to join forces with Walter. Maggie was angered by this act of disloyalty and couldn't imagine Martin paying out good wages to someone when he could have continued the long-term work-exchange with Walter. It had worked fine for years.

"Never mind," Walter soothed her. "We'll make out OK. I just hope Martin does, too."

"Who is this hired man, anyway?"

Walter and Nora exchanged glances before Nora said, "Some guy they met in the bar. They spend a lot of time at the bar in town. The guy's been a regular visitor all spring. Guess Martin decided he might as well put him to work. Name's Floyd but I've never met him or seen him close up."

"Close up he looks like a left-over hippie from the sixties." Walter explained in disgust. "Never been on a farm before. I just hope he doesn't wreck Martin's machinery."

That evening was warm and, from the window in Maggie's upstairs bedroom, she could see the dining tent clearly. At first, all four residents at Martin's, were seen to be in the tent, drinking beer. She stomped down to give Nora the information. "Sitting around drinking! Walter's still out in the field. The place will go to hell in a hang-basket."

"Hand-basket," Nora corrected. "But don't worry. I don't think Martin's that dumb."

"He married the Duchess, didn't he?"

There could be no reply to that, and Nora didn't attempt one.

When bedtime rolled around, Maggie continued her surveillance of the dining tent across the road—aided considerably by the binoculars, which she had thoughtfully brought along. Because they had rigged up some sort of a light, perhaps a lantern, silhouettes were clearly visible and, as she watched, the Battle Axe departed for the house. Shortly after, Martin rose, stretched and also went inside. Although the light was presently extinguished, Maggie knew that the Duchess and the hired man remained in the tent. Around midnight, eyestrain and exhaustion overcame Maggie and she crawled into bed.

The next morning, she related her impressions of the tableau to Nora and expressed her suspicions. But Nora was tight-lipped and only said, "Don't worry your head about them, Maggie. Things will work out. They always do."

"Work out for who?" Maggie wondered.

Within the month, she found out.

The information came via a phone call from Nora. "I think you'd better come home, Maggie. As soon as you can. Resign from Eaton's or whatever you have to do. Martin spoke to Walter last night. Evidently Floyd has absconded with the Duchess. And here's the kicker. The Battle Axe went with them!"

"Holy cow! When did this all happen?"

"A week or so ago, I guess, but Martin was too ashamed to tell anybody at the time. Now he's in a bind. Spraying needs to be done. Has to have some help from Walter. Otherwise, he probably wouldn't have told us. He's in a bad way, Martin is. Can't understand what went wrong. She cleaned out their joint account and maxed out his credit card before they all took off."

"In the Lincoln Town car?"

"In the Lincoln Town car."

"I'll be damned. The police know about this?"

"You know Martin. No police."

"I'll be home as soon as I can."

*

Although Martin was happy enough to have his sister return home, the facts behind Maggie's move back from the city were a source of shame to him. At least a dozen times a day, he slapped his forehead and cursed the day he ever met Dorinda. And, that she'd convinced him to marry her, was a continual source of wonder and regret. He denounced himself for the stupidity he'd shown in forming that alliance and allowing his bride to exile Maggie from the only home she'd ever known.

Just the memory of Maggie's awful apartment on Furby Street made him cringe. Martin's only visit had occurred after he'd taken Dorinda to the airport the time she went to fetch her mother from Edmonton. The place was in a bad area of the city, to start with. But the worst part was the dilapidated condition of the house where she lived. The 'apartment' she'd rented was on the third floor and comprised only one room with a tiny alcove for a kitchen. The bathroom, down the hall, was shared by the kind of people he didn't even want to think about. The furniture was musty smelling, and even Maggie's afghans couldn't disguise the antiquity of the sofa and chair. To her credit, Maggie had done what she could to make things cheerful and had probably cleaned and scrubbed what she could. Still, the place stank and was depressing. He tried not to think of the costly renovations taking place at the Kroeger house for Dorinda's comfort.

When he asked if she'd made any friends, she was evasive and said she knew lots of people who worked at Eaton's and she was fine. The place was convenient, she could walk to work and there was an old garage out back, which the landlord had rented to her so the pick-up truck could be safely stored. Maggie saved money, she said, by walking or taking a bus almost everywhere she went. She only used the truck on the weekends she spent with Walter and Nora and it didn't cost a lot to run.

"I know you visit them every week or so," he'd said. "Why don't you run over to see us sometimes?"

"I will when Dorinda invites me. She already said she doesn't want a third person around. I don't want to butt in."

He'd wanted to tell her she wouldn't be 'butting in', but courage failed him when he considered his wife's reactions to an unexpected visit from her sister-in-law, so he didn't pursue the subject. A third person butted in, in any case.

He should definitely have put his foot down when Dorinda moved her mother in with them and let her take over Maggie's old room. But he'd learned that attempting to thwart his new wife's schemes created such unbearable hostility and days of silence that he gave in.

The final betrayal was Dorinda's insistence that Floyd—a man they'd recently met in the bar—be installed in the household as well. He should have been bright enough to guess the relationship between his wife and the newcomer. Against his better judgement,

Martin hired Floyd to help with the farm work. That meant four of them were living in the house.

Floyd was totally ignorant of farming operations, but was devoted to beer drinking, Dorinda and a life of leisure. Perhaps in that order, perhaps not. Even before he became aware that Dorinda and Floyd were having an affair, Martin thought of his new 'hired man' as a long-haired, stupid, arrogant son-of-a-bitch But it was rather late by that time. He'd already severed his work-share arrangement with Walter Fields—the man who'd farmed with him and for him during the years following the deaths of his and Maggie's parents. So he continued the charade of regarding Floyd as his helper. To his cost, as he later learned.

The first 'accident' had happened while Martin was away at the elevator getting more seed barley while leaving Floyd in charge of hooking up the hydraulic hoses on the tractor. In spite of Martin's clear instructions, Floyd managed to botch the job, and the subsequent explosion caused the loss of all the oil from the machine. Time and money lost.

Another mishap occurred when the hired man failed to lift the teeth of the cultivator at the proper time and tore up some already-seeded wheat. But the final event, in a long line of costly and time-consuming misadventures, came the day Martin was busy changing the oil in his wife's Lincoln Town Car and had left Floyd to fill the air seeder. Later, Floyd's alibi was that he needed to run into the house to get a drink of water and it had taken longer than he expected. It must have been quite a long time, since the automatic auger kept on working long after the seeder was filled, and poured mounds of grain on the ground.

"He's real sorry," Dorinda explained. "He won't do it again."

But Martin had finally had enough.

"You're goddam right he won't do it again. I'm letting him go before he busts all my machinery and bankrupts me. I'll pay him 'til the end of the week. Three more days. That's all. Then he goes."

Apparently, those three days were enough for his bride, his mother-in-law and his hired man to empty Martin and Dorinda's joint account and to purchase items to the limit of his credit card before they left for parts unknown. They made their exit in the Lincoln—the vehicle Dorinda had coaxed him to buy for her and on which he'd paid the insurance, licensing and had kept in gasoline. "At least, it's had a recent oil change," was his absurd first thought when he discovered the felony.

He'd had to go, hat in hand, to beg Walter's assistance with the balance of the spring work and was forever grateful that his neighbor and old friend held no feelings of ill will. Walter wasn't one for asking questions, either. He'd only said, "I'm sorry things didn't work out for you. Nora and I are both sorry. "

Martin had half expected to be asked why, in the name of God, he'd married a woman ten years older than himself and whose frequent visits to the bar had caused some speculation among the locals. That was a question Martin couldn't have answered, because he didn't know. He only knew that, in the beginning, Dorinda seemed to find him attractive and amusing, which was such a novel idea that he'd been totally smitten. He, Martin Kroeger, could make a good looking woman laugh! It was remarkable.

Of course, he'd always been able to make Maggie laugh—that wasn't difficult. They often laughed themselves silly over nothing much at all. Like the times they decided on some after-dinner music with him creaking away on his father's old fiddle and Maggie chording on the piano. He could remember Maggie practically rolling around on the floor when, after hours of practicing, he finally got *The Devil's Dream* up to speed, but left out half the notes. Or when she eventually figured out the proper minor chords for *The Rakes of Kildare* and they'd both forgotten the melody.

No. Maggie wasn't hard to entertain. She didn't often complain, either, and she never went to the bar. She kept house fairly well and was thrifty but Maggie was, after all, his sister and it seemed like a reasonable thing for him to get married. Particularly when Dorinda was the only female who had seemed to find him entirely enchanting.

Maggie hadn't objected to the idea. Not at first, anyway, but that was before either of them realized that Maggie would be turfed out and then she seemed resigned to the idea. "Hawkie fly in and birdie fly out. Like in the square dance," Maggie had said, too cheerfully, when Dorinda insisted that newlyweds really shouldn't have a third party hanging about. "I understand. Sorta."

But it must have been hard for her to understand the fact that, from that time on, she was no longer considered part of the family. Martin was glad Maggie didn't know about the dust-up concerning the piano. Dorinda had wanted to sell it and use the money as part payment on the Lincoln Town Car. Martin had been firm. It was Maggie's piano; they couldn't sell what wasn't theirs. Dorinda sulked for a week— until he went out and financed the big automobile and presented it to her. But she arranged for movers to come in and shift the piano to the darkest corner of the basement as soon as he was out of the house.

This was, she said, because when the wall-to-wall carpet was laid, it would mute the piano too much and it would sound better on the cement floor downstairs. Not that there was anyone to play it, in any case. The wall-to-wall was only part of the wholesale renovations being planned and, although Martin was dismayed by the projected costs, he said nothing. Wives, he deduced, cost a lot of money. Dorinda, sensing his anxiety about finances, suggested that Maggie's salary be stopped since she certainly wasn't there to earn it any more. She also hinted that the process might be made retroactive and that Maggie should repay her last month's stipend. It would almost pay for the new dishwasher. Martin, reluctantly, stopped Maggie's salary, but held out against asking her to return any of it.

That was one of his few hold outs. Another was when Dorinda demanded that Maggie's tree house be dismantled. He ignored the order, but on she nagged. "It's an eyesore. People must laugh at that ugly thing sticking out practically from the side of the house."

Finally, when she continued to persist in her arguments, Martin had an answer. "I'm leaving it there, my love, so that our children can use it. When we have some."

"For God's sake, I'm not about to start having babies. I'm thirty-five years old." (He learned later that she was forty.)

"Still," he went on, "I can always hope."

"Hope all you want," Dorinda said and withheld the information that she already had two 'babies'. A sixteen-year-old daughter and an eighteen-year-old son. In the care of their father. Martin found out about them long after his blushing bride had departed and her children came to him (on instructions from their mother, he suspected). The ploy was that, as their stepfather, Martin should be willing to pay a certain amount of money for their upkeep.

But he wasn't that big a fool and, although it constituted another quite large outlay of money, Martin spent it on a divorce and was able to avoid any alimony payments to his ex. Money to a good lawyer was well spent, he thought, and under the circumstances, it didn't seem unfair to cease funding Dorinda's adventures.

Sometimes it seemed he would never be rid of Dorinda. Even when things returned more-or-less to normal—Maggie back in residence and he and Walter resuming their former working arrangements—there was an emptiness about the place. Maggie kept coming up with names of prospective partners, but single women in his age range were a rarity in the area. He didn't meet any who attracted him and he questioned the 'benefits' of matrimony in any case. Besides, he'd lost confidence in his ability to charm and amuse anyone other than his sister. But he was lonely.

"Come on, Martin, get over it," Maggie had said. "Get out. Socialize. Meet somebody. You're not that bad looking."

"I have a bald spot on top."

"So did Dad. The rest is curly and still black. You still have your boyish figure. And you're not all wrinkled up or anything. In fact, you like quite extinguished."

Martin laughed. "I'm not quite extinguished yet. But how about you?"

"I'm not going bald or wrinkled."

"I never said you were. What I meant was—what about you? You're not getting any younger. What about a boyfriend or husband for you? Didn't you meet any likely prospects in the city?"

"Are you kidding? Most of the ones who wanted to take me out already had wives and kiddies. And the one that wanted to move in with me only wanted a free place to stay so he could keep up the payments on his Jeep Cherokee. He worked in Eaton's, too. Men's shirts and ties. What a cathetic case he was."

"Then I guess we're stuck with each other."

"I'm not giving up yet," Maggie vowed.

But Martin thought he might as well abandon the matrimonial quest. It was too much trouble and, besides, he had a housekeeper, even if she was a bit daft at times. All in all, life could have been worse.

SANDRA'S WEDDING

Nora had been busy for the two months following Sandra's announcement that she and Nick were planning a big wedding for the end of June. She was flabbergasted at first. "It's not enough time to get the wedding cake made and set aside to ripen. You have no idea the kind of huffing and puffing that goes into making a big fruitcake—not to mention icing it and all the rest."

"So. Make something from a Betty Crocker cake mix instead. I don't care."

"You've got to be kidding! Your grandmother would have a hissy fit to end all hissy fits if we deviated one iota from tradition."

"Make it this week; it'll be OK."

Nora tried once again to reason with her daughter. "Wait until the end of August. We need time to get ready for the kind of a coronation you're proposing. "

"Mother! Teachers always get married at the end of June. As soon as school is out. Didn't you know that? And it's not a blasted coronation; it's a normal every

58

day kind of wedding. And I'll help as much as I can."

"How very generous of you," was all Nora could think of to say.

As she suspected, Nora had to pretty much go it alone. Sandra had her hands full winding up the school year, and it was all she could do to get herself to Maggie Kroeger's for wedding gown fittings. The groom, likewise, was busy finishing up his year as a high school teacher and no help could be expected from that quarter. Even if he'd had the time, Nick Kazakov was too much of a dreamer to make many concrete plans. He had, though, arranged for new positions for both himself and Sandra in Ontario. Guelph. So far away. He'd been able to swing that without much trouble, Nora thought bitterly.

She was left with making up the guest list, the wedding cake, the wedding invitations and all the other minutiae that has to be attended to. In four weeks she was tired. In five, almost totally exhausted, for the occasion had escalated to a grand affair involving over two hundred guests. On Nick's side of the house, vast numbers of people known only to his parents apparently expected to be included. And long forgotten friends and relatives kept springing into the mind of the elder Mrs. Fields who was manipulating the affair into a huge family reunion. When Walter objected to the inclusion of his cousin, Angela, and her son who lived in Florida, his mother was adamant. "They'll have to come to McClung sometime, anyway. You know, to bury the ashes of your Uncle John and Aunt Margaret."

"They died a long time ago. You mean she didn't bury them in Florida?"

"Of course not. They belong here. It would be the perfect time for her to do it."

"You mean, combine a wedding and a funeral?"

"Not a funeral exactly. An interment. Quiet. Just

immediate family. And on a different day, of course. In any case, another two guests won't be any big problem. And I already told you I was willing to pay for the wedding supper."

When Walter tried to object, his mother was exasperated. "You and Angela used to be great friends, for Heaven's sake! What's got into you?"

Walter didn't say what had gotten in to him, but thereafter gave up trying to call any of the shots.

If Maude Fields didn't have much faith in Walter and Nora's ability to draw up a comprehensive guest list, she was even less inclined to trust Nora's expertise in other matters. Her mother-in-law, evidently, considered Nora incapable of engineering such an auspicious event—the wedding of her favorite granddaughter. She phoned at least five times a day to see if they'd remembered to invite old Aunt Lizzie or second cousin Herbert or to ask if Nora had stored the wedding cake properly and had she included the proper amount of sherry? (Sherry was considered by the elderly lady to be non-alcoholic and, therefore, acceptable on rare occasions.) If Nora had been a drinking woman, she'd have drunk the sherry herself, and put grape juice in the cake. She tried to be as civil as possible but the constantly ringing telephone was beyond bearing and three days before the wedding she stopped answering it altogether.

It was on the day that Sandra had gone to visit her friend, Lori, who was to be one of the bridesmaids, leaving Nora and Maggie to embalm the tiny slices of wedding cake with Saran Wrap and then tie them with ribbons so they'd be sufficiently attractive to pass around to the guests. It was a frustrating and time-consuming job that Trevor could have helped with if he'd wanted. "Can't see why that big lout can't give us a hand now and again, instead of spending all his time in that blasted hammock," Maggie complained.

"He says his fingers are all thumbs."

"Garbage! Even as a little boy he could do stuff with his fingers that I never could. Remember when we made kites for him and Sandra when they were kids? He could do better than anybody. And when I used to baby-sit the kids, he was the one that could do that cat's cradle thing with the string. I never could figure it out. He's got real smart fingers, I know that for a fact. He's just got lazy. A lazy lout!"

Although that expressed Sandra's sentiments exactly, (and Nora, herself, was beginning to think in those terms), she wouldn't admit it. Besides, she didn't appreciate having her son referred to as a 'lout', even if Maggie had known him from a baby. But, instead of contradicting her she walked out of the kitchen, strode down the hall, and took a much-needed bathroom break. As she sat on the toilet, Nora was dimly aware that the phone rang a couple of times and then stopped.

She came back into the kitchen to find Maggie grinning to herself. "I answered the phone," she said and then laughed out loud.

"So?"

"So. It was the old troll herself. Again."

"I thought we agreed to let the darned thing ring."

"I know, but it was getting under my nerves." Then Maggie began laughing so hard she had to sit on a chair. She was holding her sides when she informed Nora, "They're fine now. My nerves."

"What on earth happened?"

"Not much." Maggie wiped her eyes on her Home Depot apron. "She wanted to talk to you like usual. I knew you wouldn't mind, so I told her you were dead."

"My God, Maggie! This is the goofiest thing you've ever done. And that's saying a lot." Nora sat across the table from Maggie and thought a moment. "What did Mother Fields say to my being dead? I mean, how did she take it?"

"She kinda gasped and then I hung up."

It took another moment for the prank to strike Nora as funny as it was apparently striking Maggie, and when it did, she laughed insanely. "Dead! Dead! Wouldn't the old girl be happy if that happened to be true. Except, she'd have to wrap this blasted cake herself. Her and the happy bride."

"Should I tell Trevor?" Maggie managed to ask.

"That I'm dead?"

"No, silly. About what I did."

This possibility sobered both women and thought of the fall-out also silenced them for the moment. Presently, Nora went to the phone, dialed her mother-in-law's number and hung up. "Busy," she said. "Can you imagine what's happening now? Who she's calling? All that."

"I guess I never thought of that. What should we do?"

"You mean, what should *you* do? It was *your* idea. Remember?"

"I guess for starters, I better go home. Almost time to make Martin's supper, anyways."

"Oh no, you don't. Your brother will just have to wait for his supper."

"For how long d'ya think?"

"I have no idea. Until Walter comes home, at least. He'll have to go tell his mother what happened—probably have to take you with him. Let's just try to finish this job and we'll see what happens."

All laughter gone, they worked in sullen silence until a police car, lights flashing, skidded to a stop in the driveway and two burly Mounties began pounding on the door.

"What's the offence, officer?" Nora asked, after admitting them.

The men looked around, as though fully expecting to see a blood-soaked body somewhere nearby. "We had a call about an unexplained death. This is the Field residence, isn't it?"

"Yes, but the call was a prank. This is Maggie Kroeger and she will explain it to you."

Nora had forgotten all about Trevor who was now standing just behind the uniformed men with his mouth hanging slightly ajar. "What in hell...?" he asked no one in particular. And then, to the officers, "Why are you harassing my mother?"

No one answered him—partly because Walter came charging into the house at that moment adding to the confusion. It was a half-hour or so before everything was explained, finally believed, and the Mounties left with the suggestion (more of an order, actually) that Walter, Nora and Maggie call on the elderly Mrs. Fields immediately to set the lady's mind at rest. They also warned Maggie that there might be a charge of public mischief laid against her.

It was not a happy occasion. Walter was furious and suggested, not too gently, that Maggie go home, to which Nora responded, "If she goes, I go and you can manage this damned wedding by yourself. Maybe you could get your mother to help you."

Walter shook his finger at her. "And don't you forget that my mother has generously promised to pay for the wedding supper. You have no right to insult her!" Before Nora could repeat that she hadn't done anything insulting, he stormed out of the house, jumped into his pick-up truck and wheeled out of the yard in a hail of gravel.

Trevor just grinned. "I presume he's going to explain to Grandmama. I kinda wish I could be there for that farce." Then he went back to his refuge in the hammock.

But it was Maggie who suffered the most indignity.

First, she was astonished that Walter—her friend, her neighbor, her idol—had practically ordered her out of his house. Not that she left, but that was Nora's doing and Walter was usually so calm. Then, even though she phoned and apologized to Walter's mother, it was not considered a sufficient penalty. Mrs. Fields Senior was not one to be easily mollified and she stoutly demanded that Maggie be banned from the wedding entirely. "She's always been a flighty, silly girl. Never know what kind of shenanigans she might get up to. Probably end up spoiling things in some way. And, you know yourself, Nora, I might have had a heart attack being told you were dead. So sudden, like that. I do not want her at my granddaughter's wedding. In fact, if she goes, I will simply have to stay away."

How Nora managed to hold her tongue in the face of such Maggie-abuse, she never knew. Over the years, she'd been used to her mother-in-law's shabby treatment but she should have stood up to the insult inflicted on Maggie. Perhaps, it was the thought of the financial help that stopped her, although she preferred to think it was because she was taking her mother-in-law's increasing senility into account. In any case, Nora spoke in a carefully measured, reasonable tone. "Maggie has always been a good friend to us. Like one of the family. She's known the kids since they were babies, she's baby-sat them and changed their pants...."

"I did that, too! You talk as though I never did anything for your children."

"I never said anything of the sort."

"I baby-sat them and changed their pants."

Nora could remember the one occasion when they'd left Sandra with her as an infant. It was also the one occasion when Maude Fields changed her diaper. And as far as Trevor was concerned, she scarcely paid him any attention. However, that was hardly the point and not worth mentioning. "Yes, Mother, you've been good to our children. We appreciate it, but this is Sandra's wedding and she'll have to be the one to make the decision about keeping Maggie from the wedding."

"Don't see why. Maggie's nothing to her."

Nora thought of reminding her mother-in-law that Maggie, a lifelong friend of Sandra's, was devoting her considerable skills to construction of her wedding dress and deserved to be in attendance, but only said, "Maggie is making Sandra's dress, you know. As her gift. It's going to be beautiful. It would break her heart not to be able to see Sandra actually getting married in it."

"Pooh! Making a dress is nothing. I could have done it myself if my eyesight was better. It's not that much of a gift."

Nora didn't trust herself to continue the conversation so she only said, with as much civility as she could muster, "Thanks for calling, Mother. Walter will discuss the matter of Maggie with you. Goodbye." She willed herself to hang up the receiver gently instead of smashing it into the base of the phone as she was aching to do, then snatched a tea towel, bunched it over her mouth and screamed as loudly as she could. It helped some.

The threat had to be taken seriously since Nora knew her mother-in-law might also withdraw her offer to finance the meal. And the infusion of some extra cash into the celebration would be a Godsend. It presented a huge problem for it was unconscionable to exclude Maggie.

A family consultation that included Maggie as well as the bride and groom lasted well into the night. It was Trevor who came up with the plan and even though Sandra was not, in theory, speaking to her brother, she had to agree that it was the only one possible. Walter was unhappy with the scheme, but couldn't come up with a better one. He had several stipulations, however. Maggie would have to make herself as scarce as possible. She would be unable to attend the rehearsal party at all and would be required to lie low at the reception—perhaps staying only long enough to eat.

Maggie would go to the wedding after all but she wouldn't be wearing the chiffon, floor-length, peach-colored dress she'd purchased at ACT 11 quality used clothing establishment in the city.

Luckily, Penguins (the costumers who were supplying the tuxedos for the groom and groomsmen) were able to outfit Maggie with a spanking white tux, complete with an elegant shirt and bow tie. A trifle fancy for an usher, perhaps, but workable, nevertheless. Maggie's brother, Martin, didn't mind relinquishing, what would have been his job. It was all for a good cause. The best they could come up with, in any case. An unsuspecting hairdresser complied with Maggie's request for a very short haircut and a dye job. A bright red dye job, as it turned out.

It was hard on her to miss the rehearsal and subsequent party and she plied Nora with questions. Maggie had also made the little flower girls' dresses and expected a detailed account of the event. "How did they look? The little girls' dresses?" she asked Nora breathlessly. And was disappointed to hear that they were wearing jeans, keeping the fancy pink organdy creations spick and span for the big day. The good news was that the tots had behaved themselves. "What about the new minister, Reverend Ferguson—how did he behave?"

The minister was another story and Nora hardly knew where to begin. Ferguson was a man who seemed ill fitted to his career, generally unhappy and unwilling to be anything more than coldly polite to the wedding party. Maggie was outraged by Nora's report that the good reverend's drill-sergeant orders scared the little girls half to death. He'd put a hand on the shoulder of the littlest one and barked, "You will stand over here by me." Wide-eyed with terror, the tot had obeyed but whimpered, "Okay, but don't pull my hair!"

Sandra and her two bridesmaids, already suffering from wedding nerves, burst into giggles which made both flower girls burst into tears. This unseemly response sent the clergyman into a cold, silent rage and he stared malignantly at each member, in turn as if to say, "Why am I continually forced to deal with fools and savages?"

Chastened, and anxious to change the subject, Sandra asked the minister, "When will Reverend Coates be back?"

"That is of no consequence, young lady." Then, relenting slightly, he added, "Mr. Coates is enjoying a bit of a holiday. We're not sure if... I mean, when, he'll be back."

Sandra's inquiry as to the whereabouts of Reverend Coates, innocent though it was, was an embarrassment to Nora since she knew the reason for his little 'holiday' but had forgotten to mention the affair to Sandra. Since Sandra was teaching at a school nearly a hundred miles away, she seldom had the opportunity to attend her home church and Nora had neglected to mention the Coates case. Perhaps she'd simply blocked it from her mind.

Reverend Coates, their previous preacher, had been quite popular with most of the congregation—especially the ones who approved of his stand on modesty and moderation—and was a distinct favorite of Mrs. Fields Sr. Until she had the misfortune to attend the town's Annual Pork Barbeque. It was during that event that Coates had come to earn his 'holiday' by getting immoderately drunk and doffing all his clothing before a stunned crowd of eighty or so McClung citizens. He was about to start a Conga line when a couple of parishioners escorted him off the premises.

So they were stuck with his replacement, who, Nora had to admit, conducted the actual marriage ceremony with dignity. "At least he kept all his clothes on," Walter remarked later. "And I suppose even preachers are entitled to a nervous breakdown at least once in their career."

The wedding day turned out to be one of the best that June could offer. Nora's expensive mother-of-the-bride dress (blue, with shoes dyed to match) fit very well, drew numerous compliments and remained unsoiled throughout the proceedings in spite of her penchant for spilling food and drink when she was nervous. Walter looked handsome and poised in his new dark gray suit. "Not at all like a farmer," Sandra had teased.

As they were about to proceed down the aisle—one on each side of their daughter, Nora glanced at Walter and, to her horror, saw tears running down his cheeks. She whispered to Sandra, "Hold up a minute," quickly located a Kleenex in her purse and handed it to him. They stood very still for a moment or two until he had regained his composure and, by then, Nora thought she might cry, too.

"Cool it," Sandra hissed. "Just cool it!" They got to the altar without further incident.

All in all, the big day had gone very well, the bridesmaids didn't giggle, the flower girls didn't cry, the bride and groom looked young and fabulous and hardly anyone recognized the slight, red-headed usher in the white tux. Certainly Maude Fields, who was awaiting cataract surgery, was unaware that Maggie was, indeed, in attendance. In any case, the grandmother of the bride was left in the care of a truly male usher on the far side of the church.

Most people seemed to think Maggie was some effeminate fellow from 'the other side of the family'. Probably, 'one of those strange Russians', in the case of the Fields clan. The Kazakov connection, no doubt, assumed the usher was one of those 'flashy Irish fairies' from the bride's mother's side of the family.

A number of people expressed surprise that Maggie wasn't there with her brother, Martin, since it was well known that the two were close friends of the Fields. When asked outright, Nora and Walter made vague reference to a flu bug that was going around. And Nora assumed that Walter's apparent anxiety had to do with Maggie's presence. He was on pins and needles all through the celebrations—particularly the reception, which was held in the church hall.

No hard liquor was allowed but a concession had been made to provide for one small glass of white wine to each adult for toasting purposes. Nora noticed that Trevor didn't drink his, but had used his water glass to toast his sister and her new husband. She made a mental note to ask him if he had a problem with alcohol and promptly forgot about it. Everyone else seemed to enjoy the novelty of actually consuming wine within the confines of the United Church and it disappeared in mere seconds.

Great crowds of people, both known and unknown, swarmed the reception hall and, while standing in the receiving line, Nora was nervous lest she forget the name of one of the Fields' relatives. It could happen, there were so many of them. As for the unknowns—friends of the bride and groom—they were no problem since Nora was unembarrassed to ask names of these young strangers. She smiled a lot and tried to forget about Maggie.

Walter, apparently, didn't forget about her, though, and kept a sharp eye on her comings and goings. Maggie had barely finished her cheese cake when it became obvious that one of Nick's pubescent nieces had become more than slightly enamored with the handsome dude in the white monkey suit. Walter rose abruptly from his seat at the head table, went quickly to speak to Martin, who, leaving his meal unfinished, took his sister by the arm and escorted her out of the room and home.

Maggie's departure was a relief and Nora and Walter were able to give their full attention to an escalating political disagreement between Nora's red-neck Texan brother-in-law, Hank, and an uncle of Nick's who held more liberal views. The subject was capital punishment, and while Nora was willing to kill them both, it was her sister, Audrey, who came to the rescue by confronting her husband with the latest news. "I was looking for the ladies' room and discovered your idiot son standing in the vestibule smoking a joint."

While liquor consumption (in moderation) was perfectly acceptable to most members of the United Church of Canada, marijuana use was not. Especially not on church property. So the argument came to an end when the Texan stomped away on his zillion dollar cowboy boots to tend to the offender. Audrey just grinned and whispered to Nora in her newly acquired Texas drawl, "Now y'all can relax and have fun."

And, for the most part, they did. Following the speeches and the toasts, the entire company moved across the street to a hall where the wedding dance was held. It was a night of dancing, visiting, reminiscing and much laughter. The bride and groom danced together and were joined by the wedding party and the parents. Nora and Walter danced with Nick's parents and then Nora danced with Nick and Walter with Sandra. Walter even led his mother around the floor in a slow waltz. Nora noticed that he had tears in his eyes occasionally. Walter would miss having his daughter around—the two enjoyed a special bond. Nora would miss her, too, for in spite of some mother/daughter differences of opinion, she and Sandra were close. Weddings were emotional affairs.

Long tables had been set up along the sides of the hall and people gathered in clusters visiting, laughing and drinking. Angela and Mario sat with the crowd at their table. At first, Nora was embarrassed by Walter's formal coolness towards his cousin and her son and remembered how unenthusiastic he'd been at the idea of including them in the invitations. Nora wondered, briefly, what had been behind Walter's objections. In any case, the two cousins seemed to be warming to each other and, since Mario had found a pretty young bridesmaid to dance with, and Walter and Angela were deep in conversation, she relaxed. There wasn't going to be a donnybrook after all. She left them to their conversation and began going around the hall speaking with guests and was too busy to wonder what was happening back at her table.

From time to time, Nora would catch sight of the bride and groom dancing or visiting with their many friends. She was proud of her beautiful daughter and hoped that, in time, she'd become fonder of Nick, too. It was just that, right then, it felt as though he'd stolen Sandra out from under their noses and was taking her so far away. She had mixed feelings about that. They were a handsome couple, though—Nick dark and good looking and Sandra a picture-perfect vision right out of Today's Bride. When it was time for them to pass the tiny, wrapped pieces of cake that she and Maggie had slaved over, Sandra and Nick performed the ritual as though they had done it many times before. They might just have escaped from a movie set—so self-assured and handsome!

Just a few more dances, a cold buffet lunch and it was time for the bride to throw her bouquet before she and Nick took their leave. Nora had a twinge of guilt thinking how Maggie would have enjoyed joining the group of squealing girls all intent on catching the prize.

Nora looked them over, half expecting to see Maggie in the line-up wearing some exotic get-up to disguise her appearance. But she wasn't there. She was almost sorry that Maggie hadn't come up with another costume in order to join the flower-catching competition. The peach chiffon Maggie had originally bought second hand for the wedding would have been fine. She would have had to find a wig, though, if fooling Maude Fields was still a priority with anyone. Now that the big event was nearly over, deceiving her mother-in-law was no longer a priority with Nora. She felt a wave of guilt thinking how they'd all let themselves be intimidated by a snooty old lady, and had allowed Maggie to be put in such a ridiculous position. They should never have counted on financial help from Mrs. Fields Sr., but made whatever arrangements they could afford in order not to be held hostage to such a mean-spirited plan. Too late now, though. The bouquet had been thrown, a winner declared and the bride and groom had departed. Nora sighed as the band began to play for the last part of the evening.

Just as Nora had been thinking these unkind thoughts about her mother-in-law, the lady, herself, appeared at Nora's elbow. She had Walter and Angela in tow. "It's been a lovely evening, my dear but I'm very tired. Walter has offered to drive me home. And Angela wants to go back to the motel."

"I've a bit of a headache," Angela explained, "but

Mario will likely stay until the end of the dance. I hope you don't mind our stealing Wally for a bit. It's been marvelous. Perhaps we can all get together before Mario and I have to leave for home." She looked around the hall. "Trevor seems to have come back. I think Mario wants to have a visit with him. Find out what this Marine Biology is all about."

Nora was surprised. "Trevor was away?"

"Just for a little while," Angela replied. "He said he'd forgotten something at home. Maybe his camera. Anyway, we're off. Thanks for a wonderful day."

Nora wondered briefly why Trevor had found it necessary to go home during the party but forgot about it when Walter's sisters demanded some of her time. She seldom saw Mattie, who lived in Barrie, Ontario and now seemed thrilled to know that Sandra and Nick would be living in Guelph, not far from them. "We'll be able to get together from time to time. That will be lovely. I can actually get to know my niece."

"You'll find that she's just as nice as she looks," Phyllis gushed—not to be outdone. "Ever since she's been a little girl she's wanted to be a teacher and work with children. Why, I remember her talking about it as far back as when she was about eight years old. Cute little thing she was, with long pigtails."

Nora wondered how Phyllis had come by that information since her visits had been so infrequent, even though she lived not far away in Winnipeg. And Sandra had never worn pigtails in her life. An odd relationship Walter's sisters had with his family. With each other, too, it appeared. Nora could sense the rivalry between them and was uncertain how to maintain a balance now that she seemed to be the catch of the day.

"John and the boys would really like to have come," Mattie confided, "but they are all so caught up in things. John is a bank manager now with the Royal,

73

as you know. And right now, things are so busy at work. I worry about him. I really do."

"Besides," Phyllis cut in with a smirk, "you said it would be awkward for him to take days off now since he'd need extra time in the fall when you go on that Mediterranean Cruise."

Mattie went on as though Phyllis hadn't spoken. "And the boys. Well, Geoff has his law practice which takes up way too much of his time."

"Which is why his marriage broke up," Phyllis added helpfully.

Again she was ignored in order that Mattie could relate the achievements of her youngest son. "Bernard has been working hard getting his chiropractor's license."

Phyllis grinned. "Couldn't make it in a regular medical school."

That was too much for Mattie. "What do you know? He never even applied at McMaster. Never wanted to be a regular doctor. Ever. He knows what a bunch of quacks most of them are! And what about your precious husband? Where is he? Do you have any idea?"

"My Harvey is away at an important conference. In Ottawa," Phyllis huffed.

"Accompanied by one of his bosomy secretaries, I presume."

"You're so full of crap!"

"And your Brenda, where is she? I thought she'd have been happy to come to the wedding of her only girl cousin. Too many heads of hair waiting to be cut?"

Phyllis, trying to regain her composure, turned to Nora. "Brenda has her own shop. This is a busy time of year. I told you that when I replied to the RSVP thing."

Nora's head was spinning but she tried to smile. "Of course, you did," she managed to reply. "Well, it's been nice hearing about all the kids but I think I'd better go and talk to some of the other guests." She turned then and left her sisters-in-law to duke it out, but not before hearing Mattie say to Phyllis, "There now, are you happy? You've done it again...."

So great was Nora's relief at escaping the warring sisters that she fairly flung herself into being the perfect hostess. She flitted from group to group, table to table like a demented butterfly. At one point, Audrey approached her. "Nora, how much have you had to drink?"

"Just the wine at supper. Why?"

"Oh, no reason. Just that your cheeks are all flushed and you almost staggered there once."

"Just tired. That's all. And these shoes! Haven't been able to buy a comfortable pair since Leahy's Shoe Store went out of business!"

Audrey laughed. "You must write and tell Da."

"He'd be pleased. Anyway, you don't need to worry about me drinking too much."

"I just wondered, that's all. I never thought a wedding could turn a person into a whirling dervish. But do your thing. Carry on."

Nora carried on. Most people seemed to be in high spirits and she laughed and chatted with them all. Danced, too. She even found herself in the midst of a group of tipsy high-steppers involved in the old Chicken Dance.

Presently, she began saying good night to some of the older guests who were ready to go home. Walter wasn't anywhere in sight and she had to do the honors alone. Some dance enthusiasts had paid the band to play for an extra hour, so it was very late by the time she was able to collect Audrey, Hank and Jason and announce that it was time to go home.

Past time, as far as Audrey was concerned, but they had hung in with Nora and she appreciated that.

Even at that late hour, Nora didn't feel exhausted. She'd long since passed that point and was now into her second wind and the sisters sat up talking in Nora's kitchen. Audrey's husband and son had retired for the night. The women were still at it at three-thirty in the morning.

The sisters' age difference, once a factor in the growing-up years, had dissolved in the time since. Because Audrey had moved to the States soon after marrying her Texan, the two had been deprived of one another's company for a long time. One evening together hardly made up for the past, but it was a help and neither noticed the late hour.

"It would have been nice if Da could have been here," Nora sighed. "We sent him an invitation, of course. But, you know him."

"A ticket from Ireland is pretty expensive and he was here just two years ago."

"I know. But his own granddaughter. His only granddaughter. You'd think he might have sprung for that."

"Da didn't spring much for anybody, did he? I mean, I don't think Mother ever had very much. No money of her own or anything. And he kept hauling her around the country—from Alberta to Ontario to Manitoba. I think she'd have liked to go back to Ireland but that was never a consideration, I guess."

"Oh well, by the time he could afford to go, she was already dead."

"And by the time he was rid of the two of us—less than a year after I left home—he sailed off to Ireland."

"There's something else," Audrey said hesitantly. Another thing. I've always wondered... I mean, did you ever wonder about how she died?"

Nora was shaken by the unexpected question, but only said, "I *know* how she died. Under the wheels of a semi-trailer."

"What I mean is, do you think it was an accident?"

Nora sighed. "I don't know. That's what they told us. That's what Da believed. Why?"

"Because I always worried that maybe it wasn't. I think maybe she knew that truck was coming when she stepped off the curb. Because I think she was maybe manic depressive. How come we never talked about it, you and I?"

"I guess neither of us wanted to believe she'd leave us on purpose."

"Well, it scares me to think I could do something like that myself. Maybe. If I was half-crazy with worry or something."

Nora was concerned. "And do you often feel half-crazy with worry?"

"Not really. The usual stuff, you know. I just wonder sometimes... I always thought that you and Da knew something I didn't."

Nora put her arm around her sister. "No. At least, I didn't know anything for sure. Maybe, Da. But I don't think so. I'm sure he loved her in his own way. Look, it's quite possible that is was an accident. She was probably distracted and didn't notice the red light. Anyway, what's done is done. There's no use in dwelling on it."

"Sorry to bring it up," Audrey said. "It crosses my mind sometimes, that's all. And Da isn't what you'd call a warm, giving type."

"But he did send Sandra some expensive Waterford Crystal. Do you think he might marry again?"

"I doubt it. Like I said, for an Irishman, Da is definitely a cold fish."

"I suppose so. He's reserved, anyway. Walter's a bit reserved, too. It's not such a bad thing."

"I wouldn't know. Reservation isn't one of Hank's strong points. I'm sure you've noticed." Audrey thought for a moment. "But I never thought of Walter as reserved, either. How do you mean? Reserved in company or reserved in bed?"

"Not in company. At least, not usually. As for bed, I'm sure I don't know. I have no one to compare him with."

"Do you ever wish you had? I mean, had someone else before Walter?"

"I'm not sure. I can't imagine it, somehow. How about you?"

"I did. Remember Richard Hayes?"

"The Hayes where you used to baby-sit!?"

"The very one. He used to drive me home after I'd been sitting. One thing led to another, as they say."

"My God! You were only seventeen or so. He had a wife!"

"And children. That's why I was there. But I thought he was a handsome brute and he knew how to flatter a girl."

"How long did that go on?"

"About six months or so. Up until the time his wife got pregnant again. He said he wasn't sleeping with her anymore. You know. The usual. But, in retrospect, it was better *she* got pregnant than me."

"You didn't tell me a thing about it."

"I didn't tell anyone. Can you imagine what Da would have said?"

"I wouldn't have told Da. Do you think Richard's wife knew?"

"I didn't think so at the time. Now, when I think about it at all, I imagine she knew something was up. Wives have a tendency to know things like that. Anyway, I got out before Da found out or *I* got pregnant."

"Good thing, too."

"And then there was Wilson," Audrey continued. "He was in my Philosophy class in University. That lasted until I came home for Christmas vacation that year. When I got back, he had another girlfriend. I was heartbroken—for about a week. Amazing how fast young hearts heal, isn't?"

"Speaking of hearts, I'm worried about Trevor. Something seems to be wrong with him but I can't think what. I just wonder if he's broken up with some-one. But he won't talk about it. Or anything. I wish he'd open up with us. Or, at least, with me. He and Walter don't seem to talk much."

"Was Walter disappointed when Trevor decided to be a Marine Biologist?"

"Some. I suppose he'd hoped his son would take over the farm someday. But he didn't object too strenuously. I remember him telling Trevor that people always had to eat. There'd always be farmers. Sometimes I have my doubts on that score. Not that people don't have to eat, but that there'll always be farmers. At least, on a smaller scale." Nora shook her head. "With everything getting bigger and bigger and all that..."

Audrey seemed shocked. "You're worried? I always thought you and Walter had the world by the tail. Are you in trouble financially?"

"Well, not exactly. Not yet, anyway. But Walter wor-ries all the time. Lately, it's been even worse. He's so distracted. Goes driving alone at night. He hardly seems to notice I'm around."

"He's probably just upset at losing his only daughter."

"Maybe. I've wondered about that. Plus, I don't think he believes that Nick will be a good breadwinner."

"Oh, honey! Times have changed. Sandra's not helpless. She'd get along even if Nick doesn't set the world on fire. And he seems like a really nice guy. I only hope Jason grows up to have such good manners. Sometimes he drives me crazy. Him and his dad! Hank has no patience at all. Gets his shorts in a knot every time Jason does something he disapproves of. Like tonight, for instance. Hank's smoked pot lots of times. It's more alcohol I'm afraid of. Some of the kids in his high school. Well, they do a lot of drinking. And so many of them are packing guns nowadays. All we can do is hope that Jason doesn't get into that. Did your kids get into pot and booze?"

"Some, I suppose. Not a lot, though. Not that we knew of. In fact, I don't think Trevor drinks at all now. I don't know why that is. I just hope it isn't because he's got a drinking problem. And he left for awhile during the party, apparently. Came home for something. At least, that's what Angela said. It wouldn't have surprised me if he'd just decided to come home to bed. But, later, he turned up again. He sat and visited with Mario and some other younger people. I'm worried about him. He seems to need so much rest I wonder if he's depressed or something."

"You always were a worrywart. Maybe he's just decided that he's going to have a different life-style. Maybe he thinks life's too short..."

Nora was thoughtful. "We've never been in the habit of keeping a lot of liquor on hand. Just when company comes, or something."

"There you go—you see—Trevor hasn't been raised in a drinking household so he's probably not in the habit of drinking much himself. Quit fretting over it. Just think of today. It was a wonderful day. You must be proud."

"Oh, I am. It's just that Trevor doesn't seem to be himself at all and he and Sandra have had a horrendous falling out. So silly. They're so silly, my kids."

After Nora went into a detailed explanation of the falling out, Audrey hugged her sister and said, "You were right. They are silly. Both of them. You'll just have to take Walter's advice. Forget it. It'll work itself out. Like I said, think of the good things—the wedding. It was beautiful. And so many people that I hadn't seen for ages. And all of Walter's relatives—I didn't realize he had so many!"

"Yeah. And at that, they didn't all come. I got a blow-by-blow of why his brothers-in-law and the kids didn't turn up. From his sisters. You should have heard it!"

Nora was a good mimic and Audrey roared with laughter upon hearing Nora's report of the Mattie/ Phyllis bout, then said, "Well, relatives aren't all as congenial as you might wish. And speaking of relatives, I finally got to meet the fabled Angela. A first cousin of Walter's isn't she? I'd always heard she was good looking, but what a knock out. I don't think I remember her from before."

"Me neither. She was gone before Da hauled us out here from Ontario. The family never talks about her much. I'm sort of surprised she accepted the invitation. It was Mother Fields' idea. Walter was furious at first but then he admitted that since all the other cousins were invited, it would have looked kind of funny to leave Angela out. Maybe they didn't get along or something. I don't think he's mentioned her twice since I've known him. Although Mother Fields has occasionally referred to her as, 'the one that got away'. Whatever that means."

"Probably just means she got out of McClung—away from the clutches of family."

"Well, her own daughters got away and she never complains about that."

"Not much wonder, by what you've told me."

"Mattie and Phyllis have never gotten along with their mother but nobody ever says much about that either. It would have been better if they'd been staying at the motel instead of with her. I'm sure the infighting goes on wherever they are and it has to be distressing for the old lady."

"You don't much care for your mother-in-law, do you?"

"Not really, but I do feel sorry for her now and then. Now, for instance! Anyway, Walter and Angela are about the same age and they must have played together as kids, so it's kind of odd that he never mentions her."

Audrey laughed. "Well, you know men. Out of sight, out of mind. Or something. But he certainly noticed her tonight. He danced with her enough times. By the way, where is the father of the bride? I haven't seen him for ages."

"I expect he came home to bed after he drove his mother and Angela home. He couldn't have known that the party would last so long. I think it's been a hard day for him. Losing Sandra and all that."

"My God, Nora! You talk as if Sandra had died or something! She only got married. It's not like she's gone forever."

Nora's eyes filled with tears. "I know that. It's just that.... Things won't ever be the same."

"Things won't be the same—things will be better. You have another son now, and maybe, someday, you'll have grandchildren."

"Sorry, I'm not usually so negative."

"I know that. I think you need a good rest. Why don't you plan on a trip to Texas? It isn't the end of the earth, you know. Come and spend a couple of weeks with me in McAllen. Meet my friends. See the country. We could take a spin up to San Antonio. Do some fancy shopping, walk the River Walk, tour the missions, do the Alamo. I love that city. God! I hated to move from there. Still, Hank had a chance to buy this really good cowboy store in the Rio Grande Valley. Only don't call it a cowboy store in front of him. It's Western Wear. Everybody dresses like cowboys."

Nora had to laugh. "You don't dress like a cowboy."

"No, but enough people do to make dressing them a thriving business. And, for God's sake stop worrying about Walter and Trevor. They're probably not worrying about you. In fact, I bet they're upstairs sleeping like babies right now."

✑

And Walter was, indeed, in bed when Nora finally retired—sleeping like a baby or, at least, pretending to, just as Audrey had predicted. Too tired to put on her nightie, Nora slipped out of her dress, unhooked her bra and went to bed in her underwear. She snuggled up to Walter but he turned his back and moved away from her. It was silly, she knew—even unfair, since he was sleeping—but she felt spurned. She bit her lip and determined to think only good thoughts.

Her mind spun through the day's events—a kaleidoscope of activities—it finally came to rest on her meeting with Angela. Angela, newly widowed, and her tall, handsome son, Mario. When Walter, somewhat reluctantly, introduced Nora to them, she immediately noticed, and pointed out, Mario's pronounced resemblance to his mother's side of the family.

Angela just laughed and said, "Really!? Most people think he's the spitting image of his Italian father."

"Oh, but surely you can see it. The reddish hair, the green eyes. Just like Walter's. Even his nose!"

"All I've ever noticed is the Minnelli in him but I suppose the Fields' genes are in there somewhere."

Poor Mario! Nora cringed at the memory—she'd blundered on as though the person they were discussing weren't even there. "Of course, I never met his father. All I can see is the Fields' features." Then, suddenly, feeling Mario's eyes on her, she took him into the conversation. "You even look a bit like our son, Trevor. Speaking of Trevor, have you had a chance to meet him yet?"

Mario seemed relieved that his features were no longer of paramount interest and smiled. "Oh, I saw him in the wedding party and Mother figured out who he was. Didn't get to meet him yet. I'd sure like to, though. Mother's never been much for keeping up a relationship with our Canadian relatives and he looks like he'd be somebody interesting to know." Even Mario's voice reminded Nora of Trevor's, but she didn't mention it.

"Well, we'll soon fix that. Walter, will you go and hunt him down?"

Walter seemed all too glad of the diversion and returned momentarily with Trevor in tow. "I had to drag him away from a couple of pretty girls," he said before making the formal introductions.

The cousins eyed one another briefly. "Real glad to meet you," Mario said. "Likewise. Will you be staying around for awhile?"

Angela had answered for her son, "We have to leave late Monday afternoon. Mario has to get back to his job as our capable restaurant manager. Or I should say, restaurants, we have three now," She looked affectionately at Mario. "He's a busy man so we only have a few days. I wanted him to meet some of his relatives, though. And, of course, to be on hand for the interment. I thought he should see where his maternal grandparents are to be buried. That's really why I had him come along up to Canada with me. And it's been wonderful to see Aunt Maude after all these years."

"She's a great old gal," Mario said.

Although that wouldn't have been Nora's assessment of her mother-in-law, she was glad that Mario appreciated her.

84

"She knows all kinds of family stuff. I'd like to get her to tape some of her memories. Just to have. To keep. I'd like that."

Angela cut in quickly. "There won't be a lot of time for that sort of thing,"

Walter cleared his throat. "But there'll be the gift opening at our place tomorrow. Mother will be there. You and Mario are both welcome to come. Everybody's welcome."

"A gift opening? What's that?" Mario asked.

"It's probably not the custom in Florida," Walter informed him, "but the newlyweds around here usually get together with family and friends the day after the wedding and open their gifts."

"Then everybody has to be fed again," Nora sighed, thinking of all the lasagna she'd stashed in the deep freeze for the event. Not to mention all the cakes and cookies she and Maggie had made and frozen, and the hundred-cup coffee maker she'd borrowed from the church.

"Before they go on their honeymoon? They open their gifts and eat again?"

"Well, yes."

"At a restaurant?" Mario asked.

Nora looked at Mario and laughed. "Unfortunately, no."

"I think it's a wonderful idea—the gift opening day, I mean. Maybe I could popularize the idea back home and encourage the families to come to our restaurants."

"Don't mind Mario, he's always looking for ways to increase business. Anyway, it's a new tradition since I got married, I guess."

"Things change," Walter said.

Angela seemed thoughtful. "I didn't know about the gift opening. I guess we'll have to have the interment the following day." She looked at Walter, "I especially

85

want you to be there. It can be in the morning, I
suppose, since our flight out leaves in late afternoon."

"That's rushing it a bit for you, Mother. How would
it be if I went on ahead—after the interment. I'll leave
for the airport right from the cemetery and you can
stay on for a few more days."

Nora left them discussing the pros and cons of the
return trip to Florida and table-hopped around the
room visiting with still more relatives while Walter
stayed on, chatting with Angela. She saw Mario and
Trevor drift away toward a table of young people and
thought again how much alike they were.

Nora finally fell asleep wondering how she would
ever get through the next couple of days. "Give me
the strength," she prayed. "And enough food to go
around."

*

With the help of Audrey, as well as Maggie and the
bridesmaids, Nora managed the 'gift opening' with a
minimum of stress. She thought she had never seen
so much tissue paper and ribbon and wondered how
the bride and groom would manage to transport the
newly acquired loot to their new home in Ontario.

"My God!" Angela said, "I've never seen such a pile
of stuff in my life. Certainly wasn't like this when I
was married."

"Me, neither," Nora agreed, and thought briefly of
the scanty provisions with which she and Walter had
started their lives together. Then she smiled. "But
we had all we needed, Walter and I. We had each
other and we managed just fine."

But it was mainly providing and delivering the food
to the fifty or sixty invited guests that occupied Nora's
thoughts and time. Luckily, since the day was fine—
warm and sunny with almost no wind—the event

went off according to plan. Adding to the success of the party was the fact that Mother Fields either didn't notice Maggie's presence or decided that, since she wasn't paying for the food, there was no point in creating a disturbance.

After the guests were gone and Sandra and Nick finally departed on their honeymoon to Clear Lake, Walter, Trevor, Angela and Mario attended to the cleanup duties amid much laughter and horseplay. Nora was happy to see her son and husband engaged in a useful activity and, apparently, enjoying it.

And after Angela and Mario returned to their motel, Walter helped Nora organize and store the gifts in Sandra's old bedroom. Following one of his many sneezing fits, Trevor excused himself and went to bed.

Nora sighed. "Now all we have to do is get through tomorrow. Thank God, we have no responsibilities concerning that. I think I'll go to bed now. You coming soon?" she asked hopefully, but Walter just grunted something she couldn't make out.

Walter didn't go out for his nightly drive, but sat up very late watching the television set. At least, that's where Nora left him when she dragged herself, exhausted, to bed.

TREVOR FIELDS

Nora watched her son, hoping he would be unaware of her scrutiny. Slightly shorter than his father, at just under six feet, Trevor still gave the impression of huskiness, but Nora was beginning to doubt that his appearance reflected the true state of his health. For one thing, the circles under his eyes had become more pronounced during the ten days he'd been home. The frantic time preceding Sandra's wedding had flown by and it seemed there had been no opportunity to have a real conversation with him.

Now it was time for Trevor to get back to his summer job in Vancouver and he was driving as they headed to the Winnipeg airport. Trevor and his father had said their goodbyes earlier, since Walter had begged off the Winnipeg trip. Privately, Nora questioned his excuse; did the hay baler really have to be repaired that very morning or was he unable to face lingering airport farewells? Walter was well known for his emotional reactions. In any event, it did give her and her son some time together. Not that much had been said thus far beyond remarks regarding the size and color of the new crops. And, at that point, Nora knew that neither of them gave a hoot about the height of winter wheat or which farmers had changed over from growing cereal crops to root vegetables.

"Yesterday went pretty well, I think," Nora said, referring to the interment of Angela's parents' ashes.

"I suppose."

"Did you get much chance to visit with Mario?"

"Some. Not much. He wasn't there long."

"I noticed you talking at the wedding dance."

"Yeah."

The conversation wasn't going anywhere that Nora could see, but she continued. "Do you like him? I mean, I know he's very interested in the family history. Did he ask you things?"

"I liked him fine. He asked me quite a lot about the family. Although why he should care is beyond me."

Nora was taken aback by his offhand answers. "Why? Don't you care about family?"

"To some extent."

"To what extent?"

"Not to the extent that you guys and Sandra think I should."

Nora didn't particularly want to get into another Sandra versus Trevor fray so, after Trevor had sneezed for about the tenth time, she brought up the health topic once more. "I don't like the way you keep doing that. I really wish you'd have seen Doctor Hughes while you were home. Be sure to see somebody as soon as you get back."

"Oh, for Pete's sake, Mother, not that again. I already told you a hundred times, it's just an allergy thing. I thought it might be better on the prairies than it's been at the coast, but it seems to have gotten worse, even though I've been taking antihistamines all along. It'll clear up in a week or so."

"Still, I don't like it. And your color is awful. Those circles under your eyes..."

"I'm just tired, is all."

"What from?"

"I don't know." Then he added a heavily sarcastic, "The excitement, maybe."

Nora ignored his tone and said gently, "Or maybe you're upset with Sandra?"

To that, Trevor just grunted and was silent for some moments before taking a deep breath and launching into his tirade. "I don't see why she has to get on her high horse all the time. Just because she's used to bossing me around. When is she going to realize I'm not her baby brother any more? I'm her grown up brother with a mind and a brain of his own." He slammed his fist into his thigh, "Damn her, anyway! I don't hate Nick, like she said. I don't look down on him either. Why should I? He's an OK guy. Only he'll sure have his work cut out for him living with that shrew."

Nora patted his arm. "There, there, don't get all upset. Sandra had a bad case of wedding nerves. She's not mad at you, particularly."

"Then she gave a pretty damned good imitation of mad. Anyway, to hell with her. At least I won't have to see her again for a long time. Maybe never," he said, grimly.

Nora bit her lip. Things weren't going the way she'd hoped and she felt a familiar wave of guilt. Somehow she should have been able to help her children over this silly fight. She'd always been able to do it before. She was close to tears. "I wish I could help you through this. Wish there was something I could do. This isn't right, you know, leaving with all these bitter feelings."

He ignored the remark. "You know what? She didn't even ask me to dance at the wedding dance. She danced with everybody else."

Nora was flabbergasted. "Didn't ask *you*?! Did it ever occur to you that it was *your* place to ask *her*?"

"I don't happen to think so. Anyway, forget it, Mother. It doesn't involve you."

"Doesn't involve me?!"

"No. Or Dad, either, for that matter. Just forget it ever happened."

Nora marveled at the insensitivity of her children. Did neither one of them realize that parents were involved all of their lives? Did they not realize that the things that hurt their children also hurt them? Perhaps, when they had children of their own....

As though divining her thoughts, Trevor said, "If Sandra and Nick ever have any kids, I hope they're the worst little buggers the world has ever seen."

For some reason, this struck Nora funny, but she had the good sense not to laugh.

"If I ever have children—and that's a very remote possibility—but if I ever do, I'll treat them exactly the same. No favorites."

This was no longer funny. Now, she was expected to deal with the subject of favoritism—or the lack of it. All she could say was. "I'm not sure what you're driving at."

"Favoritism. I think I just mentioned it. As in Sandra. She and Dad have always been such buddies. You know that. The sun rises and sets on her—not to mention that dear old Grandmama feels the same way."

Although it was true that Maude Fields doted on her granddaughter, Nora had assumed that Trevor had taken the obvious in stride, had adjusted to it. She was wrong.

"I don't know why you and Dad let her get away

91

with it. Why didn't you tell her that I was part of the family, too. You know, mentioned it from time to time. Insist on some fair play."

Nora wanted to tell her son that, over the years, she'd tried on numerous occasions to do just that, but she was given no chance to explain. In any case, her mind reeled under the attack and it was doubtful she could have formed a coherent reply.

"The money she spent on Sandra's clothes! Always some new dress. New shoes. Whatever. Nothing at all for me. You guys, too. You always made sure Sandra was dressed like a princess or something."

Apparently, Trevor remembered going through his young life in tatters, which was certainly not the case. Just keeping him shod was always an interesting financial experience. But, in Nora's flustered state, these kinds of rebuttals were not available. Nor would she have had time to put them forward.

"Dad always called her his 'Little Princess'. Did you ever hear him call me his 'Little Prince'?"

Nora sat mute and puzzled during her son's harangue. Clearly, he had a few things to get off his chest. 'Why now?' she wondered. 'What in the world has brought on this onslaught? What has happened to change my good-natured, fun-loving son into an angry, angry young man?' But for the moment, all she could do was listen and hope that she wouldn't cry out in pain or frustration.

"And she was so mean to me and you didn't care! Remember the time Sandra threw my Bic Banana out the car window and Dad wouldn't stop the car to get out and look for it? Said the traffic was too heavy. I could have found it if he'd let me look. She was supposed to buy me another one, but did she ever? No bloody way. My favorite pen that Sally Hansen had given me for Christmas. Remember that?" he demanded.

Remember his Bic Banana!!? Nora didn't know how to answer. She recalled many back seat fights, but not that particular one. And it seemed so petty.

"What is wrong, here?" she finally asked, as patiently as she could. "This is not an adult conversation."

Trevor wasn't listening, though, and ranted on. And on. It seemed that all the slights he'd ever received at the hands of his family were resurrected.

Eventually, the rant wound down and, with it, Nora's anger. She leaned over and looked closer into her son's face. "Trevor, you're really not well, are you?"

He ignored her question, so she pressed on. "Are you?"

He laughed shortly, following another sneezing fit. "Well. not exactly. Not at the moment, anyway."

"I'm very worried about you. Maybe you're overtired? Working too hard?"

"Lord, no. I mostly do filing and stuff. Those poor guys have to make out a zillion reports about every fender bender in the city. I help. Mostly sit at a desk. Boring as hell. I'll be glad to get back to University in the fall. That's what's interesting."

"You glad you decided on Marine Biology?"

"Sure. Glad enough. Better than police work any day."

Since Trevor was now in a more rational state of mind, Nora felt she could appeal to his common sense. "You really must get over all the bad memories you have. I'm truly sorry for any harm we may have caused you. Believe me, if we did things that hurt you, it was unintentional. You must know that your father loves you dearly. I don't see how you could doubt it for a moment. And so do I. And so, believe it or not, does Sandra. And as far as your grandmother is concerned... Well, she's always been a bit different. You must know that, too. She's a bit possessive, a bit overbearing. She doesn't treat me that well, either. Never did. When I think back to when your dad and I were first married! Actually, she's a mean-spirited old bitch. Always has been."

It was, apparently, the right thing to say. Trevor roared with laughter. "My God, Mother, I never thought I'd hear you say that! Never thought I'd hear the truth about the old troll from your own lips. You! You, of all people! Dad mumbles into his beard about her sometimes, but he never really comes right out and tells her off."

"Well, she's his mother. I guess he doesn't want to get too lippy."

"And Aunt Phyllis and Aunt Mattie! Aren't they the pair of witches? Serves Grandmama right to have daughters like that. I wonder how come they turned out that way."

Nora wanted to suggest that the same kind of jealousy that was causing a rift in her own family was implicated in the estrangement of her sisters-in-law, but she didn't want to be too tactless. Maybe he'd figure it out on his own. She only said, "I don't know. I've often wondered the same thing. The jealousy! It seems to drive them mad. Turns them into braggarts. Liars, even. Oh well, we're not lumbered with their presence very often. Did they offend you?"

Trevor laughed again. "Offend me? Hardly! They were so busy sucking up to me, telling me what a fine boy I was. Maybe to get in Dad's good books. Who knows? Anyway, I found it kind of interesting. A psychological mystery, or something."

Luckily, by the time they were approaching the airport, the tension between them had dissipated and when they arrived, Trevor said, "I won't bother parking in the lot. I'll just jump out at the Air Canada door, grab my bag and you can carry on. Won't take a minute."

And it didn't. Suddenly, after stopping the car, he gave her a brief kiss on her cheek, jumped out, grabbed his duffel bag from the back seat and leaned in the window to say, "Sorry if I've upset you."

All she could think to say before he disappeared through the big automatic glass doors was, "Please see a doctor as soon as you get back." Then he was gone, her last sentence, "Remember, we love you so much," still hanging, unheard, in the air.

The drive home took longer than usual because Nora had to keep stopping to cry—or, at least, to blow her nose and clean her glasses. At one point, she turned off the highway and drove a mile or so to the Assiniboine River where she knew of a quiet place to park for a time.

She had an uncomfortable foreboding. Her family, the one she'd loved and nurtured all these years, was falling apart before her very eyes. She knew of lots of places where she and Walter might have done better with the children, but they couldn't have gone completely wrong. Nora and Walter, like all parents she knew, did the best they could with the resources they had. But other people's children grew up loving one another. Or tolerating each other.

The trouble between Sandra and Trevor was, apparently, long standing and much deeper than she'd thought. Nora couldn't imagine feeling such animosity toward her own sister and, in a way, they'd had more problems to contend with than Trevor and Sandra ever had. Being trundled around the country by a father who, if not indifferent, was certainly not given to overt expressions of love, having a depressive mother who died young, and the always present lack of money were the things that made up the misery of Nora and Audrey's young lives. Perhaps, she thought, it was the bond that came out of a difficult situation that held them together. In any case, nothing of the sort seemed to be cementing the relationship between Sandra and Trevor.

All the arguments that had deserted her during Trevor's 'poor me' harangue came to her then. She might have reminded him that she and Walter had made sure that neither of the children ever wanted for the necessities of life, as well as having provided many things that were far from necessary. Trevor, apparently, chose to forget that they'd supplied him with expensive hockey and ski equipment, bicycles, dirt bikes, a motorcycle and, when he went off to university, a car. Something they hadn't done for Sandra.

Not only that, but they did the good parent thing— attended parent-teacher meetings, baseball games, badminton games, hockey games, volleyball games, provided music lessons (a disappointing waste of money), took them on holidays when they could, welcomed their friends into their home and fetched Trevor from the police station when he was caught drinking and driving. Something else they'd never had to do for Sandra.

They'd also gone to recitals and endured awful high school plays. Later, they made sure that both Sandra and Trevor had the kinds of post secondary education they wanted. Their choice. And as far as Walter was concerned, Trevor's choice was a disappointment—Marine Biology—which took him as far away from home as he could go. And Sandra! How Nora had slaved over that wedding. Not that she really minded, but still... Did the girl really appreciate the hard work she'd put into it? Not very likely!

By the time Nora turned from her river refuge and started home, she was past her weepy stage and feeling put-upon and angry. Damn it! All she'd done, and now look! What was the expression? 'Sharper than a serpent's tooth it is to have a thankless child.'

She pondered that one for a time, wondering whether it came from the Bible or Shakespeare. She finally decided upon Shakespeare.

Audrey and her little family were gone—had left the night before for their home in Texas. She wished they were still there, that she could have a heart-to-heart with her sister. It was no use trying to explain to Maggie. Maggie thought the entire Fields family was wonderful. With the exception, of course, of Maude Fields and, given time, she'd probably forgive her. Maggie was like that. She tried to make excuses for anyone connected in any way to Nora and Walter.

Nora wanted to talk to someone, but not especially to Walter who seemed to be occupying some dark space of his own. In any case, after she parked her car in the garage, she saw that his truck was gone. Lucy, her library friend, was still away on holidays. Besides, Lucy was childless and wouldn't necessarily relate to the problems of sibling rivalry. 'Lucky woman!' Nora thought bitterly. Then, because she was at a loss for an advisor, Nora undressed, took her second shower of the day, put on her old jeans and torn plaid shirt and wrote a letter to Ann Landers. Not a real one, of course. In her head, she confided:

> *Dear Ann,*
>
> *Although I have never had occasion to write you before, I now find myself in a situation that I am unable to handle. I have been happily married for nearly twenty-five years and have a recently married daughter and a son still in university. Lately, I have discovered that our son is dwelling on past grievances which seem extremely petty and destructive. Not to mention, outlandish. He is very jealous of his sister because he believes that his father and I have given her preferential treatment, which is untrue. At least, on my part. His father and*

grandmother are another matter, but time and space preclude an itemized list of their alleged crimes.

Today he attacked me verbally regarding his complaints, which date back to the time when he was eight years old and his sister threw his favorite pen out the car window while we were traveling through the city. So, as you can see, things have been festering for a long time, since he is now twenty-one. Or is it twenty-two? I think it's twenty-two.

He was just home for his sister's wedding and they had a silly falling out which, it would appear, has escalated beyond all common sense. I love both my children, but have no idea how to cope with the bad feelings between them. My husband says not to worry about it, it'll all come out in the wash. I don't think it will. I do the washing around here, and I know a permanent stain when I see one. Besides, Walter (my husband) is too distracted right now to know what is going on.

It is now half past seven and Walter is no-where in sight. No note, either. I don't know whether to start peeling potatoes, or what. (Nora decided not to mention her suspicions about him having an affair with either Fran, Ruby or Inga. No use going off on a tangent.) I will appreciate any advice you may have to offer about my dilemma.

◌

Nora couldn't decide whether to sign the letter 'Puzzled on the Prairies' or 'Miffed in Manitoba', so she went for a walk down the back road to think about it.

WALTER

W<small>HEN</small> W<small>ALTER</small> <small>MARRIED</small> N<small>ORA</small> L<small>EAHY</small>, <small>HIS MOTHER WAS LESS</small> than pleased. It wasn't that Maude Fields had all that much against his wife—although Nora was Irish—she was simply annoyed that Walter had chosen to marry at all. He was, after all, the youngest of her three children and, as the only son, she seemed to expect that he would dedicate himself exclusively to his widowed mother. And for a time it appeared as though Walter might do just that.

As to Walter's two sisters, they didn't care one way or another, for they rarely visited. Mattie had long since married and moved to Ontario with her husband and two sons. Phyllis was installed in an expensive home in the River Heights area of Winnipeg, courtesy of her husband who was an upstanding member of the Canadian Wheat Board.

Besides his two sisters, Walter had had five first cousins all living in the immediate area and all attended the same one-room rural school. He had fond memories of happy times with them—summers at the beach, wild games of Prisoner's Base, Hoist Your Sails (or Oyster Shells, as some of them insisted the game was called), Fox and Goose (in winter) and Tug of War. (He'd broken his ankle during one extra strenuous game of Tug of War and, although that game had subsequently been banned by his mother, the cousins found a good level area behind the west granary—out of sight from prying parental eyes—and continued their dangerous pastime). Like all danger-loving children, they dreamed up other perilous activities such as swinging from the rafters of the hayloft and then dropping into the hay. When there *was* hay. By early summer, the haymow was all but emptied of its contents and many bumps, bruises, cuts and sprains resulted from hard falls to the bare boards beneath. If serious, these 'accidents' were reported as having been sustained in some other, more approved, manner.

Although the rough-and-tumble play of the children was not particularly endorsed by either of Walter's parents, it was the Field farm the cousins mainly chose as their playground. And, if his mother was almost nauseated by the sight of blood, it didn't interfere with her ability to wash, treat and bind up the countless injuries that occurred on her home turf. Of these, the most serious mishap was suffered by Angela during an aerial maneuver in the hay loft which went badly awry.

That awful day Walter was the one to carry his co-matose cousin to the house. The memory haunted him for years. In a quick conference it had been decided that Walter's mother be told that Angela had fallen off her bicycle. One of the older boys helped him struggle her down the ladder. Then the other three cousins jumped on their bikes and disappeared down the back road. The terrified Walter was left to take care of his favorite girl-cousin, and he somehow managed the long trek to the house and sobbed out the lie. He was certain that Angela was dead and so, for a time, was his mother. Her face and long coppery-colored hair were running with blood from a long, deep cut on the forehead.

As with many childhood mishaps, this one looked worse than it really was and, luckily, Angela regained consciousness fairly soon. After she'd been washed and a torn strip of clean bed sheet wrapped around her head for a bandage, Walter's mother insisted her niece remain in bed for the rest of the day. Angela was not happy with the decision but acquiesced when Walter said he'd read to her from the book she'd brought to the Fields' farm with her—*Anne of Avonlea*. After a few minutes she slept, but he stayed by the bedside watching her breathe, half convinced that each breath would be her last. He prayed his first earnest, frightened prayers then. Walter and Angela were twelve at the time.

That day marked a change in their relationship—one that was recognized and occasionally referred to in a teasing manner by some of the cousins, but at the time, went largely unnoticed among the adults. Walter and Angela were in love. Not puppy love as his older cousin, Robert, contemptuously called it one day a year or so later when the two were having an argument about the finer points of football rules. How Angela's name came into the conversation, Walter had no idea but, suddenly, there was Robert taunting him.

"First cousins have idiot children, you know. It's a form of incest. Time you found a proper girl friend and quit acting like a baby."

To his embarrassment and shame, Walter wept. Heartbroken thirteen-year-old tears. What Robert was saying was not exactly news—horror stories of babies born with one eye in the middle of their foreheads or covered with fur and mewing like cats had circulated among the cousins for years. The causes behind the births of these malformed infants were thought to be many, but chief among them was the family relationship of the parents.

Over the years, the cousins had swapped and absorbed much misinformation. They believed, for example, that swallowing chokecherry pits would cause immediate and excruciating death, and that drinking milk after eating chokecherries would probably have the same effect. Even when these 'facts' were disproved, some remnants of old wives' tales lingered on and were the reason most of the cousins, even during their teen years, would not kill a spider unless rain was needed. In drought years, they sought out spiders to squash, even though it eventually became evident that sacrificing innocent arachnids never brought on the promised precipitation.

Walter gave up his beliefs that a lightning storm would sour milk, that wearing overshoes indoors would cause blindness and that a bird in the house presaged a death, but the incest taboo regarding cousins never left him. It was, he knew, more than superstition. It was a no-no, taboo, verboten. Unacceptable, at least in his family.

He and Angela continued their relationship, but secretly—or as secretly as was possible under the watchful eyes of the other cousins. In the beginning it was innocent enough and involved only the odd Saturday afternoon movie, which everyone attended, although he and Angela always managed to sit together, and often, apart from the others. When he had enough money, he bought her little presents from Woolworth's—sometimes barrettes for her hair and, once an exotic blue bottle of Evening in Paris perfume. The best that Woolworth's carried.

By the time Walter and Angela left the little rural

school and started high school in town, they were
lovers. During the previous summer they had found
opportunities to be alone. Walter had his driver's license and the use of the family car, which provided
escape from the nosey cousins even though he was
often required to chauffeur some of them here and
there. Without the constant presence of their three
younger chaperones, he and Angela were free to roam
at will and they discovered a tree-sheltered area along
a stretch of deserted beach far removed from the cot-
tages. In their seclusion, they went effortlessly from
heavy petting to actual intercourse. It was a golden
summer for both of them—secretive and magical. To
Walter, it became a sacred place, an Eden of sorts, to
which they would never return.

Angela's parents became suspicious about the activities of their only child, although, for some reason,
Walter's mother and father never spoke a word about
the affair. Perhaps, if they had any concerns at all,
they assumed the teen passion would burn itself out.
But in an attempt to sever the bond, Angela's mother
packed her off to a girls' boarding school in Winnipeg
when she and Walter were about to enter grade
eleven.

Walter felt as though an important part of him had
been amputated and he was filled with a rage he could
express to no one except Angela. Their letters flew
back and forth almost daily at first. Walter would
rush home from school and try to be first to the mail-
box, snatch the precious messages and race up to
his room to savor the words from his beloved. He'd
sniff the envelope to check for her perfume then, ever
so carefully, use the bone-handled jackknife—a gift
from Angela—to slit the flap. In the beginning, her
letters always opened with, My Dearest Wally and
were signed, All My Love, Angie.

Because Walter had chores he was required to

perform, his answers had to wait until late at night. The cows he fetched to the barn, then milked, were treated to lengthy monologues—the content of letters he was framing in his mind. In the evenings, he tried to discipline himself to do his homework before getting out his writing paper, but it seldom worked that way, and often the homework was left undone or only partially completed. Walter was a clever enough student to maintain his grades in spite of the neglect.

The content of Angela's letters changed gradually over the weeks and months from loving recollections of their private times together to accounts of her daily activities, new friends she was making and the impossible demands of her teachers. Her opening and closing remained the same, though, and Walter read Angela's news avidly and then secreted the letters in an old book bag in the bottom of his closet. As far as he knew, they remained undisturbed.

Walter's letters also cooled from mad protestations of everlasting love to more mundane accounts of the doings of the other cousins, classmates and their mutual friends. The unknown people Angela mentioned were of little interest to Walter, but he did note a frequent reference to a girl friend, Rita Martinelli. Apparently, Angela often spent time at their home. Quite a lavish home according to her descriptions.

Angela spent very little time at her parents' home in McClung, but Walter was never quite sure whether it was a rule of the school or because of orders from her mother. On the few weekends that she was allowed home, her parents made sure that her time was entirely taken up with activities that did not include Walter. Once, he heard from a cousin that she'd brought her friend, Rita Martinelli, home for a visit. Many times, Angela had been and gone before he even knew about it.

Once, though, during Christmas holidays, they'd been able to steal time together. Both he and Angela had been invited to party at the home of a mutual friend. There was no drinking, but a flurry of games kept the fifteen or so guests occupied and, during an increasingly silly game of charades, Walter and Angela escaped to a bedroom. They were gone no more than twenty minutes or so and the few guests who noticed their return to the rec room seemed unconcerned. No other cousin was there to do any reporting.

Walter had high hopes that the affair was back on track—if it had ever left it—and the correspondence picked up momentum again. Then it slowed. Walter understood the difficulty of sustaining a long-distance relationship via the mails and the infrequency of Angela's letters didn't worry him too much at first. Then, with some alarm, he noticed the change in her greeting from Dearest Wally to Dear Wally and the closing with Love, Angela, instead of, All my love, Angie. But what worried him the most, was her habit of mentioning the Martinelli family so often. Now, not only Rita's name appeared, but also that of her brother, Paul. 'The big brother', Angela called him. 'If I'd had a brother, I'd have wanted him to be just like Paul.'

Well, a big brother wasn't so bad, Walter guessed. Summer would come eventually and he and Angela would pick up where they left off. But summer was nearly over by the time Angela got back from Moncton where she'd been sent by her mother to visit relatives on that side of the house. Toward the end of August, Walter ran into Angela in the McClung Hardware. She seemed happy to see him but turned down an invitation to attend a wiener roast some of the cousins were planning for the coming Saturday night. "Come on," he pleaded. "Your mother can't be mad at me forever. Anyway, she might not even find out that I was there."

"Sorry," Angela said and it seemed as though she was.

"What gives? They used to let you hang out with us."

"Oh, it's not that." She hesitated before deciding to tell him the truth. "It's just that Paul Martinelli has asked me to go to a play with him that night."

"I see," Walter said angrily, "the 'big brother'. Have you been going out with him?"

"Now and again. But it's not really a steady thing or anything like that. He's a lot older than me. Twenty-five. And Rita often comes with us."

Walter was in a frenzy of jealousy and not concerned about who might overhear his words. "Twenty-five! And you're...?"

"Eighteen next birthday. In case you've forgotten."

"Are you sleeping with him?!" Walter demanded in a loud voice.

Angela whispered through clenched teeth, "I'd slap your goddam face only old busy-body Emmy Norton is right behind that display listening to everything we say and I won't give her the pleasure of seeing a fist fight into the bargain. Besides, you have no right to tell me who I can go out with and who I can't."

"He's rich, I presume," Walter said bitterly.

"Right up there with the Bronfmans," Angela spit out before turning on her heel and stalking out of the store.

Walter followed her outside, then stopped and watched through tears of rage as Angela's coppery pony tail bounced in time with her angry footsteps and disappeared around a corner.

Forgetting why he'd been sent to the hardware store in the first place, Walter sped home without buying the special screw-nails his father needed. He left a rooster-tail of dust hanging in the air when he pulled into the farm yard, rushed into the house, up to his bedroom and slammed the door. His father was angry, but no amount of cajoling by his mother would elicit the information behind the aborted mission. In time, his parents forgot about that hot day in August. But Walter never did. He was wounded beyond words by Angela's infidelity. For that was how he thought of it.

By grade twelve, Walter was busy playing football, baseball, helping on the farm and dating other girls. Angela sent him a birthday card signed only, Your Cousin, A. It was an insult, far worse than nothing, so he ignored her birthday. She also sent him a Christmas card, which he ignored as well. They almost never saw one another although both attended family reunions and funerals. Angela missed a day of school to travel from the city by bus to attend Walter's father's funeral. It was in March when the elder Fields succumbed to a heart attack and it was a cold, blustery afternoon when he was laid to rest at the cemetery near the farm.

It was a terrible time in Walter's life. Everything changed so suddenly. All at once, he became 'head of the house', or so his mother said through her tears. He hadn't realized, either, how much he had loved his father—the man who had gone about his business with dignity and quiet concern for his family. As the family stood around the stark gravesite, the wind keening through the bare maple trees, Angela came and hugged him. They both wept. She whispered in his ear, "Look after yourself. I love you." Then she was gone again.

He quit school to devote all his time to the farm but he never forgot Angela's warm hug and her profession of love for him. He thought of her when he was bedding down the cattle, milking the cows or tending the pigs and chickens. The amount of labor involved in running the farm became instantly clear when he was left on his own to do it all and he felt closer to his father than ever.

Walter had little spare time for social activities and, besides, felt he had nothing left in common with the people who had been his friends in high school. He became, for many months, pretty much of a loner. At Christmas, for the first time since the funeral, he was elated to learn that he would see Angela again. He and his mother were invited to a party at Angela's parent's home. His hopes rose again and, almost giddy with excitement, Walter managed to tame his curly red hair into a more mature-looking style. But excitement turned to outrage when he discovered that the big occasion was in honor of Angela and Paul Martinelli's engagement. All the relatives, as well as half the population of McClung, were in attendance, but had Walter known the reason for the celebration, he most certainly would not have accepted the invitation. To his embarrassment and shame, he acted badly.

Angela's parents had provided a punch—one to which no liquor had been added. They also had numerous bottles of good Italian wine on hand—compliments of Paul's parents. This was an unusual occurrence, as liquor wasn't something ever served in that household of teetotalers and was a concession to the prospective in-laws. And Angela was nineteen—all grown up. Walter often indulged in the odd beer with his pals, but had no experience with the insidious properties of wine. It was considered by the young people of his acquaintance to be fit only for drunks who couldn't afford good Canadian rye whiskey, and was usually encased in a brown paper bag. In any event, he appropriated a bottle for himself and proceeded to consume it as quickly as he might have put away a bottle of beer. He had

almost finished the entire contents when Angela came
to him and asked, "Aren't you going to wish us well?"
He stared hard at her for a moment, almost as if he
hadn't understood her question. Then he said, "Go
to hell," turned on his heel and walked into a wall.
He had to be helped home and his mother was furious, but not half as furious as he was with her for
not having told him about the reason for the party.

Angela and Paul's wedding was scheduled for mid
June and he didn't see her again until about two
weeks before the big event. It was the kind of day
that made him ache for childhood's carefree days in
the rich Manitoba summer. He had just showered
and was preparing to go to town to buy a part for the
sprayer when a strange car pulled in the driveway.
He watched in surprise as his cousin got out and
walked towards the house. She was barefoot, as he
so often remembered her, but the white blouse and
yellow skirt reminded him that she was no longer a
child. Angela was more beautiful than ever. He met
her on the front porch and greeted her uncertainly.
"I was just thinking about you."

"Hi, Wally, you look all fresh and clean. Did I catch
you going out on a date?"

He swallowed and shook his head. No one else but
Angela had ever called him Wally and the use of her
old nick-name made his throat tighten. "Mother's not
home," he said, stupidly. "She went to Brandon for
the weekend. To visit Aunt Mary."

"That's OK. I didn't come to see Aunt Maude. I came
to see you."

"I can't imagine why you'd want to see me."

Angela sighed and looked at the floor. "I'm sorry if
I've hurt you, but you know as well as I do that it has
to be this way. Nothing could have happened for you
and me." Walter could think of no reply. "Well," she
said after a moment, "aren't you going to ask me in?"

Wordlessly, he held out his arms to her and led her indoors. It seemed inevitable that they'd cling together after their long separation and she made no objection when he led her up the stairs to his bedroom. With nothing spoken of her upcoming marriage or of the fact that this could never happen again, they lay together making love throughout most of that long afternoon. Then, she rose, dressed quickly, kissed him on the forehead and slipped quietly out of the house. Walter listened to the sound of her car fading in the distance and lay in his bed dozing and half-dreaming until after sunset before he thought to get up, do the milking and make himself some supper.

Later, he sat in front of the television for an hour or so, but if anyone had asked what program he'd seen, he wouldn't have had the faintest idea. Presently he came to himself and wondered if the entire afternoon had been some kind of strange dream. When he finally retired for the night, though, Angela's musky perfume still clung to the sheets and pillows. There was no doubt about their earlier tryst. But what, he wondered, had been her purpose in coming?

The next day, he found out. Angela phoned to ask him if he would be prepared to give the toast to the bride. Her voice was business-like and she made no mention of the previous afternoon. Perhaps someone was listening. It surely couldn't be that she'd forgotten about it! Walter simply said, "No," and hung up.

During the days before Angela and Paul's marriage, he tried to think up excuses to forego the event. Because of his mother's pleading, however, and her wails of, "How will it look?" he forced himself to say he would attend.

Getting ready to go was a nightmare. He cut himself shaving, he'd forgotten to get himself new shoes and he needed a haircut. Although Walter's mother had bought him a new white shirt, neither had thought to have him try on his only sport's jacket and, in the year or so since he'd worn it, it seemed to have shrunk. His last growth spurt and the muscles acquired during the past year's hard work, had increased his size considerably and made the jacket almost unwearable. But it was the only one he had. He looked despairingly in the mirror. The sleeves came well above his wrists and there was no possibility of closing the front buttons. The garment seemed to have been made for someone else. Someone who didn't have any clothes sense at all, someone who looked like a half-wit, someone who would have been totally unworthy to be the golden Angela's lucky groom. Even if the fates had ordained that union to be possible. He left the house feeling like a hobo.

Although Walter's mother wanted to sit in a pew near the front of the church, he insisted that they sit as far back as possible and still appear to be part of the celebration. He made it through the ceremony— the march down the aisle, the exchanging of vows, the signing of the register and the final, triumphal march of the bride and groom up the aisle, but he knew that was as much as he could tolerate. There was no possible way he could stay to extend congratulations to the happy couple so he whispered to his mother that, since it was a calm day, he had to get the last of the spraying done. She was furious with him again. "Nobody's paying attention to your jacket. Stay and see the day through. It won't kill you. Besides, how will it look?"

Walter wanted to tell her that he already felt half dead and that any more time spent listening to Angela and Paul's professions of undying love might just finish him off. He was also on the verge of saying he didn't give a hoot about how it might look, thought better of it, and simply slipped quietly away as the bridal couple was posing on the church steps for photographs. Five minutes later, Walter couldn't have told anyone what the bride was wearing. He'd scarcely given her a glance. He went home and got on the tractor.

The following years blurred in Walter's mind and were marked by dim memories of this girlfriend, that girlfriend, good harvests, poor harvests and the year he decided to sell the livestock and concentrate solely on grain farming. In this decision he was encouraged by Archie Kroeger, the neighbor with whom he shared the seeding and harvest work. The move relieved him of much of the day-to-day labor of animal care and he had more free time. Along with a bachelor friend he even did some traveling. Once, they went to Florida and he had a wild notion to visit Angela and Paul in Naples. He knew they were living there and that they had a son. Good sense prevailed, however, and all he did was look up their name in a phone book. He didn't call.

Meanwhile, the Leahys moved to McClung and opened up a shoe store. The local bachelors, at first delighted by the addition of two attractive females to the town, had been put off by Robert Leahy's inquisition of one of Nora's suitors. Or at least, that's what was being ground out in the local rumor mill. Walter wasn't particularly interested, anyway.

That all changed the day his mother shamed him into buying a new pair of shoes, and he went into Leahy's store for the first time. He'd seen Nora around, of course. There weren't that many pretty girls in McClung, and he'd noticed her the odd time in the bank or coming out of the library. But he'd paid scant attention until they came face to face. He was so struck by her honest face and fresh complexion that he bought the first pair of black oxfords she brought to him.

He introduced himself and, on impulse, invited her to accompany him to a fowl supper and dance the following Saturday night. She blushingly accepted, but her father who, just moments before, had come in and loudly plunked some letters down on the counter, had obviously heard the invitation. He frowned and inquired of Walter's age, occupation and intentions. Walter was so taken aback that he answered all Robert's questions—even the one about his intentions.

Of that, he said, "My intentions are quite honorable, Sir. I just thought your daughter might like to get to know a few of the younger people around town."

"She already knows quite a few."

"I hardly know anybody," Nora contradicted. "Just a few who've been in to buy shoes and all I know about them is their shoe size."

Her father, apparently, chose not to hear her. "Anyway, you're a fair bit older than Nora."

Walter wondered where Mr. Leahy got that information. His age wasn't stamped on his forehead as far as he knew. "Twenty-six isn't considered that old in these parts."

The older man took off his spectacles, carefully cleaned them on a snow-white handkerchief and harrumphed a couple of times before speaking. "Even so, Nora's only twenty and not accustomed to keeping company with older men."

Nora intervened. "For heaven's sake, Father, we're not eloping, we're just going out."

He ignored her and continued to speak to Walter. "Nora's sister, Audrey, might like to go out, too."

"Fine," Walter said, "she can come along with us if she likes." He was not used to being treated like a third rate Casanova and was beginning to feel angry, but had no notion of backing down from this heavy-handed tyrant.

113

"We don't even know if Audrey will want to go," Nora said to her father.

"She'll go," he retorted and disappeared into the storage room—a small man immaculately dressed with a back stiff as a poker. Not a man about to allow his daughters to run around with just anybody.

Nora pulled a face. "He thinks I need a chaperone, I guess. He's been so overbearing since Mam died. Thinks he has to watch over us like a mother hen all the time. Anyway I guess we'll both be your dates on Saturday night."

That was the start of Walter and Nora as a couple. Audrey tagged along with them sometimes, but likely as not, she'd find something else to do with her own crowd of outlaws as soon as the three of them were beyond range of Mr. Leahy's piercing blue eyes.

Walter didn't feel the same degree of passion for Nora as he had for Angela but he loved her for herself. She was intelligent and pretty. In appearance, Nora was almost Angela's opposite—she was shorter with dark hair and wide-set sparkling blue eyes that crinkled around the edges when she laughed—which was often. He admired the fact that she could laugh at all, given the hours she spent in the shoe store with her dour father.

Walter had no idea why the elder Leahy disliked him so heartily even though Nora told him not to take it to heart, that he was that way with most people, and for no reason that she could discern. Probably the cause, she said, behind the family's frequent moves. Business didn't exactly thrive when the owner was distant (or even rude) to customers. Still, Walter wished he might be welcomed into the family since he had more-or-less made up his mind to ask Nora to marry him.

It wasn't only Robert Leahy who was apprehensive about the couple. Maude Fields seemed equally concerned, although Walter knew her motive. "You seem to be seeing a lot of the shoemaker's daughter," she said to Walter one Saturday night as he was getting ready to go to town.

"He's not a shoemaker. You know that. He's a shoe retailer and his name is Robert Leahy. But you know that, too, don't you?"

His mother was in a sulk. "You don't have to talk down to me. I'm not senile. Just taking an interest."

"Robert Leahy has two daughters. Nora and Audrey. You've seen them both. Nora's the one I've been dating for months now. So it can't really be news to you, can it?"

"Leahy sounds Irish."

"I believe it is."

"I hope they're not drinkers like the Haggertys."

"No, Mother, they're definitely not drinkers." Walter said this through clenched teeth as he headed out the door.

"Don't be late, son. You know how I worry."

It was probably Maude Fields' last remark that brought Walter to a decision. He would ask Nora to marry him that night. After all, they'd been seeing one another for almost a year and she seemed ready to settle down. He was weary of his mother's possessiveness and anxious to start on a new chapter of his life. She would just have to get used to it.

Since there was no question of asking Nora to share a household with his mother, Walter had already thought about what he would have to do and had recently checked out housing prices in town. His father's will had stipulated that Maude Fields could continue to live on the farm as long as she wished and that Walter could do so as well. The financial arrangements were a 40/60 split of the net farm income with Walter getting the larger share as payment for his labors. Crops had been good for the past few years and they could easily afford two residences. If his mother refused to move off the farm, he and Nora would simply have to live in town and he would commute to do the farming. It wouldn't be as easy, but either way would work.

Whether Robert Leahy was really as concerned about his daughter's welfare as he made out, Walter never knew. Perhaps he was just reluctant to give up his source of free—or almost free—labor. In any case, he made Nora's life a misery for a couple of weeks before he'd give his consent to her marriage. Not that his consent was needed, it just seemed like the decent thing to do.

Nobody asked Maude Fields' consent. Fortunately, for she would not have given it. Upon hearing the bad news, Walter's mother protested vigorously; she couldn't live by herself, she had to have someone around to help her, her daughters didn't care about her—in fact, nobody cared about her.

To give him credit, Walter took her complaints as he'd always taken them—with a grain of salt. He bought a small bungalow within walking distance of the stores—although his mother could, and still did, drive a car—then he asked her which home she preferred. A fair enough proposition since he and Nora were agreeable to living in either place. To cause greater inconvenience and in an attempt to exert her unraveling control over her son, Maude Fields waited until two weeks prior to Walter and Nora's wedding before making her choice known. She'd give up the only home she'd known for over thirty years and move to town. She might, just might, find some neighbors who would be kind to her.

"Not unless you're kind to them," Walter told her.

"What do you mean, kind? I'm always kind."

"Not to your neighbors, necessarily."

"I don't know what you mean."

"I mean the Kroegers, as if you didn't know. They've been neighbors for years and I don't see you being very neighborly to them."

"Rubbish! I visit Mrs. Kroeger occasionally."

"You mean, Vera. I call her Vera, why don't you? You call her husband, Archie."

"Well, I see more of him. Especially when you're doing the seeding or harvesting together and he's here for meals. I don't see her very often."

Walter sighed. "That's what I mean. You haven't been very friendly with her." Maude Fields sniffed. "I don't believe in living in people's pockets. Especially with close neighbors. You never know when they might take advantage."

"Them take advantage of us?! I couldn't have managed to run this place without Archie's help after Dad died. We'd have had to sell the place or rent it out."

"Of course, he's been a big help. I'd be the first to admit that. But I was afraid she might have tried to get too cozy. And that daughter of theirs...!"

"Maggie? She has a name, you know. It's Maggie."

"I know. Silly nickname, Maggie. Don't know what's wrong with plain Margaret. Anyway, she runs around barefoot and in overalls. Nothing on underneath them, as far as I can tell. Saw her tearing through our yard just the other day. Wild as a hare. I'm not sure she even owns any proper clothes. Anyway, Mrs. Kroeger and I don't seem to have much in common. They don't belong to our church or anything." She drew herself upright and said disapprovingly, "I'm not sure they belong to any church."

Walter could barely keep from snorting in disgust. If she'd taken the trouble to get to know Maggie, his mother would realize that the little girl's free spirit was something to be treasured. And her implication that non-church-goers were an inferior breed was intolerant, to say the least. If she'd cared to look around at the congregation in her own church pews, she'd have found any number of adulterers, cheats, gossip mongers and at least one felon. The Kroegers were the most moral people Walter could think of, their non-adherence to any religious denomination notwithstanding.

And mention of her aversion to 'living in other people's pockets' was truly laughable. His mother and her sister, Mary, had lived in one another's pockets ever since he could remember. But then, that was family. People not related by blood or marriage counted for little in Maude Field's estimation and were always thought of as strangers no matter how long or intense their acquaintance. His mother's people were a family of huddlers and, therefore, for the most part, ignorant and intolerant of others. His sisters escaped from it as soon as they could, and although he had to live in close proximity to his numerous relatives (many of whom he truly liked), Walter hoped to avoid the claustrophobic clan attachments of his elders. Closeness with his cousins was fine when they were young but he had no desire to maintain the chummy relationships once they were adults.

He knew from experience that argument with his mother was pointless so he just sighed and gave up. "Oh, never mind about the Kroegers. Let's just figure out what kind of furniture you'll be needing."

*

So it was accomplished that Walter and Nora were married and Maude Fields moved into a house in town. Not that it was an easy transition for any of them. In a fit of possessiveness, Maude demanded most of the furniture from the farm home in addition to many new items. When Walter asked his mother why she needed to have the sofa and chair from the farm as well as the new ones they'd bought for her, she was huffy.

"Since the basement is finished in my new house, I decided to furnish it. Anyway, those things are mine, you know. I'll also be wanting all the furniture from the bedrooms as well as the dining room suite. Including the sideboard."

Walter was dumbfounded. They'd already furnished her house with new pieces after a shopping spree that left him breathless and practically penniless. Now, it seemed she wanted to plunder the farm house as well.

"Let her have the stuff," Nora said. We'll do without until we can afford to replace it."

"That may take a while," Walter worried. But he went along with his mother's demands. All except for the bedroom suite from his room. "It's mine and I'm keeping it," he told his mother. "Where did you think Nora and I would sleep, anyway? On the floor?"

"Nora will want all new stuff, anyway."

"We can't afford it. Not now. You know our financial situation as well as I do since you're part of it."

"You should have thought of that before you rushed into this marriage. You hardly know her. The Leahys," she continued scornfully, "just moved into town and now they walk around as though they'd been here for generations. Mark my words, she's only after you for your money."

"Then she's going to be in for a disappointment, isn't she?"

*

Luckily, Walter and Nora had planned a small, inexpensive wedding with only immediate family and a few close friends—about twenty people in all—and the dinner was held at a local hotel.

Nora's sister, Audrey, was bridesmaid. "It was a beautiful wedding," she told Nora and Walter later. "Quiet and dignified. And probably the best looking couple in the province!"

Maude Fields wasn't so appreciative, though. "I'd have thought a prominent businessman like Robert Leahy could have provided a better wedding for his eldest daughter," she sniffed privately to Walter later. "Nora didn't even have a proper wedding gown. Imagine getting married in a suit."

"They only spent what they could afford, and Nora and I were very happy with everything."

And they continued to be happy in spite of the shortage of household furnishings. They were able to make-do with what they could scrounge, and acquired some things at auction sales. In order to build up savings for newer, more appropriate acquisitions, Nora continued to clerk at her father's store. Walter drove her to town in the mornings and collected her at six o'clock. This arrangement was short-lived because Nora's morning sickness put an end to it within three months. The pregnancy was unplanned, of course, and would make their situation tighter, but neither of them was too distraught by the development.

Sandra was born within four days of their first wedding anniversary and her birth softened, to some extent, the breach between the couple and Walter's mother. The new grandmother was on hand with all sorts of advice about the care and feeding of newborns. Arrival of the new infant also served to loosen up the older woman's purse strings and she presented them with a number of items for the nursery—including a crib, a high chair and a baby carriage.

Not only that, but she began returning many of the things she'd taken from the farm house the previous year—things Nora and Walter had replaced or done without. In any case, they were things the young couple no longer needed or wanted. "What in hell are we supposed to do with another dining room table and six chairs?" Nora demanded of her husband. He had never seen her in such a temper and was a bit taken aback.

"I suppose we could sell the suite we got at the second hand store. Maybe they'd even take it back."

"Not on your life. I'm used to that set now. I want to keep it. And, anyway, I don't want any of her stuff. What if she gets in another huff. She'd take it all back again and then where would we be? Out combing the stores for used furniture again, that's where. Tell her to take it back again and not to send out any more."

Walter wasn't keen on telling his mother anything.

"If you won't, I will and it won't be a pleasant discussion."

Walter tried to tell Nora that his mother was attempting to atone for her past treatment of them, but Nora wasn't appreciative. "She's trying to buy us off. As if that could make up for everything. And I really wish she didn't interfere so much with the baby. I'm not an idiot. I can manage."

Nora was not an aggressive sort of person and had never before made her feelings known to her mother-in-law. Walter knew she'd stand firm this time, though, so he was forced to deal with his mother himself.

"We really don't need the things now, Mother," he told her. "Anyway, you said you were going to put any of the extra furniture in your basement."

"There's not room down there. You know that."

"We also knew that when you were hauling the stuff in."

"Why didn't you say something then?"

"I believe I did. On a number of occasions. But they

121

were your things, Mother. You could do with them as you wished."

"Well, I now wish to give them to you."

"Maybe some of the others might like them."

"Your sisters have all the furniture they need. They don't want my old things. I can't see why Nora doesn't appreciate this. All the trouble I've gone to. Hiring a truck. Movers."

"You might have asked us first."

"Never mind. I guess all we can do is put it in storage until you decide what to do with it."

"That will cost money."

"No doubt it will. I'll look after it."

So that situation was more-or-less resolved and wasn't spoken of again. They tolerated Maude Fields' frequent visits and tried to ignore the expensive gifts she lavished on her granddaughter.

Two years later, Trevor made his appearance but his birth prompted no special treatment from his grandmother. A brown plush teddy bear was about the most he got from her. Sandra, with her dark curly hair, was always the favorite. Trevor was colicky, cranky and subject to projectile vomiting—not an easy infant to have around.

But they grew and thrived. Except for the usual childhood diseases and complaints, the children gave their parents little trouble. The farm prospered and Nora settled into the community life with apparent ease. Not that there was a lot of socializing involved, but they took part in the 4H Club activities and other neighborhood projects as they arose. Nora did volunteer work at the hospital and at the library in McClung as well as taking the occasional adult education course. Walter kept busy with the farm and sometimes hunted or fished with male friends. He also belonged to the Elks Lodge and the Lions Club in town. They kept busy.

Walter was fond of Nora, often proud of her and secretly pleased that, locally anyway, they were thought of as a handsome couple. They had a good sex life. Normal, as far as he knew. Whatever normal was. He'd never consciously compared her to Angela and that part of his life suited him. Nora never turned her back on him. He thought of Angela less and less often.

ANGELA

Although Walter thought of Angela less frequently, she was never entirely out of his mind. However, when his mother suggested that she be invited to Sandra's wedding, the idea struck him as ludicrous. Or, perhaps, dangerous, since he wasn't sure how he would handle it. In the end, because Angela had recently written the elder Mrs. Fields saying that she felt it was time she brought the ashes of her parents back to be interred in the McClung cemetery, it was apparent a visit was imminent in any case.

"It makes perfect sense," his mother said. "I've always thought Annie and Jim's ashes belonged in Manitoba—not Florida. Good thing she never got around to having them buried there. Anyway, while she's here, she might as well go to the wedding. It would be a sort of family reunion for her. Maybe she'll bring along her son, Marian, or whatever his name is. Now that she's a widow, she'll have some free time on her hands."

Walter knew that Angela was a widow since she'd

sent a notice to his mother two years before informing her of Paul Martinelli's untimely demise. The news
was passed on to Walter, of course. Mrs. Fields, in
the assumed role of Family Matriarch, prided herself
on keeping abreast of all the births, deaths and weddings of the large extended family. She maintained
quite a large list of relatives to whom she unfailingly
sent Christmas letters with a rundown of family news.
In this way, Walter and Angela were kept reasonably
current as to the basic information about one
another's lives. Walter, for example, knew that Angela was widowed with a grown son while she,
presumably, knew that he and Nora were still married and the parents of a son and a daughter.
Statistics, really, were all he got concerning Angela's
life.

"Okay, I'll mention it to Nora although you've already complained about the list getting out of hand."

"Well," his mother huffed, " the addition of one or
two people on our side of the family isn't going to
hurt. If Sandra wasn't marrying the huge Russian
family, the list wouldn't be nearly so long and there
wouldn't be any worry."

Walter laughed. "It's okay, Mother. I'm sure Nora
will agree to invite Angela and Mario. His name is
Mario, not Marian, remember? And, don't make it
sound as though Sandra is marrying the entire Red
Army Chorus; there aren't *that* many of them!"

And Nora didn't object to including two more on
the list. He almost wished she had said, "No! No
damned way do I want that woman around!" But she
would have had no reason to react that way. To Nora,
Angela was just another cousin in a long string of
cousins and, with so few relatives of her own, she
never objected to taking on a few more of her
husband's. The invitation was sent, and accepted.

During the weeks before the wedding, Walter

vacillated between wishing Angela had declined the invitation and wondering how he could tolerate the wait before actually seeing her again. His picture of her was of a youthful, rebellious, auburn-haired beauty and, try as he might to imagine how she might look now, no strands of gray appeared in her hair, and no extra flesh gathered about her midriff.

It was a spring of apprehension and, occasionally, outright dread for the father of the bride. Coupled with Sandra's wedding jitters and Nora's frayed nerves, the household was in a constant state of flux. He tried to stay away as much as possible—away from the frantic wedding preparations. Walter wished his daughter happiness, of course, but he also wished she and Nick had just eloped, saved the money the event was costing and put it to better use. His attitude didn't go unnoticed by either his wife or his daughter and Sandra had told him several times to "lighten up." Once, she added, "or I'll get Martin Kroeger to give me away." He laughed although he didn't think the threat was either funny, or in good taste. He did, however, understand that he desperately needed to lighten up. The question was, how?

He began to spend more time chatting with the 'Fact Finding Females' as Nora referred to Ruby and Fran. They came walking by every morning—not always on cue, but regularly enough that he had little trouble waylaying them and trading bits of gossip. The fact that Walter invented his contributions to the rumor mill escaped the women entirely. As he told Nora, "they wouldn't recognize a joke if it bit them on their rumps."

Nora warned him that his little charade would most likely get him in trouble but he rather enjoyed the silly game and kept hoping to find at least a trace of wit lurking somewhere in the minds of the walkers. So far, nothing had emerged to give him the slightest hope of that.

Then there was Inga who lived just up the road and who occasionally joined Ruby and Fran for the last leg of their jaunts. Inga was a nice looking woman—divorced, he understood, although she never said as much, and managed to make it clear that she was not looking for a new man in her life. All she needed, she said, was the occasional helping hand from someone who knew how to look after her sewage system every time it went on the blink. Which was often enough that he was called to her rescue on several occasions. Inga, at least, had a sense of humor and he wondered at her bothering to have anything to do with Ruby and Fran. Loneliness, probably. He could relate to that, although he couldn't have said precisely why a busy farmer with a family currently going through prenuptial frenzy should suddenly find himself lonely.

One day, Inga phoned to ask if he had a chain saw she could borrow to remove a dangerously weakened branch on the big maple tree in her yard. "It's hanging right over the dog house and the run. I've got a brand new litter of pups and if it fell..."

"I never loan my chain saw to ladies in distress," he said, "but I'll come and do the job for you." When he finished and climbed down the ladder, she invited him in for a cup of coffee. He accepted and immediately wished he hadn't, for he found himself uncomfortably aware of the intimacy of the occasion.

Inga, sensing his discomfort said, "Don't worry about the hunters and gatherers, they've been and gone."

Then he dared to ask, "How come you're friendly with Ruby and Fran? They don't seem like your kind of folks."

"Thank you," she said. "Nice that you realize that. Anyway, it's a way to pass some time, get me

127

outdoors. You know... I'm totally fascinated by the trivia that passes for intelligence in their little heads. I'm a writer, you know, and I get some useful ideas from them sometimes, just listening to them blather on. Weird, but occasionally useful. And I never tell them anything I wouldn't want to see headlined in the McClung Sentinel."

"Good thinking! Or, the other thing you could do is, you could always make up crazy stuff to pass along. That's what *I* do, sometimes. Like, a while ago, I told them that my daughter's groom-to-be comes from a family of eighteen children—all boys—and that they toured Saskatchewan as two baseball teams with the father acting as umpire and their mother driving the bus." He laughed, "They bought it!"

Inga wiped the tears from her eyes, "They would! No doubt I'll hear about it soon. I haven't walked with them for a while. Been busy with the pups. The gals will be practically giddy with excitement to have some fresh dope on your family."

"Pretty interested in us, are they?"

"You'd better believe it."

"I guess I should be more careful. Nora says I'll get myself in trouble."

"She could be right but it would be a shame to spoil your fun." Then, in a serious voice, Inga continued. "You know, I quite like your wife, what little I know of her. I think she might be somebody I'd enjoy knowing."

"You would. I mean, Nora is a very nice person. Intelligent. Witty when she wants to be. Certainly a good wife and mother. Why don't you invite her over for coffee sometime?"

"I've thought of that, but I don't think she likes me very much."

As Walter tried to protest, she interrupted. "No, don't pretend. I think, maybe she's worried that I have my claws out for you. I *don't*, you know."

"I know."

The lengthening silence disturbed Walter and as he rose to leave, he suggested, "Invite Nora down to see the puppies. She loves puppies. She might be happy to get out of the house for a little while, too."

"Good idea. I'll do that. Soon."

"Just don't send her home with one of the little blighters. We don't need another dog. Nora might think so, but as long as old Sam is still in the land of the living, he figures he's head honcho at our place."

So the short interlude with Inga was another little break in Walter's day. When he left her place, he went straight to the coffee shop in town and was in time to meet with the last of the afternoon's coffee row hangers-on. He not only forgot about Inga immediately, but also forgot to take his power saw with him when he left her place.

Nora was busy and still in her housecoat when Inga arrived the next day just before noon bearing Walter's saw. "Your husband left this at my place yesterday. Just thought I should return it."

"Oh, thanks," was all Nora could think of to say and didn't add that she had no idea he'd even been at Inga's the previous day. Nora was completely distracted. She'd been tearing her hair out since seven, re-doing the guest list one more time and trying to figure out a way to stay more-or-less within budget. The budget Mother Fields had laid out when she offered to pay for the wedding dinner. She hadn't even showered or combed her hair. Nora glanced at the clock, "I really must stop doing this."

'Stop doing what?"

"Running around half the morning before I stop to get dressed. Please excuse my appearance."

"Is there anything I can do to help?"

"Oh, no thanks. Not unless you're a magician or

something."

Inga hesitated, "Sorry, I left my bag of magic tricks at home and I'm useless without it." But the look of incomprehension on Nora's face was a clear signal that her small joke was not appreciated. Or even noticed. "Okay then. Where should I leave it?" Inga asked, uneasily.

"Leave what?"

"The chain saw. You see, Walter cut down a tree limb for me because I was afraid it would break off and hurt the puppies. It was hanging by a thread right over the dog run and...." Inga knew she was babbling but the woman before her looked completely unhinged and probably hadn't heard a word she'd said. "Guess I'd better get going," she finished. "Tell Walter thanks again. I'll just leave the saw right here on the step. He'll see it when he comes home."

"Fine," Nora said. "I'll see that he gets it." Then she closed the door.

When Walter appeared for lunch, Nora had showered, dressed and worked herself up into a bit of a lather. "Well, you missed the bleached blond," she said before even saying hello or asking where the hell he'd been all morning.

"The who?"

"You know, your Scandahoovian girlfriend."

"My what?"

"Don't be so coy. She returned it."

"Returned what?"

"Your chain saw. You practically tripped over it coming in the house."

"I wondered what it was doing on the step. I guess I left it at Inga's yesterday."

"Brilliant deduction."

"What else have you left at Inga's?"

"My God, what goes on here? I do a favor for a neighbor and you act as though I was some kind of a criminal."

"I don't see you doing favors for anybody else. Just Inga."

Walter was flabbergasted. "Just for Inga! What a load of crap! I do favors for Martin all the time. Not to mention, Mother."

"Why not mention Mother? There's no possible way we can invite all the people we have to invite and stay within the price limit your mother has set for the dinner."

"Is this, so called, conversation about girlfriends or money? Because, at the moment, I don't have a surplus of either."

And the argument dragged on until Walter went out to the shop to sulk at his work bench.

Recalling the row later, Walter knew he should have realized that Nora was just fatigued beyond endurance and done something about it—like take her out for dinner or offer to lend more of a hand in the wedding proceedings. He was reasonably sure that Nora knew there was nothing between him and their blond neighbor, but there was no question that she suspected something was going awry in their relationship. He sighed and wished the wedding and Angela's visit were behind them and he could get back to feeling normal again—or, at least, a bit more relaxed. He almost hoped that Angela would turn up at the wedding with a second husband on her arm and he could forget his fantasies. But, no, the invitation reply clearly stated that it was Angela and her son who would attend. Walter had no idea what to expect—of himself, or Angela.

✑

Walter was amazed by how easily he and Angela slipped into their old relationship and how quickly the years fell away, almost as though they had never been. The situation had gone completely out of control almost immediately. He couldn't believe what happened the night of Sandra and Nick's wedding. Or rather, he could believe it, he just found it difficult to imagine what turn his life was going to take. For it was certain that, one way or another, his life would never be the same again.

It was as though he and Angie had never been apart—the old love or lust, or whatever had been between them, blazed as hot as ever. He knew it the moment he set eyes on her at the wedding and, later when they danced, he held her close, breathed in the smell of her hair and whispered, "I never stopped loving you." It was the truth. He held her as though he would never again let her out of his arms. As though she belonged there, belonged to him.

They gazed into one another's green eyes and suddenly both laughed. "Remember how Aunt Mary used to say we might as well have been twins, we looked so much alike?" Angela said. "I don't know how close twins are supposed to feel, but *I* feel that I'm actually a part of you. Part of your body, you know?"

"I know, "he said.

Somehow, Walter was able to get through the evening. He remembered that he smiled and laughed a lot and visited with as many people as possible. Although all he wanted to do was keep Angela in his arms, he danced all his 'duty' dances and still managed to know exactly where, and with whom, Angela was at any given moment. Luckily, some part of his brain had been aware enough to keep a close eye on Maggie and have Martin take her home when it appeared she was attracting too much attention, and astute enough to pour oil on some waters that his arrogant brother-in-law had managed to stir up. The astonishing thing was, that even as his mind occupied

some strange and magical space, it was able to func-
tion on several levels and guide its owner through
the routines involved in maintaining his dignity as
the host and father-of-the-bride.

He hung on until after Sandra threw her bouquet
and the newly married couple said their farewells
and left the hall. After that, the musicians went into
their rock mode, the volume increased alarmingly
and many of the elders made going-home noises.
Including his mother who approached him with,
"Please Dear, if you don't mind, would you drive me
home. I'm afraid I'm tired right out. I think Angela is
about ready to leave, too, and Mario seems to be busy
with those young folks. Perhaps you could drop her
off at the motel."

It was as easy as that! Walter might have told Nora
where he was going, and again, he might not have.
He was never quite sure. In any case, he dropped his
mother off first and then he and Angela went to her
motel room. Before the door was even closed or
locked, they began undressing one another. There
was no shyness. It was as though they'd been doing
this for the past quarter century. In less than five
minutes they were in bed. He felt as though he'd come
home. His precious Angela in his arms where she
belonged!

After about an hour with Angela—maybe more,
maybe less, Walter never really knew, Angela gently
suggested he really must go or people would start
wondering. He was reckless enough not to care, but
she insisted. After another long, lingering kiss, he
rose, dressed slowly and left without a backward
glance or a goodbye. It didn't seem necessary.

He wondered later if anyone had missed his presence at the remainder of the dance. He couldn't
believe he'd actually done what he'd done—ignoring
his family duties and doing what *he* wanted to do. To

a point, anyway. What he really wanted to do was spend the rest of his life in bed with Angela, but even at the time, he realized that was asking a bit too much. No one seemed to question his disappearance—particularly as he was back in his own bed when Nora came home. Dumb luck, he told himself.

Although their private meeting that night was unexpected, the news Walter got from Angela was even more unexpected and he still hadn't decided whether it was good or bad. Certainly, it put a new light on things. After the first frantic love-making, Angela had said, "I am probably still somewhat fertile. I hope you didn't get me pregnant again *this* time." Then she giggled. It was a moment before the import of her words took effect.

He raised himself on one elbow and looked into her green eyes. "What do you mean pregnant again this time?"

"You didn't know? You didn't guess? Mario is yours, my darling. No wonder your wife noticed such a family resemblance."

Walter fell back, stricken. "Why didn't you tell me you were pregnant?"

"I didn't realize it until after Paul and I were married."

"And you're sure the baby wasn't his?"

"Very sure. And wonder of wonders, Mario turned out to be quite normal. Not deformed in any way. Not feeble-minded, in spite of what they used to say— you know, about first cousins."

"Christ Almighty! *We* could have been married. I had no idea. Does Mario know? Did Paul know? Does anyone else know?"

Angela laughed again. "I'm sure there's been speculation—particularly by my mother—but no, Mario doesn't know, Paul didn't know—or, at least, I'm pretty sure he didn't know. As far as I'm aware it's a closely guarded secret."

"Why do you think your mother knew?"

"Oh, she kept mentioning the fact that at least some of Paul's genes should have made it through, and giving me odd looks. That was in the beginning, when she and Dad first started coming down to Florida for the winters. After a few years, she seemed to give up on the idea and, after they moved down permanently, I never heard any more about it. I suppose she realized that, even if she was right, bringing it to Paul's attention wouldn't have been such a hot idea."

"Why didn't you and Paul have any more children? I mean, any of your own?"

"I didn't want any of Paul's children. I went on the pill. He never knew."

"So," Walter mused, "I have two sons." What would they think if they knew they were brothers?"

"Half brothers," Angela corrected. "They might be happy about it. Who knows?"

"More importantly, what would Nora think about it?" Walter wondered.

"I doubt if she'd be thrilled."

"She mustn't ever find out."

"Do you love her a lot?"

"I guess I do. I suppose I do. It's not like with you, though. You I adore, but I guess ours was a once in a lifetime thing, not fated to work out."

Angela pulled him to her and gazed directly into his eyes. "What if the fates changed in our favor? What if it still could work out?"

"I don't see how."

She snuggled against him. "Maybe the fates will change in our favor."

He held her close and shut out everything but the miracle of her nearness.

🖋

Later, back home in his own bed, Walter was unable to sleep. During all his married years, he'd never slept with anyone but Nora and, even before his marriage, Angela was the only one who'd mattered. He was overwhelmed by conflicting feelings. Awe, excitement, happiness, guilt.... There was also the little matter of Mario. Guilt, however, was way down on the list. There hadn't yet been time for real, debilitating Presbyterian guilt to work its way to the top.

It did, eventually, though. Particularly on the day he let Nora go to the airport alone with Trevor. He should at least have gone with them—said goodbye properly to his only son. 'My youngest son,' he corrected himself—and not without some pride. But he had other things on his mind. Angela, to be precise. The day before, directly following a short family committal service for the ashes of Angela's parents, Mario had left to go back to Florida.

Before he left, however, Walter heard him ask his mother, "What do I tell Stewart if he wonders why you didn't come back when you said you would?"

Walter was so startled, he didn't really hear Angela's reply. Stewart?! Who the hell was Stewart? A boyfriend? Already? He felt the old familiar gut-burn. Had Angela found herself a replacement for Paul? For him?

Walter did, however, catch Angela's next remark to her son. "Tell *all* my friends that I've decided to stay on in McClung for a short visit. That's all they need to know."

Her decision to stay on came as a surprise to Walter and he had been in a state of hyper anticipation ever since hearing of it. What was even more interesting, was that Angela had decided to keep her room at the motel even though his mother had invited her to move into her house for the balance of her visit. Since Mario had driven their rental car back to Winnipeg where he caught his flight home, Angela was now without wheels. Also an interesting development. Walter would get to provide transportation—or, at least, that's what he hoped.

Therefore, on the day Nora and Trevor went to the airport for Trevor's return trip to Vancouver, Walter made an excuse to stay home. He didn't even remember what the excuse was, but apparently it was satisfactory, for no one questioned it. He was free to see Angela.

She phoned him from his mother's. "I'm glad I caught you home."

"Nora took Trevor to the plane. I stayed home."

"I thought you might. Your mother invited me for lunch so I walked over here to her place. Now she's having her nap. What are you doing?"

"Up until now, I've been waiting for you to call."

"Then I didn't disappoint you, did I?"

Walter chuckled. "My love, you never disappoint me. At least, not lately, you haven't. Listen, Mother sleeps for a couple of hours every afternoon. I'll pick you up right away. We'll go for a drive or something."

✐

Their tree-enclosed area of the beach where they used to make love, was now occupied by a three-story 'cottage'. "Times are looking up," was Angela's reaction to their discovery. "Who'd have thought anyone would build a mansion out here? Even if they could afford it."

"I haven't been out here for so long I had no idea this was going on. It's not a place I ever came to without you."

"You never brought other girls out here?"

"No."

"Not even Nora?"

"No."

"I don't know why that pleases me, but it does. Strictly our place, then, wasn't it?"

"I'm afraid so. Do you...? Did you ever think of it?"

"Many times. But life goes on."

Suddenly, Walter needed to know. "Who is Stewart?"

"Just some guy I've dated a few times. Why?"

"Do you plan to marry him?"

"The subject *has* come up?"

"That's not what I asked."

"Then the answer is, 'that depends'."

"Depends on what?"

"On how I feel about things when I get home."

Without any further discussion of Stewart, or of anything else, for that matter, Walter drove them back to town to Angela's motel. Neither gave any thought to who might have seen the two of them entering her room or who might have noticed that Walter didn't emerge until two and a half hours later. After all, they were cousins and there'd been a great deal of coming and going for a week or so. Probably, not one person in McClung would have thought a thing of it. Perhaps not even the Fact Finders, Ruby and Fran.

What Angela told his mother, Walter never knew, only that it would be believable and she would be believed. At any rate, he felt no concern over what anyone might think for he had pretty much made up his mind about what was going to happen with the rest of his life. The only problem was how he could make it happen without hurting too many people. The situation was complicated—spousal and financial.

By the time Walter got home that night, it was past sunset and Nora had worked herself up into a towering rage. He could almost believe she knew how he and Angela had spent the afternoon. But that was impossible. Anyway, it was the evening she was angry about.

"Where have you been all this time? Why do you have to roam around like a nomad all the time and leave me to take Trevor to the airport alone? I didn't know where you were. Why can't you ever come home for supper? I get lonely, you know."

Nora's lip was trembling and he knew she was making a valiant effort to stave off tears. He felt a rush of sympathy. Not love, particularly, but a kind of affectionate sympathy. He knew all about loneliness. "I'm sorry, I should have come home sooner. Called, at least. I'm sorry you're lonely," he added, patting her head.

"Don't pat me. I'm not a mangy old dog! I need a hug, at least."

So Walter hugged his wife, ate some cold fried potatoes and ham, then turned on the television set where he sat watching whatever came on, not seeing or hearing any of it.

LEAVING HOME

After Angela went back to Florida, Walter was distraught and lonesome to the point of anguish. He'd already made up his mind to follow her when he could. In fact, he'd pretty much made her that promise. But he needed to look after getting the hay baled and ready for sale. It would provide some extra money. And before he could possibly leave, definite arrangements had to be made—arrangements for someone else to take over the farming operation. He owed Nora that much.

Martin Kroeger could do it he hoped, although he hadn't as yet had the nerve to ask him. Martin and Maggie had a special relationship with him and Nora, and Walter's leaving would be hard for them to understand or accept. Martin often spoke about acquiring more land, so that might allay any feelings of disloyalty *he* might feel towards Nora.

Nora. That was another matter entirely. Walter had no idea what to do about her. A month after his decision to leave, he still hadn't told her, although there was no doubt she knew their marriage was in trouble. 'Coward,' he told himself. And Angela was pressuring him to get on with it.

"If you keep putting it off, you won't ever go through with it, will you?" she'd said, accusingly, during their last phone conversation.

They talked when they could, and his last opportunity had been the night of Martin Kroeger's birthday party when he'd made some excuse to go home by himself. "I'll do it. I promised you, and I'll do it. It just has to be the right time, and I still haven't got arrangements made about the farm. By the way, has your friend, Stewart, been around?"

"He's called a couple of times."

"Shit," was all Walter could think of to say. Then, "I'll get things looked after as soon as I can, but there'll still be harvesting to get done."

"Surely somebody else can drive a combine. I'm getting lonesome, you know."

"Lonesome! You're not the only one. I miss you so much. I promise, I'll get things sorted out as soon as I can. I love you." After he hung up, Walter got into his truck and drove around until nearly midnight wondering if he was going crazy or if this was a normal kind of thing men go through. He had to do something, and soon.

That was over three weeks ago and nothing had been settled. Nothing had been said! Finally, he found the courage to cross the road to the Kroeger place and found Martin in the shop working on his ride-on lawn mower.

Martin straightened up, shoved his greasy John Deere cap back and greeted Walter with: "Damned glad to see you. I think this thing is beyond fixing and Maggie's mad as a wet hen because the grass is a foot high. Wants me to buy a new one, but they cost an arm and a leg. Says she's sick and tired of trying to herd this one around the yard. Steering seems to be shot. What do you think I should do?"

Walter was aware that some answer seemed to be required, but he couldn't for the life of him, think what it was Martin wanted. Instead, he just blurted out his news. "I've decided to leave the farming business. Would you like to take over for me?"

Martin just looked at Walter blankly. Then he laughed. "Leave? We'd all like to pack it in—leave the farm to the goddam gophers. Not to mention the hail and the drought and the piss-poor grain prices. I've got enough problems of my own without taking on yours. What's the joke?"

"It's no joke."

Martin studied him for a moment. "You're not fooling, are you?" Then, alarmed, "Are you sick or something?"

"I suppose I am, in a way."

"Have you seen a doctor? What does Nora think?"

"Nora doesn't think anything. She doesn't know yet. Anyway, it's not the kind of sickness anyone around here can do anything about."

"You got some rare disease and you're going to a clinic in the States, I bet. The Mayo Clinic or somewhere?" He put his arm around Walter's shoulder. "Come on, you can tell us. Come into the house and I'll get Maggie to make us some coffee."

"Thanks, but no thanks. And I'm not ailing in a physical way. Or, at least, it's not incurable. I hope."

Martin scratched his head. "I don't know what in hell you're talking about. Beats me. What would you do? Where would you go?"

"I'd go to Florida. But not to a clinic."

"Florida? What's there then?'

"The woman I love."

Martin seemed more confused. "Does Nora want to move to Florida?"

"I'm not taking Nora."

"But you said... I mean, about the love thing. I don't understand..."

So Walter tried to explain as best he could about the situation with Angela.

Martin was appalled. "And leave Nora?" he kept asking. "She's the best woman I ever met. Why? Are you crazy?"

"I don't think so. I know it's hard for you to understand, but I've been thinking about it for a long time—ever since Angela came to Sandra's wedding."

"That's not so long ago. That's not a very long time."

"I realize that, but sometimes a person just knows when the time has come. And maybe I was even considering it before then. I think I might have been."

Martin scratched his head again and looked at the ground. "Well, I sure as hell can't figure it out."

"I don't expect you to. Just believe me when I say I'm leaving and I'd like you to have a chance at running our farm."

"I can't believe what you're saying. Me? Run your place?" Then after a pause, "Maybe Nora could run it. She *could* do it. Hire people. All that. She's one smart lady."

"I doubt if that would work. She doesn't know all that much about the operation. It would be simpler if you'd just rent it, work on a crop-share basis, or something. Maybe you'd be interested in purchase, later on. All I know is, I'm leaving. I'll tell Nora tonight."

"I think that's rotten."

"I'm sorry you feel that way." Walter walked to his truck but, before getting in, turned and said, "Let me know by tomorrow what you've decided."

Martin just stood, shaking his head. "I still don't understand... What am I gonna tell Maggie?"

"Nothing yet. Not until after I've told Nora."

"You son-of-a-bitch. I've known you all my life and

143

I never took you for a guy that would dump the best woman in the world."

"I wish it didn't have to be like this. Really, I do. I'm sorry."

"It don't have to be like this, you crazy ass."

"Yes, it does. I'm sorry. I've already told you I'm sorry."

Walter got in the truck, turned on the ignition and wondered if he'd have to spend the rest of his life saying, 'I'm sorry.'

He had no flair for shocking or disappointing people and he left Martin knowing that he'd managed the conversation and farm proposition very badly. The outcome of their exchange was plain, though. Martin loathed what Walter was about to do. It was discouraging, but not much different from what he expected. Quite probably there was no one who could possibly appreciate his position, to sympathize and tell him he was doing the right thing. There was no one who could appreciate what he felt for Angela. Certainly not Nora.

Walter made up his mind to be as gentle as possible with Nora. He drove around for a couple of hours until he thought he could face her with his decision. But all of his rehearsed speeches, all his good intentions went up in smoke. It happened without his reckoning. When he got home for supper, the table was set but no food was in evidence. He sat at the table.

Nora was not in a good humor. "You're here. Finally. We've got some stew I can heat up or we can have bacon and eggs. What do you want?" There was a long silence before she repeated, "What do you want?"

His answer amazed them both. "A divorce," he replied, simply.

So it was out.

Nora sat abruptly and stared at him. "You're not kidding, are you?"

"No."

"Inga?"

He almost laughed. "No."

"Who, then?"

"Angela."

It seemed to take Nora forever to comprehend his announcement. Finally she looked at him and said, tonelessly, "I figured there must be somebody. But I never even thought of Angela. How stupid of me."

Walter could think of nothing to add that would make his wife feel better and there was another long silence during which Nora appeared to be turning his stunning revelation over in her mind. As though coming to some solution, Nora finally said, "But these things happen to men sometimes. They get bored with what they have—their work, their wives. Mid-life crisis, it's called." She put her hand on his arm encouragingly. "We can work it out." She sounded surprisingly cool, as though the bad news was not unexpected and she was half prepared for it.

But her remark angered him, made it seem as though the love between him and Angela was a tri-fling, temporary thing that he'd get over in time. He removed her hand and his voice was harsher than he intended. "No," he said, "Sorry, but it's nothing that can be worked out. At least, not between you and I. I've made up my mind. I'm going to Florida as soon as I can get things arranged." Then he went out driving in his truck.

When he got back an hour or so later, she was still sitting where he'd left her. No sign of tears, although her cheeks were blazing red and she was shaking.

"And what am *I* supposed to do?" she raged. "Have you given that any thought?"

"I think Martin will take over the farm. Rent, I suppose, once he's thought it over. He knows. I talked to him today. Whatever arrangement we come to, I'll make sure you can stay on here in the house."

Nora leapt to her feet. "How very generous of you. You bastard! You're goddam right I'll stay on in the house. I'll run the farm, too. I'll figure out how things are done. It can't be too hard—you've done it all these years. No way you're going to rent it to Martin. I'll need all the money I can get from the place. We *are* still paying for our son to go to university. Or have you given Trevor any thought at all? You son-of-a-bitch! And don't expect to get any money out of this place to spend on yourself or your precious Angela. You low-down, dirty son-of-a-bitch!"

Walter had no idea his wife could curse like that. He was able to block out a lot of the tirade, but distinctly heard her accusation, "Mario is yours, isn't he?"

He took a deep breath. "Yes."

She jumped up and came toward him with fists raised as though to strike. "You son-of-a-bitch!"

"You've already mentioned that." Then, Walter put his hands up to ward off the potential blows. "I didn't know before, or I would have married her. I would never have believed those old wives' tales about children of first cousins being idiots. I would never have got you involved in the situation."

"Would never have married me, you mean." Nora lowered her fists and produced a sneering laugh. "What a mercy that would have been! Then maybe I might have married a man who took his marriage vows seriously." Her face was white and she sat again. "What do you propose to tell your *legitimate* children?"

"I have no idea." Then, after a moment. "I thought it might be best if.... Maybe you could tell them...."

She flared up again. "No bloody way! That's your responsibility. And what about your mother? What do you intend to tell the old witch?"

"I have no idea."

"Maybe you'd better get some ideas. And soon."

✐

But ideas of how to tell his children and his mother about his impending flight didn't come easily to Walter. In fact, they didn't come at all. He'd made such a mess of dealing with first Martin and then Nora that he was completely paralyzed as far as dealing with anyone else was concerned. He simply couldn't face up to anyone who might accuse and berate him or try to make him see where his duty lay. So he put the matter of telling Trevor and Sandra out of his mind.

After the confrontation with Nora he took his usual truck ride and a mile and a quarter from home, he ran out of gas. Unusual for Walter to forget to fill the tank, but then everything in his life was unusual and his thoughts were constantly scattered. They were more focussed, though, on the walk home to fill a gas can and the subsequent walk back to the vehicle. To keep his thoughts from becoming gloomy, he concentrated his thoughts on Angela and the dream of having her, once again, in his arms. It was late when he finally parked the truck in the garage and went indoors.

Nora was no where in sight, but all the suitcases they owned were piled neatly in the kitchen. Walter looked inside them to check. They were filled with his belongings. He took the cordless phone into the back shed and dialed Angela's number. It would be God-only-knew what time in Naples, Florida, but he didn't hesitate.

When Angela finally came on the line sounding half-asleep and worried, she asked, "Where are you?"

"At home. Well, in Manitoba, anyway."

"Are you drunk or something?"

"No."

"Why are you calling at this hour?"

"To tell you I'm leaving for Florida."

"When?"

"Right now. Tonight. I didn't think I could get it together this soon, but it'll be tonight all right."

"Have you told Nora?"

"Yes. Tonight. Earlier."

"How did it go?"

"The worst day of my life."

"Sorry about that. When should I expect you?"

"When you see me, I guess. I'm driving. I'll keep in touch. I love you."

Walter could see the lights of McClung when the truck stopped—out of gas again. He banged his head on the steering wheel and cursed his forgetfulness. There was no all-night gas bar in McClung. He'd have to wait in the cab until morning. Then the entire township would know he was leaving. All anyone had to do was look in the back of the truck to see the suitcases tossed in there helter-skelter. Since there was no chance for sleep, he tried to review his situation more sanely. First of all, he had only about forty dollars in his pocket—not much more than enough to get him to the US border. He'd have to walk to town and wait somewhere until the banks opened. Then he'd have to get some gas for the truck. Also, it would be a good idea to see if the hardware store had a tarp he could purchase to cover the suitcases in the back of the truck. He spent until nearly dawn pondering his moves when an early morning milk tanker stopped to see if he was in trouble. It was driven by a young man he knew slightly, but who asked no questions and paid no attention to the truck's contents. He offered Walter a ride into McClung and it was gratefully accepted.

It was still very early in the morning—too early for any businesses to be opened, so Walter got the driver to drop him at his mother's house where he took refuge in her garage. At five to nine, feeling like a thief, he slipped out of his hiding place and walked to the hardware store using his credit card to purchase the only tarp they had in stock. A bright yellow, eye-catching one. Then he put it under his arm and walked to the nearest gas station where he persuaded the surly young attendant to fill a gas can for him. All he had to do after that was to wait until someone he knew came along to give him a ride to his vehicle.

It was accomplished more quickly than he anticipated when another young man of his acquaintance came by for gas and agreed to do taxi duty for ten dollars. Then all that was left to do was drive back to town, return the gas can, fuel up the truck and go to the bank. He took only as much money out of his and Nora's joint account as he thought was fair— three thousand dollars—not a huge amount. After all, she'd have to have cash for household expenses. And to finish the farming operation for the season. After that, she should have some money. What he, himself, would do for money after his cash ran out, was something he didn't concern himself with. He was going to see Angela. That was all that mattered.

Before ten o'clock, Walter was in his truck heading for the border and Interstate Highway 29. He was too tired to feel much of anything.

⬭

When Nora reeled into the kitchen in the morning she was still in a daze from the sleeping pills she'd taken the night before—after packing Walter's belongings. She had considered getting drunk but she had no taste for whiskey and knew it would only produce an unappetizing vomiting session. After rummaging through the medicine cabinet, she found some pills that had been prescribed for Walter after one of his hernia operations. She took two to be on the safe side.

Therefore, it was nearly noon when she came to and began to ponder the previous night's activities. She hadn't heard Walter's return. The suitcases were gone, though, and so, she suspected, was Walter. It took two cups of strong coffee to bring her around enough for the rage to return. She looked around. "Jesus Christ!" she shouted to the blank bulletin board. "The son-of-a-bitch didn't even have the decency to leave a note!" It wasn't until then that she cried.

*

When Martin Kroeger came over around two-thirty that afternoon, he peeked in the kitchen window and saw Nora sitting, hunched over the kitchen table, surrounded by wet tissues. She was fast asleep. He opened the door and quietly went to her side, reached out to touch her hair and then stopped. He had no words of comfort ready, so he continued to stand until she, sensing a presence, jumped up suddenly, toppling the chair.

"Sorry," she said, "I'm so nervous." She had one hand on the table to steady herself. "I didn't know anybody was here. I thought at first it might be Walter."

"No, just me," Martin said as he took a moment to right the chair and put off the time when he could no longer avoid her eyes.

Nora took Martin's arm and forced him to turn and look at her. "Did you know what was going on?"

150

"Not until yesterday."

"He really did a number on us, didn't he?"

"Looks like it."

"Maybe he'll come to his senses. Come back.... Do you think he might?"

Martin shook his head sadly, "I doubt it. He seemed pretty determined."

"I can't help but hope, though. Maybe Angela won't want him." She laughed shortly. "Maybe she'll get sick of him and send him back."

"Maybe."

"Maybe he'll have an accident and get killed. My God! What am I saying?!" she sobbed.

Martin took her in his arms then in an awkward, brotherly hug. "It'll turn out all right. Don't worry, Maggie and I will look after you."

"But what are we going to do? What am I going to do?"

"Right now, just go and get dressed. Then pack a bag."

"Whatever for? I'm not going anyplace."

"Just to our place. Until you get yourself together. Maggie is making those biscuits you like. She brought up some chokecherry jelly from the basement to have on them. I don't suppose you've eaten. I told her to give us half an hour." He released her. "Go. Get ready."

So Nora, not knowing what else to do, showered, dressed and threw an odd assortment of garments on the bed before rummaging in the closet looking for a bag. Then she remembered that she'd used every suitcase, piece of hand luggage and tote bag in the place the night before. They were all stuffed with Walter's things, in the back of Walter's truck, on their way to Florida.

That knowledge brought on a fit of hysterical laughter and when she ran downstairs with her collection of underwear, jeans and tee shirts tumbling out of her arms, Martin looked terrified. "Are you OK?"

She rushed past him into the kitchen. "I'll have to use a shopping bag!" Then, wiping her eyes, "I must get hold of myself."

Martin followed her and watched a she rifled through the pantry, tossing out bags of various shapes and sizes until she found what she wanted— a large plastic Wal-Mart bag—and began stuffing her clothing into it. "Walter always joked that an Irishman's idea of matched luggage was two Eaton's shopping bags. Now, Eaton's is long gone. And so is Walter. Funny, eh?"

"Here, you dropped this," Martin said, handing her a black lace nightgown.

Nora took it and held it up. "Why would I pack a thing like that?"

"I have no idea."

"Walter gave it to me on my fortieth birthday. I only wore it once or twice. When we went away on trips I took it. It didn't seem like me. Too elegant, some-how." She dropped the gown in the garbage "I'll just run up and get my cotton nightie."

"Aren't you going to lock the door?" Martin asked when Nora finally completed her packing operation.

"We hardly ever lock doors. Only if we're going to be away for awhile."

"Well...?"

"It'll be OK for a little while. I don't think Walter has a key with him and if he should come back..."

Martin didn't argue and they started off across the road. In a moment, he noticed that she was carrying the cordless telephone. "You won't need that, Nora."

"I just thought. You know. If Walter should decide to call..."

"Nora, it wouldn't work at our place, anyway. And he isn't going to call."

"How do you know?"

"Just a feeling, that's all."

"You're probably right," she said, throwing the phone into the ditch.

Martin retrieved it. "No need to throw it away, though. You'll need it later. When you go back home."

"I may never go back home."

"Whatever."

Maggie was waiting on the steps when they arrived. She was red-eyed and obviously upset, although she had on a blouse, skirt and frilly apron—not Maggie's usual form of apparel. This meant she was going to try to pull herself together and play the gracious hostess even if it killed her. "Welcome," she said. "You can stay as long as you like." Her bottom lip trembled. "You can take your things up to Mother and Dad's old room."

Martin frowned. "Not yet, Maggie. We'll eat first. Anyway, she only has this little bag of things."

"Yes, only a little bag," Nora said.

Nobody seemed to know what to do or say next. The transition from being the elder, protective neighbor to an extremely needy grass widow was not going to be easy.

"Well, come on everybody. Sit in," Maggie invited, and held out a chair for Nora.

The table was set with the Kroeger's best silver and china and, even in her despair and confused state of mind, Nora was flattered. She reached for the teapot. "Would you like me to pour the tea?"

"God, no!" Maggie practically shouted.

Nora was taken aback. "Sorry. I didn't intend to interfere."

"Not interference. Exactly. It's just that Momma always said that if you let somebody else pour tea in your house you'd get pregnant."

Martin was embarrassed. "Oh, Maggie. Such crazy superstition!"

"Well, I'm not going to take any chances."

"The chance you'd have to take wouldn't be with a teapot," her brother teased.

"Oh, bugger off!"

"I've heard that teapot thing, too," Nora said to soothe Maggie. "That, and plenty of others. The Irish are great on superstitions. I wouldn't pay any attention to who pours your tea."

"No, well..."

Conversation languished. Martin had, apparently, extracted a promise from Maggie not to talk about Walter's defection and Nora had no desire to do so. She was too tired to do much beyond drinking her tea and eating a few bites of Maggie's biscuits. Finally, when it became clear that she was having difficulty staying awake, Martin suggested that Nora go lie down for a nap.

⌀

Either the sleeping pills from the night before had not entirely worn off, or Nora's mind and body were clamoring for escape. In any case, she dropped into a drugged sleep. There was a reddish glow in the sky when she wakened and was amazed that she'd slept until sunset. It was some moments before she realized where she was and her reason for being there. She lay still for a few moments, not remembering whether the bedroom window faced east or west. A few muffled sounds drifted upstairs form the kitchen and she assumed that Maggie was preparing supper, so after a hurried trip to the bathroom and without even looking for her comb, she slipped downstairs.

Martin was sitting at the kitchen table stirring his coffee and Maggie was busy making toast. They both turned at Nora's approach. "Good morning," they said in unison.

"Morning! I thought it was suppertime!"

"Nope. Morning. We never have toast for supper. Martin has to have more than just toast for supper."

"Why didn't you wake me?"

"We were going to," Martin said, "but you were sleeping,"

"Sleeping like a hog,"

"Like a log, Maggie, not a hog," her brother corrected, then shared a glance and a grin with Nora.

'I can still smile.' Nora thought in wonder, 'Maybe I'll live after all'.

Martin cleared his throat. "Guess we're gonna have to do some talking. Make some decisions."

"But you told me I couldn't say anything...."

"It's all right, Maggie. I'm feeling some better. A little rested, anyway. And I'm not that fragile, I won't break."

Maggie turned away quickly to hide her tears. Martin ignored her. "Maggie and I.... Well, we've talked it over and we're willing to help in any way we can. If you want us to rent, we'll rent. If you want to do some kind of a share thing, we'll do that, too."

Maggie blew her nose. "What if Walter changes his mind and comes back? He might, you know. I think he's sick, that's what I think. No other way would he just up and leave us. Leave *you*, I mean. He's not that kind of a guy."

Martin gave Maggie a dangerous look. "Remember, I told you we have to leave personalities out of this as much as we can. We can't depend on Walter to come back. Just put a sock in it, OK?"

"Why do you have to be so bitchy in the mornings? Martin is always bitchy in the mornings," she explained to Nora.

"I'm feeling kind of bitchy, myself. But you're right, Martin, we have to figure out how to keep things going." Then she went and hugged Maggie. "Walter's not coming back. We have to get used to it."

Maggie struggled free, shrieking, "How do you know? You can't be sure! He's just sick. I know it in my bones. He'll come back to us!"

Martin and Nora watched sadly as Maggie fled to her bedroom.

"She's taking it pretty hard. Almost as bad as you, I think."

"At the moment, I have no idea how I'm taking it. Not gracefully, that's for sure. I can't believe it yet. Really. But it is becoming clear, even to me. Even to stupid old Nora."

"You're not the least bit stupid," Martin said, angrily banging his coffee mug on the table. "It's that low-down, son-of-a-bitch that's stupid!"

"But you told Maggie we had to keep personalities out of this."

"I know, I'm sorry. It's just that I'm so goddam mad."

"Me, too. But it won't help. Gotta keep cool, that's what we gotta do. First, I have to figure out how to tell the kids. And the ever-loving mother-in-law."

"Why? That's his job."

"He won't do it."

"Want me to?"

Nora sighed and put her head in her hands. "No, I'll have to do it. Somehow, sometime, someway."

There was a short silence before Martin rose and said, "Guess I'd better get out and do a bit of work."

Nora looked up in time to see tears glistening in Martin's eyes. "OK. Fine. I'll be OK. Thanks for everything," she said, as he went out the door.

ALONE

Nora didn't stay on with Maggie and Martin as long as she thought she might. For one thing, there were chores at home that needed attention—her roses, her indoor plants and, of course, poor old Sam who had alternated between whining at the Kroeger's door and pacing around in the garage where Walter used to park his truck. He'd reluctantly followed Martin as he coaxed the old dog across the road to be fed, but Sam obviously didn't relish the idea of taking his meals from a strange dish beside a strange doorstep and would leave as soon as he ate. He was a one-family, one-dog-house mutt and was enormously happy to see Nora returning home with her Wal-Mart bag of belongings three days after she'd left. He almost wagged his tail off.

"I wish I could be as happy as you are, old boy," she murmured, kneeling down to accept a wet welcome home kiss.

Once indoors, Nora pondered her first chore. She went directly to the telephone and called her mother-in-law. As she expected, the elder Mrs. Fields was full of complaints—notably her inability to reach Nora or Walter. "I've been calling for days. Where have you been for land's sakes?"

"Here and there. Busy, you know. But fine, otherwise."

"How is Sandra, have you heard from her?"

"Not for a while, but I'll be in touch with her again soon. I'm really calling to see if you might have Angela's phone number in Naples."

"Why? Did she leave something behind?"

"Not exactly. She got away with something that didn't belong to her."

"What was that?"

"Nothing too important. I'll be talking with you again soon. If you wouldn't mind now, I'd like the number. I'll explain later."

When she'd carefully written down the number, which Maude Fields had to repeat twice—Nora poured herself a tall glass of cold water from the fridge and sat for a moment, gathering strength.

It took three attempts before she succeeded in getting through. When Angela came on the line, Nora was unable to say a word. Not even hello, although Angela kept repeating, "Who is there? I know somebody is there? Can you hear me?"

Nora hung up, went to the freezer and pulled out a couple of left over pieces of Saran-wrapped wedding cake. She had to have a sugar fix. Or something. Alcohol didn't appeal to her. Never had. Then she made a big pot of Kona coffee, a gift from friends who had been to Hawaii, and a special treat. When it was ready, she got down her fanciest bone-china mug and poured herself a steaming pick-me-up. After adding two teaspoons of sugar, she settled down beside the phone and called Angela's number again.

This time, she was ready when Angela answered.

"Is Walter there?" Nora asked in a voice she didn't recognize as her own.

"Why? Who's calling? Who wants to know?"

"His wife."

"Then why doesn't she call?"

"She *is* calling. This is Nora. May I speak to him, please."

There was some background conversation, which Nora couldn't catch. Then Angela was back on the line. "Sorry, he can't come to the phone right now."

"So he *is* there?"

"Yes."

"I need to speak to him."

There was more background mumbling before Angela came back. "Sorry, he doesn't want to talk right now. He's very tired. He's had a hard few days."

"That's a pity. Poor Walter. Poor tired darling." Nora was beginning to lose it, she could feel her head beginning to pound and her hands were sweaty. "Then, ask him for me if he's told his mother yet."

"He hasn't told anyone."

"Ask him when he intends to tell his mother. The children, too."

It was an even longer interval before Angela came back. "He says you'll have to look after it. He says you're much better at these things."

Nora had the foresight to hang up before she started swearing. "Fine, then," she screamed to the dead and dying daisies that stood on the buffet. "I'll tell the old troll! I'll tell the children! I'll tell the whole goddam world!" Then she threw the bouquet through the kitchen window—brown vase and all. It was quickly followed by the china mug, which splattered coffee in a wide arc across the kitchen.

Sam carefully made his way through the broken glass and came to scratch and whine at the door. She rushed to open it. "And you, you old bitch! You don't have to look so high and mighty!" Then she sat down and tried to get hold of herself. Never, never had she ever before carried on like a raving maniac. It wasn't Sam's fault. She could hear his continued whining, but when she went to apologize to him, he turned and limped towards the Kroegers, tail between his legs.

"I'm sorry, Sam," she called after him. "I'm so sorry." He stopped, looked back twice and continued on his way. Nora ran after him, which increased his speed slightly. When she caught up with him, she fell to her knees and hugged Sam to her. "I can't afford to lose you, too." Then she cried.

Martin, who hadn't wanted Nora to go home alone in the first place, was at her side in a moment. "There, there. Things will work out."

She wiped her eyes and nose on her shirttail. "I don't see how."

Martin located and handed her a crumpled Kleenex, then knelt down beside her. "They will, they will. Things always get better. What can I do?"

"I would have said 'go after Walter', but he's already in Florida."

"He called?"

"I called Angela."

"You should have let me do that." Martin said, retrieving the damp Kleenex to mop at the place on his face where Sam had bestowed a wet kiss.

"No need to put you through that." She rose unsteadily and he put his arm around her.

"I'd have done it."

"I know. But *I* had to do it." She bit her lip." "Maybe there is something you *can* do, though."

"Anything. Anything at all."

"Come with me to the lion's den. Or the lioness's. Whatever."

"I take it she doesn't know."

"No. Angela said that Walter said I have to do it."

Martin let go of Nora and began pacing furiously. Then he exploded. "That dirty low-down son-of-a-bitch. I'd just like to beat the piss out of him." He slammed a fist into the air as though it was Walter's nose. "Him and his goddam girlfriend." He danced around in a small circle while throwing several more air punches. Then he threw his hat in the air and, when it fell to the ground, jumped on it like *it* was the errant Walter.

Confused, Sam gave up on his tail wagging and slunk off in a northerly direction.

Calm, reliable, unflappable Martin was having a major tantrum. Even the most crucial machinery breakdowns had never elicited such fury. Nora, suddenly seized with the absurdity of his uncharacteristic performance, broke into wild laughter. She was doubled over when Maggie came running out of the house.

"What's happening? Somebody tell me what's happening!"

"Martin just ruined his hat," Nora gasped before bursting into still more laughter.

"That greasy old thing? He's got lots more in the house. Daddy used to do that all the time, only his were the straw kind. Pretty much buggered them up. What's the big deal now?"

"The bastard expects Nora to tell his mother."

Maggie stood twisting her flour-covered Home Depot apron. She shook her head sadly. "He's gotta be sick. Like I said before, Walter's gone off his rocket. That's all there is to it."

Nora and Martin were silent for a moment, pondering the possibility of an insane Walter—departing on a rocket ship.

"No," Nora said, finally, "not insane. A bit nuts. Maybe temporarily nuts, but I doubt it. Anyway, he's gone. For good, I figure."

"But to leave us like that. *You*, I mean. Leave *you*. Up the creek without a saddle... How can you stand it?"

"I'll just keep on keeping on. Martin said he'd help me. *You* said you'd help me. You may as well stop the hand wringing, Maggie. It won't bring him back."

Martin, who had subsided a bit after that hat-stomping incident, took Nora's arm. "Why don't we all go into the house and figure out what to do next?"

Maggie had made a fresh batch of biscuits and there was some of her homemade apricot jam to go with them. Fresh coffee was brewed and Nora and Martin sat at the kitchen table discussing the next move. Maggie didn't sit. She seldom sat. Sometimes she perched on a stool or turned a chair backwards and straddled it. Today, she paced around the kitchen wiping up spilled flour from the counters, sweeping up bits and pieces from the linoleum and even making a rushed trip outdoors to shake the mat. Finally, she paused, poured herself a mug of coffee and stood leaning against the doorjamb. "Sounds like you might need some company. Telling the old lady, I mean. I could go with you," she offered, hopefully.

"Oh, no!" Martin and Nora said in unison.

"Why not? I'd love to go," Maggie pleaded. "I'd love to give her a piece of my mind. The old bag."

"I can understand that," Nora said gently, "but I think maybe it would be better if just Martin came with me." When Maggie was about to protest, she continued. "You know. Because of the wedding thing. Telling her that I was dead. You know. She might still resent that."

So Maggie reluctantly agreed to stay home while Martin and Nora delivered the bad news.

"I'd really appreciate having you for moral support, Martin, if you're sure you don't mind."

"I don't mind. That's not it. It's just that I hope I can help. I'm so crazy mad."

"I know all about mad. It doesn't work."

"Like smashing the kitchen window?"

"Right. You saw that?"

"Heard it. I was standing, sort of behind the caragana hedge. I heard the glass break. Don't know how you did it, though."

Nora's voice rose, "With that ugly brown vase that Walter's mother gave us for our last anniversary."

Maggie seemed astonished by the revelation. Nora, in a fit of rage? Throwing things?! "Really?! Did the vase break?"

"I expect so. I sincerely hope so. Never liked the bloody thing, anyway. I liked the china mug, though. If I had it to do over again, I'd keep the mug."

Maggie came and patted her shoulder. "Maybe you should go have a nice little lie down before you do anything else."

"Oh, I won't do anything else, Maggie. You won't have to hide your good dishes. I won't break anything else. Don't worry."

Martin rose. "I'll go measure the window for new glass right away. And why didn't it have a screen on it?"

"It was torn. Walter took it off to fix it before the wedding. Never got it done, though. I guess he'd lost interest in the house by then."

"We can get a new screen too, then. Pick it up while we're in town. When did you want to go?"

"Anytime, I guess. After I change my clothes."

They crossed the road together and Martin patiently cleaned up the broken glass and measured the window while Nora tried to decide what to wear. She eventually settled on her navy blue suit and white blouse.

When she came back down to the kitchen, Martin

163

seemed a bit doubtful. "Pretty dressed up, aren't you?"

"Maybe. Yes, I guess so, but this outfit always makes me feel organized and efficient. Sort of unflappable. Brave, maybe. I wear it to funerals."

"And this feels like a funeral?"

"More or less. Let's go."

It was past three o'clock when Nora and Martin rattled into Maude Fields' driveway in Maggie's old truck. Martin's was on loan to another neighbor and couldn't be spared for the occasion. Neither had thought of using Nora's car. They sat for a few moments after the vehicle had shuddered to a stop. The question of how to broach the subject to the elderly lady of her errant son's departure was occupying the minds of both. "Why don't we start off by just saying that Walter's gone away for awhile? To think things over. Give her some time to get used to the idea that something's wrong," Nora suggested.

"You told me you had your 'brave' outfit on. Don't chicken out. From what I know of her, the old gal's not that frail. I vote we dump the whole load. Right off the bat. She'll have to get used to it. Just like we did."

"And tell her about Angela?"

"Of course, Angela! She'll have to know why he left. What's got into you, anyway?"

"I don't know. I suddenly feel sorry for her, I guess."

"Shit, Nora, she's about as fragile as a jack hammer." Then, turning his head towards the door he added, "don't look now. She's on deck waiting for us."

"Do you suppose she knows already?"

"She'll find out soon enough," Martin said, grimly,

as he turned off the ignition and went around to open Nora's door."

The elder Mrs. Fields waited on the step until Martin and Nora were just a few feet away. She squinted at them. "My land, Nora! You're all dolled up. What's the occasion?" She stretched out her right hand to Martin. "Have I met this young man before?"

"Many, many times," Martin said, ignoring her gesture. "I'm Martin Kroeger, your old neighbor. Nora's neighbor."

"Oh, yes. You help Walter a bit, don't you?"

He ignored that remark, too.

"Well, don't just stand there. Come on in. It's your lucky day. I've just put the kettle on. I've invited Mrs. Albertson from up the street over for tea."

Nora hesitated. "Perhaps we should come back later, then."

"Oh, no. It will be fine. She's not at all particular. Come, right this way." And she led her two impromptu guests down the short hall to her small living room."

Nora was nervous, but not so nervous that she missed seeing the dust that had been collecting for some time on the furniture—also the unusual amount of clutter and disarray. The abnormal state of her mother-in-law's home indicated a growing lack of vision on the part of its owner and Nora was struck by the fact that she hadn't visited her for a very long time. She felt a tiny wave of sympathy and cleared her throat to speak.

Martin, perhaps sensing Nora's mood, spoke first. "I think it might be a good idea if you *un*invited Mrs. Albatross."

"It's Albertson," Maude Fields intoned carefully. "Albertson. But whatever for? She's my best friend."

Before Nora could speak, Martin again took the lead. "Because we've come on some private business."

"Oh. I wondered what brought you here. Most

unusual. Most unusual. Very well, then, I'll call her."

During the few moments it took for her to ring her neighbor from the kitchen, Martin and Nora exchanged uneasy glances. Martin scratched his head. Nora bit her lip, half grinned and whispered, nervously, "I loved the Albatross thing."

Martin was embarrassed. "You would! It was a mistake. An honest mistake."

"Never mind, I like mistakes like that."

"So I've noticed. Maggie amuses you all the time, doesn't she? I mean, like yesterday when she said..."

But Maude Fields was back in the room. She sat gingerly on the white leather recliner chair, smoothed down her skirt and said, "I gather it's bad news. Walter? Sandra?"

"Walter," Nora and Martin said in unison.

"Dead?"

"No. Not dead. Gone away," Martin said.

"Where to?"

Nora was barely able to speak the word, "Florida."

"To Angela?"

Nora could only nod.

"I was afraid something like that might happen."

"You were?! Then why in God's name did you insist on inviting her to the wedding?"

"I didn't insist. Only suggested. I just assumed that after all this time..." She smiled ruefully. "You know me—how I like to get all the family together when I can."

There was a long pause which, apparently, Nora was expected to fill with a commiserating response. But she just gazed, stonily, at her mother-in-law and waited for her to dig herself in even deeper.

After a few uneasy moments, Maude Fields blundered on. "If I'd given it more thought I wouldn't have bothered. Or, at least, I'd have insisted that Angela stay with me and not at the motel. That way, I could have kept an eye on her. Kept things in hand, so to speak."

Martin made a rude noise, which sounded very much like 'bullshit' but apparently, it went unheard by the elderly woman, for she went on to excuse herself from the affair. "Anyway, I expected that Walter and Angela would be over that puppy love thing by now, for heaven's sakes. Unfortunate. Very unfortunate."

"To say the least," Martin said crossly.

But Maude only sighed and went on in a reminiscent tone. "If Angela's mother hadn't been so pig-headed all those years ago this would never have happened. They would have got married and, and..."

Nora gripped the arm of the rose plush armchair until her knuckles whitened. "And I would never have come into the picture?"

"Something like that." Maude smiled condescendingly, Nora thought, before bestowing the compliment. "It's not that you haven't been a good wife, dear. You've been very good for Walter. Always kept the house clean, the lawn mowed. It's just that..."

Nora was able to unclench her teeth long enough to finish her mother-in-law's thought. "Just that Angela would have been better?"

"That's not exactly what I meant."

"What, *exactly*, did you mean?"

"That you wouldn't have been hurt like this. I'm sorry. You might not believe this but I'm truly sorry."

Martin made another 'bullshit' sound, which was once again ignored.

"I am also not surprised. That old wives' tale about first cousins marrying is rot, you know. My grandparents were first cousins. No idiots issued from that union."

Nora clearly remembered stories about Walter's great uncle Amos and his curious escapades. She had to restrain herself from commenting that her mother-in-law's complacent 'no idiots in the family' remark might be a matter of opinion.

"All upstanding citizens, my family were," said Maude Fields as she straightened her spine, smiled and assumed her regal pose.

Maude's resemblance to the late Queen Mother was not lost on Nora and, had she been wearing a big hat and holding a glass of gin, the likeness would have been almost perfect.

Martin made another noise which seemed to come from deep in his throat and caused Nora to fear he might be preparing to make an unpleasant remark. In any case, she was unwilling to hear any more about Walter and Angela, or even first cousins in general, and stood as though to leave. Martin, she could tell, was agitated, but remained seated until Maude got awkwardly to her feet and crossed the room as if she were the one planning to end the interview.

Then, he also rose and asked, "Don't you want to know what Nora is going to do? How she's going to manage without a husband?"

"Nora and I will talk again soon. Discuss details. Privately."

Again, Nora felt a white-hot flash of anger. "This is as private as it's going to get, Mother Fields. Martin will be in on all our meetings. He's standing by me. Even if you don't."

"I'll stand by you, dear! Whatever makes you think that I wouldn't?"

"Past experience."

The noble facade was suddenly replaced by her usual wheedling tone. "Oh dear, oh dear! You have to forget past difficulties. I, myself, have forgiven you. I still remember certain things but... Forgive and forget, that's what I always do."

For the life of her, Nora couldn't recall any crime

she might have committed against her mother-in-law that required any great forgiveness. On the contrary, it was Nora who'd had to do all the forgiving—the mean-spirited slights, the outright insults, the interference with almost everything she and Walter had tried to do. The list was endless.

Once again, Nora was so floored by the elderly woman's stupidity, and relentless selfishness, that she could only shake her head.

Maude Fields appeared to be panicking. "I always had your best interests at heart. You must know that. I don't want to lose you!"

Still, Nora stood, speechless, remembering the removal of all the furniture when she and Walter moved into the Field family home.

"I will see you again, won't I?"

"Of course. We'll have business to do. You'll get your share of the farm proceeds " And then, almost under her breath, "If there are any."

"And the children! You won't turn them against me, will you?"

Nora gazed directly into her mother-in-law's eyes and said, 'No, *I'd* never try to influence anyone's feelings. Anyway, they're grown-up now. Old enough to make their own judgements." Softening a little as she turned toward the door, added, "I'll see they keep in touch with you."

"Oh, thank you, thank you. I knew you would do the right thing."

As usual, Maude Fields had to have the last word and just as Martin and Nora were leaving, she bent to Nora and whispered, "Mario is Walter's son, isn't he?"

Nora nodded.

"I thought he might be. And he's no idiot, is he?" she said, before closing the door.

Martin practically ran to the truck, hopped in

without first opening the door for Nora and shouted, "Jesus Christ, Nora! I heard that! Is it true? Is it true?" he shouted again over the roar of the engine.

"Apparently."

"Shit! What are you going to tell Sandra and Trevor?"

"Good question. What do you think?"

"Don't tell them. Not about Mario, at least. They'll have to know about Walter and Angela."

Unexpectedly, Nora began to cry.

"I suppose you wouldn't consider marrying me?"

Nora shook her head

Martin reached over and patted her hand. "I didn't think so." Nothing more was said on the trip home.

⬧

Maggie had supper ready when Martin and Nora arrived back. She'd made a tuna casserole at home and carried it over to Nora's kitchen wrapped in an assortment of bath towels and an old parka. It was still hot and tasty. "Did you remember the glass for the window, Martin? And the screen?"

Nora and Martin looked at one another blankly. Nora answered, "We didn't have time, Maggie. Tomorrow's soon enough."

"Bugs, though. And mosquitoes'll be along any time now. I'll find some cardboard."

When Nora went upstairs to bed she absently noticed the pile of cast-off clothing she had tossed there before choosing the afternoon's navy suit. Too weary to hang anything up, she stripped off the suit, added it to the heap and crawled in underneath it. Her good neighbors were still downstairs, in the process of cutting up a cardboard carton to jam into the empty window space. She hadn't said thanks, or even, goodnight. They didn't seem to expect it.

Nora woke at four A.M. and stared at the wall. In Guelph it would be an hour earlier. Sandra and Nick were still on summer holidays. In three hours she would phone them, she decided, before falling into another restless sleep. When she woke again it was from a dream in which Walter was calling her to come and help him with some job or other in the garage and she was soaking wet. She jumped up in response to his request, then fell back onto the damp bed in despair.

The bedside radio clock was now standing at five forty-five. Six forty-five in Guelph. Nora staggered downstairs, found Sandra's number and phoned. No answer. "Damn, damn, damn! Where can they be?" she asked the refrigerator. "I really must stop talking to inanimate objects." She listened until there had been ten rings before giving up.

Trevor, then. She should call Trevor. But it was only just near five o'clock in Vancouver. Too early. Or was it seven o'clock? No, that was Ontario. She'd call both children later. After some coffee and bran flakes.

The sun was well-risen by the time she finished eating and thought about feeding poor old Sam. Sam, however, was nowhere to be found. At least not in her yard, so pulling an old jacket of Walter's over her night gown and poking bare feet into a pair of duck boots to ward off the morning dew, she set off for the Kroegers. Sam didn't appear to be at their place, either. She called softly from time to time, but no dog appeared.

Phone calls to the children took a back seat to the search for Sam. Nora, along with Martin and Maggie, searched every nook and cranny they could think of. "He's gone somewhere to be by himself," Maggie ventured, as she prepared to crawl into the shallow space under one of the granaries.

"Oh, no! To die, maybe?" Nora wailed.

"Not Sam, he's not ready to die yet," said Martin, as he gazed distractedly toward the nearest field. He had been heard to say, during the morning's hunt, that it was almost time to harvest the winter wheat and the machinery needed attention. It was not really in the nature of a complaint, but the concern was in his voice. Nora was concerned, too. After the winter wheat, the other crops came in quickly and they had, as yet, no extra help.

"Look, Martin, you go on and do what you need to do. Maggie and I will carry on by ourselves."

By suppertime, Sam had not turned up and Nora suggested they call the search off for the time being. "OK by me," Maggie said. "It's time to get something on the table for me and Martin. You can come over too, when you're ready. I have a big pizza in the freezer and some salad stuff. Not much use you trying to get a meal for one person."

"You're too kind. But, yes, I'll be happy to come. I don't know if I'll ever be able to cook just for myself."

While they were eating, Nora had a thought—perhaps Sam had gone much farther afield than they had expected. She didn't say anything, but when she excused herself, went home for a long sleeved shirt and some mosquito repellent. Armed against the bugs, she headed north to a bushy area, which was large enough to conceal a herd of elephants. She had just started to thrash her way through the undergrowth when she heard dogs barking in the distance—Inga's dogs.

Cursing herself for not having thought of it before, Nora covered the half-mile in record time. She was out of breath when she strode into Inga's yard and spied Sam coming toward her from around the corner of the large dog run. He didn't go into his customary trot. He didn't even hurry, but limped hesitantly in her direction as though a scolding might be in the offing. When she knelt, Sam's tail began to wag and he greeted her with the usual sloppy kisses. "What's wrong, old boy? Got a sore foot?"

He gave her an accusatory look, turned and went back to wherever he'd come from.

Then Nora heard Inga calling to her from the back porch. She was busy brushing the coat of one of her Samoyeds. "Hi, neighbor. I figured you might come looking for Sam. He's been here since yesterday. I've been trying to get you on the phone all day yesterday and again today. No answer. Figured you were away for a couple of days and Sam was lonesome so I fed and watered him."

"Not away, really. Just in and out a lot. But, thanks ever so much. I didn't think he would have gone that far, and I never even thought of him coming here."

"Oh, he comes around once in awhile to check things out. Did you know he had a sore paw? He got a piece of glass in it from somewhere."

"Oh dear! My fault."

Inga looked at Nora curiously. "Nobody's fault, I'm sure. Anyway, I got it out, fixed him up. It'll be sore for a day or so though, I imagine."

"How can I thank you?"

"No thanks necessary. Here," she handed Nora a fistful of white wool she'd just removed from the dog she was grooming. "Want to make some mitts?" She grinned.

Nora hesitated before reaching for the combings. "It's too hot for mitts right now. Maybe in January."

"Or maybe not." Inga laughed. "I had someone I know spin some of it into yarn once and made some mitts for my little niece. She didn't like them. Said that whenever they got wet the other kids told her she smelled like wet dog. Anyway, now that you're here, why not come in for a cup of herbal tea. Or

173

something. Maybe coffee if you'd rather."

Nora couldn't think of a polite way to decline the invitation so she followed Inga into her little home. She had no idea what to expect, but wasn't prepared for the coziness of the place. One stepped directly into the kitchen/living area from the doorway and a few clotheshooks attached to the wall beside the door held Inga's outdoor jackets and a sun hat. There were no cupboards as such but an antique buffet and hoosier graced the wall on either side of the sink. Above the window, over the sink, hung tied bunches of dried material Nora assumed were herbs.

"Sit, sit," Inga invited, indicating the antique rocking chair which sported a colorful granny square afghan. Nora was quite ready to sit and admire her surroundings. Tall vases of wild asters and goldenrod stood on tables and shelves while small bowls of pansies were scattered here and there. She picked one up to admire the smiling little faces.

"My favorite flower," Inga said. "Aside from the wild flowers, of course. And did you see the lady's slippers? There were oodles of them around in June."

"I guess I was too busy in June."

"It's a busy month, June is. All that planting and watering."

Inga put the kettle on. "Come with me, I'll show you the rest of my mansion." Nora followed her host, first into a tiny dining room that had been turned into an office with a desk and computer. Shelves lining the walls were filled with books and many others spilled over onto the floor. The wallpaper was light with a rather indistinct pattern suggestive of shrubbery, and three paintings hung on the walls—two landscapes and one beautiful watercolor of a young girl. Rather good ones, Nora thought. On top of the bookshelves were photographs of two teenaged children—a boy and a girl. Together and separately.

"Yours?" she asked.

"Mine. Four or five years ago. Jason and Lizbeth. High school pictures, but I like them. I don't see the kids very often. They're back in Ontario. Stay mainly with their father. I visit them a couple of times a year during holidays when I go east. They never come out here, although Liz says she'd like to. Might come out this way in the fall. I sure miss them."

"Sorry," Nora said.

"It's OK. They're busy people. Their father has all the money. He's a doctor and Jason is in pre-med at the moment."

"Lizbeth?"

"Still trying to 'find herself'. Or that's what she says. She's a good painter. Those landscapes are hers."

"Is she taking Fine Arts?"

"Only did the one year, but her father didn't approve, so she quit. He said there were already too many artsy fartsy people in the family." She laughed. "Meaning me, of course."

"You paint?"

"I write. You must have noticed my litter."

"Not really, I was looking at other things. I didn't notice the filing cabinets at first."

"Hard to miss them. I can't shut a few of the drawers. Too much paper, too little space. Anyway, bedroom next."

Nora drew her breath. "Wherever did you get such a beautiful quilt?"

"It belonged to my ex's grandmother. She liked me. I liked the quilt."

"And the hardwood floors all over the house, and the braided rugs! They're so warm and homey."

"Thank you. I like them. I had a ball fixing up this little place the way I wanted it. First time I ever had any say in choosing my surroundings." She laughed. "First my mother and then my husband. You know

175

how it is. Or do you?"

"Sort of." Nora had another flashback of her mother-in-law stripping the house before they moved in. "We had to do with odds and ends when we first set up housekeeping."

"But at least you got to choose them?"

"More or less," Nora admitted. It was true, Walter had always deferred to her judgement regarding the house furnishings and decorating. She didn't have Inga's flair, though, and wondered briefly what Angela's home was like. Probably very posh if her taste in clothing was any indication.

"I think I hear the kettle boiling. Back to the kitchen. Time for tea. Let's sit at the table this time," she said and pulled out a chair painted in Pennsylvania Dutch design. There were five others, all decorated in the same style, but in assorted shapes and colors. The effect was charming. "Painted them myself," Inga said. "First I had to go to hell and back to find the right chairs, though."

"You did a good job. A good job all over as far as I can see."

Inga handed over a mug of some unidentifiable herbal beverage in a china mug decorated with purple violets.

Nora examined it, turned it around. "Your birthday in February?"

"How did you guess?"

"The mug. I had one exactly the same. My daughter gave it to me for my birthday one time. A February birthday. I quite liked it. But yesterday..." Nora could feel her eyes filling. "Yesterday," she began again. "Yesterday, I chucked it through the kitchen window. Probably how Sam cut his paw." She put her hand over her mouth to cover her trembling lips.

"It's OK, it'll heal. We all have our moments. I've sure had mine." Inga joined her at the table. "You

176

can tell me if you like. Or not, if you like. Nothing goes out of this room in any case."

Nora hadn't planned to get into a personal discussion and she was amazed by the temerity of her first question, "Did *your* husband leave *you?*"

Inga put her hand on Nora's shoulder. "I thought it might be something like that. When did he take off?"

"Four or five days ago. Maybe six. I'm a bit confused right now."

"No doubt you are. And, since you ask—no, *I* left *him*. Not without a lot of agonizing, though. Can you tell me about what's happened to you?"

And Nora did—as best she could. Inga was a sympathetic listener.

Three pots of tea later, Nora sat, half-listening as Inga related the events leading to her own marriage break-up. Of how she had tolerated her husband's series of girl friends, his lies, his interfering mother, as long as she could stand it. She described leaving the children she loved, an editorial job she was good at and her eventual flight to the wilds of Manitoba.

She ended her story with, "So, you see, life can begin again. And it will. I know this is a terrible time for you, but take heart. You just sort out your problems as they come up and get on with things."

"There are several problems, actually. The main one at the moment is telling the kids. He refused to do that. We, that is, Martin Kroeger and I, told his mother yesterday."

"That must have been fun!"

"No worse than I thought. It was a strange interview."

"How did she take the news?"

"Well, she wasn't surprised. Upset, though, I think. But it's the kids that I dread telling. I started to phone them early this morning and then, for some reason or other, it didn't get done. Oh, I remember now! It was because I went on the hunt for Sam. Could it be I'm losing my mind?"

"Not likely, but it may seem like that occasionally."

Nora looked at her watch. "Nine-thirty. Almost dark. My God! I've lost all track of time. I must get going. Martin and Maggie will be frantic."

"You're lucky to have two such good neighbors. I don't know them well, but I like what I know of Maggie. At least she doesn't put on any airs. Not like a couple of busybodies I know."

"Would their names happen to be Fran and Ruby?"

"Whatever makes you think that?"

"Just a lucky guess."

The women laughed and Nora opened the door and called Sam. Then turning to Inga, said, "I'm sorry I didn't make the effort to get to know you sooner. Walter always said I should invite you over. This is embarrassing, but you know, I had it in my head for a while that Walter was kind of soft on you. That it was you he was mooning around about. And that episode with the chain saw.... I must apologize for that."

"No need. And I was never Walter's girlfriend. Or anybody else's come to that."

"I know that now. I'll be off."

Inga gave her a brief hug. "Take care."

"I will."

*

Nora got through to Trevor right away. "I've been trying to get in touch with you off and on for the past few days, "he said. "Where have you been? I've been worried."

"I've been out a lot," she told her son. "What's up?"

"Nothing much. I've just been wondering about you and Dad, is all."

Nora caught her breath. "Why would you be wondering that?"

"No particular reason. Coming up harvest time and all. How do the crops look?"

"The crops?" Nora said as though she'd never heard of crops.

"Yeah, crops. You OK?"

Now that she had an opening, she was unable to pass on the news of Walter's departure. Some instinct told her that the timing was wrong. "Oh, I'm fine. How are you? That's the burning question. Did you ever go to see a doctor?"

"Not yet. But I have an appointment for next Thursday."

"Still not feeling up to scratch, I take it."

"Not really. So damned tired all the time, that's the worst part. Otherwise, I can't really say I feel that sick. Besides the everlasting sniffles, of course. Oh yes, and some kind of foot thing. Itchy. Sore. Stubborn."

"Athlete's foot?"

"That's what I thought, but I've tried all the over-the-counter remedies and they haven't worked. That's really why I figured I should see a doctor."

"Good idea. Let me know what he says."

"I will. By the way, have you heard from Sandra?"

"Not for a week or so. I was going to call her today. Maybe later on tonight. Why?"

"No reason. I just wondered, is all. Dad around?"

"Not at the moment."

"Say hi to him for me. And tell him he'll wear that damned pick-up out if he doesn't give it a rest."

It was not a satisfactory conversation at all. There'd been no way Nora could tell him about Walter. Especially when she felt that there was something going haywire with her son's health. The nagging worry she'd felt when Trevor was home came back. She felt guilt over becoming so immersed in her own problems that she'd almost forgotten about his. 'When I hear from him on Thursday, I'll tell him.' She thought. No need to upset the boy just yet. But there was still Sandra.

Before Sandra's phone had begun to ring, Nora hung up. She couldn't give her the bad news before she told Trevor. Sandra would be devastated, and even if she was asked not to say anything to her brother, old habits would take over and she'd call him right away. If only to accuse him of something. Suggesting that Trevor might be ill wouldn't work. Sandra had made it clear at the time of the wedding that she considered his lassitude to be sheer laziness.

Nora put on a pot of coffee, noticing as she did, that there was a new pane of glass and a screen in the window. She looked around. The coffee stains on the walls had been wiped clean and the curtains washed. For no reason at all, she began to weep.

DECISIONS

THE PHONE RANG AS NORA WAS HAVING HER BEDTIME SNACK of Cheerios with a sprinkling of ground flax. Inga had supplied the flax. It was just after nine o'clock, way past the time when Trevor should have called. July thirtieth—a date she would always remember.

She lurched to her feet and nearly tripped over Sam in her rush to the phone. The dog had been so whiny lately, she'd allowed him inside the house for an hour or so in the evenings. A bad idea, she knew, but still, Sam was getting on in years and seemed perpetually disgruntled.

"Mom?" She scarcely recognized her son's voice.

"Are you all right? I've been waiting for you to call. How are you?"

"Mom?" Trevor's voice wavered. "Is Dad there? I'm not so good. I just wanted to tell you both at the same time."

"Not at the moment. What is it?" Her heart sank. 'What is it?" she repeated.

There was such a long pause, she thought he'd

hung up. "Trevor?"

"It's leukemia."

Nora tried to steady her voice. "You're sure?"

"CML—Chronic Myelogenous Leukemia." He spelled it out for her. "That's what the doctors say. They left me some information. I'm in the hospital right now. St. Paul's."

"My God! How did this happen?"

"Nobody knows, apparently. Been coming on for a while, that's all they said."

Nora's throat was dry and she was shaking. "What else did they say?"

"Not much. Nobody says much. My GP sent me right over here for blood work. Then I went home. About four-thirty I got a call. Was I alone? Was anyone with me? Could I come back right away? Don't even think of driving myself."

"My God! What did you do?"

"Bruce was here. Luckily. Usually he's away on the Island doing his tree-planting thing. Today he was home, though, and he drove me. Anyway, the doctors said later that the reason I shouldn't drive myself was because my white cell count was so high I was close to having a stroke."

Nora couldn't speak. Her baby boy having a stroke! It was unthinkable.

"Mother? Are you still there?"

"Yes," she whispered. "Go on."

"They've started me on some stuff that'll bring the count down right away. A kind of chemo, I guess. I think I'll have to take it every day. A temporary treatment. I'll be OK. For a while. I'll get out, go back to the apartment tomorrow."

"And then what?"

She knew he was close to tears. "I don't know. Go to a hematologist every few days for blood tests. Maybe a bone marrow transplant. Sometime. Later.

I just don't know."

"God in heaven, you don't deserve this!"

There was a long silence before Trevor was able to continue. "Look, I'll be OK, Mom. Don't worry. I'll call you tomorrow. Maybe Dad will be home then." He hung up.

Was there never to be an end to this summer of sorrows? What to do? Who to turn to? Walter? Should he be told? What about his mother? Sandra? Maggie? Martin? Inga? Meantime, there was only Sam. She kept him in the house over night while she tossed restlessly in her bed unable even to weep. The dog lay on the hooked rug by her bed and licked her face from time to time. And he smelled bad.

At four-thirty, Sam had to pee. Urgently. He wouldn't have bothered her otherwise. No use going back to bed. No comfort there. No sleep either. She prowled the house wondering where to start. There was no doubt she had to go to Vancouver, and soon. No suitcases. Damn! Damn! Damn! She'd have to borrow something from the Kroegers.

The Kroegers. How on earth could she leave now that harvest was approaching and so many things had to be done, to be settled? They'd have to be told right away.

Nora didn't stop to get showered and dressed for the day, but remained in her tattered dressing gown, going about household tasks. Feeding Sam, watering the plants, washing up her few dishes from the night before, sweeping up crumbs from the toaster. Wading through water in a dense fog, she might have said, had anyone asked. Everything gray. Colors draining away as she felt her life force draining away.

Her subconscious informed the part of her brain involved in moving body parts from place to place, and soon Nora was back in her bedroom. She rooted through her closet heaping garments helter-skelter on the unmade bed, sorting them into piles, discarding dingy or worn out underwear. Six-fifteen. Martin would be up. Maggie, too, likely. She was vigilant about Martin's having a good breakfast and taking his vitamins. A good sister, a necessary part of that household.

"My God! What's the matter?" Maggie asked when she answered the door.

Nora was still in her robe, hair uncombed. "Couldn't sleep much," she said. "Martin around?"

"Just getting washed up. Coffee's on. What's the problem?"

"Bad news from Trevor."

"He get some girl into trouble?"

"I only wish."

But Maggie was excited, not listening. "He's not even married! But he could *get* married. Lots of people get married young. Why not Trevor?"

Just then Martin entered the kitchen, shaving foam still in evidence on his chin. "What's up? Did I hear somebody's getting married?"

"Maybe Trevor," Maggie said.

Martin grinned, "Do we get an invite to the wedding?"

"Nobody's getting married. Somebody's sick."

"Trevor's sick? Why didn't you say so?"

"I didn't really get a chance. I confused Maggie, I guess."

"It happens," Martin said. "But tell us, what's the problem?"

So Nora told them about Trevor's phone call. His distress. Hers. "I have to go to him right away. I'll get a flight out today or tomorrow. Whatever I can manage. In the meantime, I'll have to borrow a suitcase or two, go to the bank. All kinds of things. I really hate to be asking for your help all the time, but I don't know what else to do."

184

"It's no bother," Martin said. "But this is awful. Will you tell Walter? Sandra?"

"I guess I'll have to. Sometime. Not until I see Trevor, though. Find out how serious this thing is."

Martin scratched his head. "Leukemia. I don't know much about it."

"That's what the Smith girl died of," Maggie supplied helpfully.

"There's treatments, though, I'm pretty sure of that." Martin was being hopeful.

"A bone marrow transplant somewhere down the road. At least, that's what Trevor said might have to happen. I guess we'll find out more about that."

"Bacon and eggs," Maggie said gazing into the fridge. "You need some. We got some. I'll make up a batch now."

"Maggie always thinks food can solve things." Martin glared at his sister, then softened and smiled. "Sometimes, she's even right."

"Oh, I couldn't eat a thing." Nora said, but when she was served a large helping, she found she was hungry. Ravenous, in fact. Things, it seemed, were coming back into focus. Things like the farm work. "But what will you do? I mean, with harvest coming on and all, I should be here to help."

"We'll manage," Martin assured her. We've managed worse things than this. Maggie can drive a tractor. Done it before."

Maggie looked dreamily out the window. "Vancouver. I always wanted to go to Vancouver. Wish I could go with you."

Martin gave her a warning look. "After harvest, Maggie. Maybe. If Nora's still out there. Anyway, this isn't going to be any pleasure trip."

"I know. I was just talking nonsense. As usual. Anyway, I have to stay here and work."

Nora felt a stab of guilt. "Maybe we can find a hired

man. Maybe I won't have to stay too long. Maybe I can bring Trevor back to Manitoba."

None of Nora's 'maybes' was feasible. She really hadn't expected them to be. Other arrangements were made, though. When she'd gone to explain the situation to Inga and to say a quick goodbye, her friend was more than sympathetic. She was helpful and hopeful. Inga brewed up another herbal concoction to soothe Nora's jangled nerves and mentioned two successful bone marrow transplant patients whom she knew personally.

"It's one kind of cancer they *can* do something about. Once the transplant has taken—no more cancer. Quite common now, I understand. Try not to worry."

Nora sipped her drink, which was much more palatable than some others she'd been given. "I'll try," she said. "But it's hard. Hard even to leave right now when I really need to be here. Martin will have so much to do. Without Walter..."

"I know. I was just thinking that. I have lots of time on my hands. The dogs don't need my attention every minute. My writing seems to have ground to a halt right now, too. I can help. How can I help? I don't know how to run farm machinery."

Nora gave the matter some thought. "Well, if Maggie has to be out in the field, somebody has to do the cooking, running errands, things like that. You know, running to town for parts, kind of thing."

"I think I'd be equal to that."

"You'd be paid, of course,"

"I'm not concerned about that."

"I know. But, what the hell, you're hired."

Since Inga also offered to keep Sam, that was another worry off her list. He'd be fine. He enjoyed being around his Samoyed pals.

Martin and Maggie also pleaded with Nora to stop

worrying about the farm. "Things will work out. They always do," Martin assured her.

"And about the worry thing," Maggie said. "I know what you should do about that. See, you make a list of all the things you worry about. Then, when you don't want to worry about a certain thing any more, you just get out the list and look at it."

Nora and Martin exchanged puzzled glances.

Maggie caught the look and defended her method. "Well, it works for *me*."

VANCOUVER

THE APARTMENT THAT TREVOR HAD BEEN SHARING WITH BRUCE
for the past year was in a well-maintained three-story
building on Harrow Street, just a short distance back
from False Creek, the Sea Wall and the terminal for
the tiny ferry to Granville Island. It was owned by
Bruce's aunt who was in a nursing home in White
Rock. Aunt Annie, as the boys called her, was well
past making any decisions for herself, but nevertheless refused to sell her condominium on the grounds
that she'd be back any day now, body and brain in-
tact. To avoid having the apartment sit empty and to
accommodate Bruce's need to be in Vancouver, it was
arranged that he should live there. Bruce's parents
lived in the Kootenays and his father, who was Annie's
brother, had power of attorney, so the arrangement
had been accomplished without fuss. Bruce and
Trevor were friends from university and Trevor was
invited to share Bruce's good fortune. The 'rent' was
minimal but it covered the condo expenses and provided both boys the opportunity to live cheaply in a

high-class neighborhood.

Bruce was away for much of the summer and, when he was in the city, spent most of his free time with his girlfriend. He was, however, on deck to meet Nora at the airport the Sunday following Trevor's Thursday phone call home. Nora wore a red carnation pinned to her blue denim dress so he could spot her with no trouble. The carnation was Maggie's idea. It was, as everybody knew, what you wore when you were about to meet a stranger.

The blue denim was Inga's suggestion. "You look nice in it. It's practical. It won't wrinkle much on the plane. It's a happy looking dress and, when I think of you, I'll remember how you looked the day you left on the Great Adventure." She had tears in her eyes. "Please, Nora, think of it as an adventure."

Martin looked doubtful, but assumed the women knew what they were talking about. All four had been sitting in the Kroeger kitchen discussing the details of Nora's departure. Martin couldn't afford to take a day off and he needed Maggie around to help him with various jobs, so Inga did the taxi run to the Winnipeg airport.

In the car, Nora sat with her hands clenched tightly. Inga reached over and patted them. "If you want my advice, which few people do, I would advise you to tell Trevor right away about his dad. Nothing to be gained by keeping it secret. Sandra, too. She needs to be told right away. They'll have to deal with it sooner or later. Might as well be sooner."

"I know," Nora said. "You're right. I'm just trying to figure out how to do it."

"It'll come to you."

"I hope so." They were entering the curved area leading to the departure area. "There's a parking spot right in front of the Air Canada sign. Drop me off there. My suitcase is light." She tried for a laugh,

"Or, rather, *your* suitcase is light! No need to bother trying to park in the lot."

"Whatever you like."

Inga stopped the car, Nora got out, took her luggage from the back seat and both women said, "Take care," at the same time. They smiled and waved goodbye to one another.

Bruce met her at the Vancouver airport. "Hi. You look younger than I expected. But, hey, my folks are kinda old so that's what I'm used to. I guess."

"How is he?" Nora asked as soon as they'd collected her suitcase from the carousel.

"Not too bad today."

Bruce was at least six feet tall and she had to take two strides to every one of his. It was difficult to keep up. No further conversation was possible until they got in the car—Trevor's car—for the drive into the city. When they were underway, Bruce spoke hesitantly, "Mrs. Fields?"

"Just call me Nora."

"OK. Nora. Listen, don't expect Trevor to be his usual self. I mean, he's angry. Very, very angry. He's goddam furious, actually. Excuse me."

"No problem. It doesn't surprise me that he's angry. The 'why me?' phase, do you think?"

"Maybe. I don't know much about these things. I just wanted to warn you, is all. He'll be awful glad to see you, though."

And Trevor *was* glad to see her. Other than his color, which was paler even than when he'd been home in June, he didn't look much different. He still towered over her and he didn't appear to have lost weight. He also didn't appear to be as angry as she'd been led to believe.

He hugged her. "Good to see you, Mom. Dad really busy in the field?"

"Not exactly. There've been some problems. I'll tell

you about them later."

Bruce tossed Trevor the car keys. "Hey, I'm going for a run on the seawall. I won't be back for supper. I'm meeting Jenny at the Kettle of Fish around six. I'll probably spend the night at her place."

"That's OK. Mom and I might just go for a short drive."

They were sitting on benches by a huge outdoor swimming pool in Kitsilano when Trevor brought up the subject of a transplant. "I talked about it with some doctors on Friday. I didn't tell you on the phone. Too complicated. Anyway, I don't want to have to have one. They pretty well kill you before you get the new bone marrow. Actually, they do kill you, or at least, your marrow—before they give you the donor's marrow. That is, if they find a matching donor. They radiate you and poison you with chemicals until there's nothing left. If you didn't get the donor's stuff right away, you'd die from all that crap immediately."

Nora swallowed. "I didn't think it was that drastic."

"It's drastic all right. I'd rather go to Mexico. Try the clinics there. I don't want to risk a goddam bone marrow transplant."

Nora had no idea how to allay her son's fears, and all she could say was, "I've heard lots of them are successful."

"And lots of them *aren't*. A sibling's the best bet but, even then, there's only a twenty-five percent chance of a match. I doubt if Sandra would want to give me any of her marrow even if it did happen to be a match."

"We should have had more children," Nora said, thoughtfully. "Three or four, at least. Better odds."

Trevor actually laughed. "Too late now."

"Later than you think."

Something in her voice diverted his attention from his own situation. "You don't mean because you're too old, do you?"

"No. It's because I no longer have a husband. I'm sorry to have to tell you this, but you do have to know."

"But what...? Why...?"

Nora told him as much as she thought he could handle—about Angela, the renewal of the childhood sweetheart affair and Walter's subsequent defection to Florida. She didn't mention Mario, even though his name flashed through her mind when Trevor was discussing sibling donors. She might mention the half-brother relationship later. Or she might not. It depended upon whether Sandra would be a suitable match, and she had no doubt that Sandra would be more than willing to donate if that were the case. Nora also had the sinking feeling that, despite Trevor's misgivings, a bone marrow transplant was in his future. She needed more information. They both did.

Meantime, she had no idea how he would react to the news of his father's leaving, but was surprised that there was no immediate angry response. It was almost as though he'd been expecting something of the kind.

After a long silence, Trevor mused, "You know, I'm not surprised. He was acting really weird when I was home. Do you think he's kind of... you know, flipped out or something?"

"That's Maggie's take on it. She figures he's gone completely out of his mind."

"What do you think?"

"I'm not sure what to think."

"Driving around in his truck all the time... keeping the crops under surveillance... not Dad's thing at all." Trevor began pacing. "I never thought of a girl friend, though. Hard to believe."

"I think I've nearly come to terms with the situation."

"Really?!"

"Trevor, I don't believe that your dad's lost his mind or anything like it. I also don't believe that he'll be coming back. Ever."

Nora noticed the red flush suffusing Trevor's pale cheeks as he jumped to his feet. "He'll be back. After I get through with him, he'll be back!"

Nora, keeping pace with her son, took his arm, but said nothing. He seemed to unleash his anger in silent, body-wrenching spasms. Then he collapsed on the grass and wept uncontrollably.

Nora drove them back to the apartment, getting across the Burrard Street Bridge safely and negotiating all the correct turns to Harrow. In spite of concern over Trevor's agitated state, she felt a slight swell of pride over her driving feat.

Back in the apartment, Trevor pleaded a headache and went to his room while Nora searched the refrigerator and cupboards for enough food for their evening meal. There wasn't a lot to choose from—four packages of Kraft Dinner, two cans of Heinz beans and pork and a can of Dole pineapple chunks in the cupboard, while the fridge yielded a half dozen ageing wieners, a jar of pickles, three eggs, a few cheese slices, some stale bread and a part tub of margarine.

She sighed and decided to find a grocery store. In the lobby, the caretaker of the building seemed to be doing something with the mail boxes and, upon questioning, told Nora there was a small convenience store fairly close by on Beach Avenue. "Or," he allowed, "if you don't want to be ripped off, there's a Supervalu up on Davie Street." He looked at her—suspiciously, she thought. "You new here?"

"Well, yes, in a way. I'm Trevor Fields' mother."

"On holidays?"

"In a way."

"Gonna be here long?"

"I'm not sure."

"Your husband with you?"

"Not right now."

"You got a car?"

Nora found his questioning irritating, if not insulting so she merely said, "Thanks for the information," and left, forgetting to ask if the bigger store was within walking distance. She didn't know how far 'up' Davie street was, nor which direction to turn once she got there. In reality, she didn't even know where Davie Street was. Opting for the convenience store, she found it easily and quickly and purchased some tinned ham, a few of the fresher looking vegetables for salad and some milk.

When she had prepared their meager meal, Nora called Trevor from his bedroom and he came, reluctantly and sleepily, to the table. "Thanks for the supper, Mom. You didn't need to. I'm not really very hungry. Mostly tired. That's the hell of it. Partly."

"You have to eat."

"That's what Bruce keeps saying."

"Then why on earth doesn't he buy some groceries?"

"He's hardly ever here. Never eats here. My responsibility."

"Never mind. We'll shop properly tomorrow. The caretaker told me about the convenience store."

"So you've met the Gestapo?"

"I guess. He sure knows how to ask questions."

"What are you going to do?"

"Avoid him, if possible."

"I mean about Dad? About the farm? About *me*?"

"I can't do anything about your dad. The Kroegers are looking after things at home. And I'll stay on here with you as long as you need me."

Trevor pushed his plate aside. Apparently, he'd eaten all he had stomach for. His face crumpled. "I

194

don't know what to do. I should be at home helping out with harvest. All that." He sat with his head down.

Nora went around to put her arms around him. "Everything's looked after. No need for you, or me, to be there. Martin and Maggie are not incompetent, you know. Or, incontinent, as Maggie would say."

Trevor produced a half-laugh. "I know that, but how will we manage?"

"We'll manage just fine. Getting you well again is the big thing. After that, we'll see what happens."

"And Sandra? How does she feel about Dad running off?"

"She doesn't know yet. I thought we'd phone her tonight. We have to tell her about you, too."

"Jesus! She'll be furious about Dad and give *me* shit for being sick. This is about the worst day of my life."

"She'll be furious about your dad, that's true, but you underestimate your sister. She'll be very upset to hear about your... your problem."

"My problem is, I have no future. I know that much. Whatever happens, I have no future. Just when I thought things were finally going my way, too."

Nora could feel the tension in the air, the approaching storm. When it came, it was loud, violent and brief, accompanied by curse words Nora was unfamiliar with. The rage was directed mainly at Walter. Trevor finished the tirade with "I never want to see him again. I don't want him to know I'm sick. I don't want the old bastard pretending to be sorry for me." Then he slammed into his bedroom—spent, Nora knew, from the outburst.

Trevor was down for the night, she guessed, so Nora wandered around the apartment, straightening and dusting. Aunt Annie had had a good eye for decorating and the furnishings were expensive. The living room was large and airy with a white leather sofa, love seat and recliner. But she'd provided lots of color in mauve and sage green pillows and an 'occasional' chair in sage green plush. Good paintings hung on the walls. At least, Nora assumed they were good. Pleasing to the eye, at any rate.

In the corner, stood a well-preserved and highly polished upright piano. Nora examined the photographs perched on top. A stylized portrait of a dark-haired, middle-aged woman dressed in dark colors and wearing enormous strands of pearls dominated the gallery. Very handsome. Aunt Annie, herself, Nora presumed. It was a black and white production, obviously many years old. The others were newer and included several children and another, older man. It was interesting to speculate who these people might be. Family members? Was the older man a lover? Maybe married? Aunt Annie was single, apparently, so she might have had a married lover.

The romantic image brought Nora to imaginings of Walter and Angela's affair—thoughts that she had tried time and again to stifle. Did he hold her hand in movies, as he'd always held hers? Did they *go* to movies? Did he deliver playful pats on her backside while she was cooking a meal? Did Angela even cook meals or did they dine in fine Italian restaurants? What did they do in bed?

Nora was shaking when she opened the sliding doors and stepped out to the balcony. It was just dusk, and from the northwest corner, she could just get a glimpse of water. Tomorrow she'd find out what the body of water was called. It seemed important to be able to name things. Things like, leukemia, divorce, heartache...

Her bedroom had obviously been used by the older woman as a storage room, for there were a great many hat boxes stacked neatly in one corner. The dresser and chiffonier drawers were crammed with clothing—all clean, but well-worn, and the tops of the teak furniture were also piled high with various sized cartons and knick knacks. The closet, too, Nora found to her dismay, was almost completely filled with assorted articles, including a mink coat that should have been in storage. It was difficult to find room for even her modest wardrobe, so she hung only a few articles and decided she'd have to leave the rest of her belongings in the suitcase which had to remain on the floor at the foot of the large bed.

A large back plastic bag, stuck in one corner of the closet and filled with men's clothing was the only evidence that Bruce occasionally used this room as his own. Oh yes, and two empty beer cans on the floor by the night table. There was no room on top. It would seem that her appearance on the scene would not put anyone out to any extent. And if Bruce did arrive for a night or two, there was always the sofa. She could sleep on that.

A heavy ivory-colored damask bedspread was the only covering on the bed, Nora discovered. Tomorrow, she'd find some sheets, but for the first night, she could only crawl under the spread and hope to get some sleep.

To her surprise, when she awoke, her wrist watch read eight o'clock. She could hear Trevor stirring in the bathroom next door, so she hurriedly rose, threw on her old cotton duster and went to the kitchen. Her son appeared, hair uncombed and wearing only jockey shorts. He looked very tired, as though he hadn't slept for weeks. Perhaps he hadn't.

"Hi, Mom," he said, giving her a quick hug. "Why are you up so early?"

"Early? It's eight o'clock!"

"Six, Mom. B.C. time, remember?"

"Of course. I keep forgetting. I must reset my watch.

197

I'll make us some breakfast."

"Nothing for me. I already had a piece of bread. Have to take these pills. Can't do it on an empty stomach."

"Maybe some toast? Not much else around."

"Sorry. We'll shop when the stores open. I have to go to the hematologist for more blood work later this morning. We can get groceries after that."

"Meantime, I'm going to try Sandra's number." When Nora could hear the call going through she asked Trevor, "You got another phone?"

"Yup. In my bedroom."

"Pick it up."

Nora let it ring five times and she and Trevor were both on the line when Sandra answered. At first, Nora tried to keep the conversation light, but when she realized that her brother was there as well, Sandra became suspicious.

"Something's wrong, isn't it?"

"I might as well be honest. A couple of things are wrong. I should have told you before now, but I wasn't sure how to do it."

Sandra took the news of her father's leaving calmly. At least, that's what Nora assumed since she didn't rant and rave the way Trevor had. A period of silence on the line stretched into an unreasonable length before Trevor cleared his throat and Sandra jumped to the conclusion that both he and their mother were in Manitoba.

"So," she said, "you going to stay on with Mother over harvest, or what?"

"No. I mean, Mom and I *are* staying together. She's with me in Vancouver, though, not at home."

Between Trevor and Nora, Sandra was told of Trevor's illness. No doubt, the reports were confusing and Sandra was clearly alarmed by the news. "Jesus Murphy! I'm coming right out. Soon as I can get a flight. Don't worry, Trevor, Mom. I'm coming."

There were simultaneous "No's" from Nora and Trevor. Then Nora added, "I mean, not right now. We're OK so far. We may need you at some time, though. If things are... I mean if Trevor has to have..."

"A bone marrow transplant," he finished for her. "The doctors say that's the way to go. I don't believe them. I figure there's gotta be some other way.

Nora put the question gently "But if he has to have one...?"

"I'll donate, of course."

"You might not even match," Trevor said.

"But I'm your sister!"

"Doesn't necessarily mean we'll be a match."

"I'm sure I'll match," Sandra said. "Don't worry, brother dear, we'll match."

But Trevor wasn't so sure and when they got off the phone remarked to Nora, "Well, she'll donate. How about that?! She'll come out here like a knight in shining armor and save her little brother."

"I told you she would."

"I hope to God it doesn't come to that. It'd be better if she didn't match. Then, if I end up having to go through with a transplant, I'd have to go with an unknown donor. One less thing for her to hold over my head."

Later, Nora went with him to meet Dr. Raymond, the hematologist, who seemed concerned and grateful that a family member was on hand to bolster his cause. "Your son seems to think there are other ways to combat leukemia. Other than a bone marrow transplant, that is. If there is, we have yet to hear of it. We can, however, keep him going for a few months with medication. Not forever, though. Think about it," he said as he stuck a tiny plastic patch over Trevor's needle mark.

Trevor rolled his sleeve back down. "We'll think

about it," he answered gruffly and rose to leave.

"Just a minute. You have a daughter, I understand?" he asked Nora.

"Yes, and we've spoken to her. She's agreeable to donate if she's a match."

"We need to have her checked as soon as possible. Just in case things progress more rapidly that we think they will. Always that possibility. We do need to know and these things take time. How may I contact her?"

Trevor strode angrily out of the room while Nora remained to provide Sandra's name and phone number.

So the tug of war was on. Should he or shouldn't he? Would he or wouldn't he? It was the subject of so much dissention between mother and son that they were both in states bordering on nervous exhaustion for days.

Over the next couple of weeks Nora phoned the Kroegers and Inga as she'd promised and spoke with Sandra every few days. Trevor would not hear of informing his father, and forbade Sandra to do so. "Not the grandmother, either, or I'll wring your bloody neck!"

"Why not tell Grandma?" Sandra asked Nora. "I don't understand why this has to be kept such a big secret."

"I'm not sure, either, but we have to respect your brother's wishes in the matter."

"He hasn't smartened up any, has he? Anyway, we should soon have some results from the blood tests. They took a heck of a lot. By the way, it's not the blood type that has to match, it's proteins or something in the blood. Six, I think. I'll find out more about it soon."

"Yes, I guess we're all finding out way more than we ever thought we'd need to know."

In a small, very un-Sandra-like voice, her daughter continued, "A twenty-five percent chance of a match isn't very good odds, is it?"

"No. We can only hope, that's all."

Although Trevor continued his bi-weekly visits to Dr. Raymond, no news was forthcoming regarding Sandra's suitability. After three weeks, though, he reported to Trevor that Sandra's tests had been done but were inconclusive. More blood work was required. More time. Luckily, he told Trevor, things were going along better than he expected and not to worry. No emergency was expected.

A nurse involved with leukemia patients suggested to Trevor that he attend the Hope Clinic for cancer patients and, if Nora hadn't been with him at the time, she would never have known about it. It took about a week of gentle persuasion to get him to agree to attend. He was still reluctant as they drove along Sixth Avenue looking for a parking space. Trevor was in a bad humor, as usual, and the meeting didn't go well for him. Nora, however, became interested in the other people present and made the acquaintance of a single-mother with a twenty-year old daughter who was also suffering from CML and awaiting a bone marrow transplant.

When they returned home, Trevor announced that it was a first and last for him. "Too depressing. All those sick people. I'm not that sick. I don't need it. What I need is healthy people around me." Then he slammed out the door after informing her that he was going to visit a friend.

"Well, maybe you don't need it my hard-headed son, but I certainly do," Nora said to the inside of the refrigerator. She was checking the inventory again.

Since Trevor had decided to go on a vegetarian diet in hopes of a cure, she was in a perpetual agony of indecision. What vegetables went together to provide an adequate diet? How many beans and lentils could people eat before their insides exploded? How does one convert tofu into an edible substance? What do they put in those unappetizing vegetarian wieners, anyway? The books she'd bought on the subject were helpful. To an extent. They didn't, however, explain how to overcome meat-cravings. Nora thought that if she had to make one more spinach lasagna, she'd scream.

Instead, she phoned Inga hoping for some information from this valuable health-food resource. "He's not turned vegan, I hope?" Inga asked.

"Not yet. Any day now, though, probably."

"Don't let him. He needs eggs and milk and cheese. Things like that."

"I'll do what I can."

Nora told her friend about the Hope Clinic and about the mother and daughter she'd met there. "I got their names and phone number. Trevor won't go back, but do you think I should give them a call? Might it seem too pushy? Or something?"

"I don't see why. Anyway, you can give it a try. It seems to me you need some support yourself. They might help." Before ending the conversation, Inga promised to send along some recipes in the next mail.

Nora fished around in her purse until she found the paper with Colleen Andrews' address, and after having a cup of tea and Coffee Crisp chocolate bar she'd squirreled away in the back of a cupboard, she dialed the number. It was Jocelyn, the daughter, who answered. Her mother was out, apparently, and Jocelyn seemed to have no interest in having a conversation. She did, however, recall meeting Nora and Trevor. Nora was so nervous she had no idea what to say, and only asked that Colleen call her back when she got home.

"I've done the wrong thing again, dammit!" Nora was having a discussion with inanimate objects again. This time, the microwave oven where she was re-heating her tea. She didn't tell Trevor about her call, afraid he wouldn't approve.

Trevor seemed to have secrets of his own. After-noons, after his blood work at the hospital, he'd go into his room and, perhaps, nap for awhile. She could hear him talking on the telephone, as well. Other days, he simply left in his car shortly after he was dressed for the day. She had no idea who he spoke with on the phone or who he saw when he was off on his own missions. Discreet questioning brought no answers. He was as bad as his father.

Walter. He was never far from her mind. Nora was desperately lonely, but there were only so many long-distance charges she wanted to rack up on their phone bill and, in any case, she couldn't call Walter. But, oh, how she needed to! Even knowing she had the support and love of the Kroegers and Inga, as well as Sandra, it wasn't enough to keep the empti-ness and fear at bay. Often at night, alone in her gigantic teakwood bed amidst Aunt Annie's belong-ings, she'd waken and reach for the comfort and assurance of Walter's warm body. She ached from the need of him. Those were the times when she had to deliberately restrain herself from calling Angela's number and begging him to come back to her. On the night that she could stand the loneliness and grief no longer, crept into the living room and dialed Angela's number, she had the good sense to hang up before anyone answered. She never did it again.

Every day was at least a week long, and Nora knew she had to take matters into her own hands to keep from being overwhelmed by the isolation she felt. She began a walking regime, which took her to uptown Vancouver where she'd often end up at the huge Pacific Centre Mall. Sometimes she took a solitary noon meal at a restaurant there. Often, she'd stroll down Davie Street, or go up to Robson and window-shop all the expensive stores there. The sea wall, too, was an attractive place to walk, but she liked that route better at sunset. There were always so many young people. Strong young people. Young people without leukemia. Sometimes it almost made her cry to look at them and she adopted her own way of dealing with it. "May you always be as healthy as you look today," she'd whisper to the unheeding ones as they passed by. She always smiled, for in her view, a blessing should always be accompanied by a smile. Occasionally, someone returned the smile and she felt better.

The Granville Market was another destination, but only if they needed fresh produce. The fee for using the tiny ferry-boat was fifty cents each way and her frugal approach wouldn't allow her to spend the money just to ride over to the island and look around. She had to have an errand. But the errands could run into several hours if the day was warm. The smells that sometimes issued from the Emily Carr Art Institute were invigorating, and Nora wished she could draw or paint—at least, it would be something to do. Jewelry shops, craft shops, gem shops, boutiques and the like were interesting enough, but she never bought anything at them, although the clerks came to know her and were friendly. The place she liked best was a very large Toys R Us store frequented, of course, by children and young families. They were almost always happy. Nora liked that.

Nora's Granville Island tour always ended at the huge market where she'd spend at least an hour choosing fruit and vegetables from the masses of displays. Once in a while, she also bought some flowers to arrange in Aunt Annie's crystal vases. All these items had to be stashed in a large canvas bag she'd purchased for the purpose and, almost always, she bought more than she could comfortably carry. This was reason enough to stop to rest just before reaching the ferry terminal. She'd sit on a bench watching the sea gulls and pigeons for a few minutes before hoisting herself and her purchases onto the tiny craft for the return trip. The last leg of the journey—up a very steep hill—made her swear to keep her buying under control next time.

Once, Nora returned from one of these marathons to find Trevor at home entertaining a friend. She hoped she'd been able to hide her surprise at finding a guest in their apartment—the first one since she moved in. Trevor seemed more relaxed and happy than usual. "This is Pierre, Mom," he said. "Pierre's dad works with me at the Cop Shop."

Another surprise. "Works with you?"

"Yes. I've been working. Some."

"You didn't tell me."

"I thought you wouldn't want me to."

"I want you to do whatever you feel up to doing. You should have known that."

"Maybe, but you know…" And then, to Pierre, "Mom overreacts to my little allergy attacks." He stressed the last words.

So. Leukemia hadn't been mentioned.

"Anyway, Pierre has problems that way, too. He's been to a homeopath and he advised him to use wheat grass. For the immune system."

Nora was intuitive enough by now to accept the wheat grass theory and wondered if they'd chew it like a cow.

"You drink it, see. Pierre bought a special juicer. For doing the grass. We got a crate of the stuff at a health food store and just finished juicing it." He handed her a glass with a tiny bit of poisonous-looking green liquid in the bottom. "Here, taste it."

The young men watched as she sipped and gagged. Trevor looked at Pierre questioningly and said, "Maybe if we added some water?"

Nora saw the worried look in Pierre's big, brown, sad eyes. "Yes, I think, if we diluted it, it might be better."

The wheat grass juicer stayed on the counter beside the other, larger, juicing appliance and the plan was that Pierre would come to the apartment when he needed a fix. Trevor was already in the habit of using the big, expensive, juicer and pounds of apples, carrots, celery, onions, beets, turnips, leafy vegetables, ginger and garlic disappeared into the noisy monster and were transformed into liquids. Sometimes all at once. The results were horrific. Nora could tolerate only apple and carrot juice. Trevor drank whatever resulted and proclaimed it tasty. And nourishing, of course.

Well into the third week, Pierre was a fruit and vegetable juice convert, too. Nora warned, "You might turn an orangey yellow, you know. All those carrots!" But both men agreed that their health was improving daily and orange wasn't so bad. Green would be worse, but so far, the wheat grass had turned neither of them green.

But the best thing that came about from the juicing experience was that it had brought Pierre into their fold. He was funny and warm. Nora liked him and wondered if he secretly knew that Trevor's problem wasn't what he claimed it to be. How, for example, did Trevor explain his many visits to the hematologist?

And then another good thing happened. Colleen Andrews phoned. She'd just come across the note her daughter had written asking her to call. Nora was so surprised and pleased, she had to sit down to talk. They began their relationship with a date to meet uptown at The Elephant and Castle for lunch the following week. Jocelyn and Trevor would not be with them.

ℐ

Colleen was a widow, she told Nora while they waited for their meals. Her husband had been killed in a car accident two years before. Jocelyn was their only child.

"I'm so sorry," Nora said. "It must have been terrible for you."

"Thank you. It was. For Jocelyn, too, of course." Colleen spoke shortly. Then, "I wish I could have the burger, too. And the fries. But my cholesterol, you know."

"I probably shouldn't be eating them, either, but I'm so starved for meat. Grease, too, I think. I could live on junk food for the rest of my life."

"Your son been put on a diet?"

"He put himself on one. Vegetarian. I'm so sick of tofu I could puke. Excuse me."

Colleen laughed. "That's OK. I'm tired of the stuff, too."

"Jocelyn into health food?"

"She was for awhile, but we both got so depressed we started to cheat a little. You know—a bit of chicken here, a salmon steak there.... Still, I figure it's no worse than the crap we were eating before. Excuse me."

This time both women laughed.

"It's so long since I laughed, I thought I might have forgotten how," Colleen admitted. "Laughter is hard to come by in our house. Or rather, in my brother's house."

"You're staying with your brother?"

"For the time being. He's just recently divorced and says he doesn't mind the company. He doesn't mind having a cook on hand, either." She hurried on in case Nora got the wrong impression. "I sure don't mind making meals and often he's not even home. An obstetrician, on call at all hours. We're real lucky to have a place in Vancouver to stay."

"I feel that way, too," Nora said and explained about Trevor's living arrangements and her own. "It doesn't cost much and it's a nice neighborhood. It's just that... Well, I get so lonely sometimes. Trevor isn't very communicative and I don't really know anybody in the city. I do have an old school friend in White Rock, though. I haven't called her yet. Trevor forbids me to tell people about his illness. His leukemia. He acts as though it's a disgrace or something. I haven't got it figured out."

"Funny situation, isn't it? Jocelyn is something the same. Her friends back in Saskatchewan know about the CML, but as far as I know, she never discusses it with them. In fact, she hardly ever talks to them. Or to anybody. Her doctor at home put her on Prozac, or something like it after her dad was killed. Not that it's helped much."

"She still depressed over losing him?"

"I suppose so, but it isn't just that he died. It's that he had his girlfriend with him when the accident happened. She survived. Jocelyn can't accept either fact."

"And you?"

"I've learned to live with it. I'd lost him before the accident but I didn't know that. I might have suspected, though. And, apparently, everyone else knew. Anyway, he could have helped with Jocelyn's situation if he'd been around."

"Trying to go it alone isn't easy, I know. Trevor misses his dad, too, I can tell. Although he's so furious with him, he still needs him."

"Are you divorced?"

"No. Not yet. It's just happened. A few weeks ago."

"Another woman?"

"Yes," Nora replied and went on to give her new friend an abridged account of Walter and Angela's affair.

"I'm sorry to hear that. Doesn't seem fair. And even when they're older, kids seem to want to know that their fathers are reliable—especially in an emergency. That's one reason I moved in with Ron. I thought maybe he could be sort of a father figure for Jocelyn, although it hasn't worked out that well because she refuses to accept him as anything other than a rather remote uncle. He had no kids of his own so he's sometimes a bit awkward with her. Not that Jocelyn is a kid, but you'd think, being an obstetrician and all, that he might have more empathy. How about you? Do you like Vancouver?"

"It's a nice city, but it's a far cry from being at home. I mean, where you can be close to friends and family."

Nora reached for the bill, but Colleen managed to retrieve it first. "My treat today. Next week, it'll be yours."

"Next week!"

"Any day you choose. Any place you choose. You decide. I think friends should meet at least once a week. Call me. And, by the way, call me anytime."

Nora walked home with a lighter step than usual. Never mind that it was downhill all the way in any case. Her heart felt a little lighter—easier to transport. She had a friend. One whom she liked and felt she could trust. And one who knew precisely the kind of hell leukemia inflicted on a family.

Also, she had someone she could feel free to call

without paying long distance charges. It was, however, Colleen who called her first. Could she and Trevor come for dinner on Saturday night? It was Jocelyn's twenty-first birthday and she was planning a surprise party. "Well, just a small dinner party, really. I thought, you know, she and Trevor might just get along. After all, they have a lot in common and we really don't have anybody else out here to celebrate with. Except, Ron, of course. And with just the three of us... Well, what do you say?"

Nora hesitated. "I'd love to come. It's just that Trevor is so damned moody right now. Excuse me," she said and they both laughed.

"I don't know why I'm laughing. He's just impossible. Refuses to go back to the Hope Clinic. Won't listen to a thing I say, keeps on harping about what a terrible person his father is, says he doesn't want a transplant from anybody, even if his sister is a good match. Which, by the way, we don't even know yet. Why is it taking so everlastingly long? He's sick, of course, so I just try to roll with the punches." Nora was out of breath by the end of her rant.

"Wow! Trouble everywhere. By the way, Jocelyn won't go back to the Hope Clinic either. Sounds to me like you need a night out. Both of you."

"Well, I'll ask him, but I sure can't guarantee anything."

"If he won't come, then come on out by yourself. I'll give you directions. Do you think you could get to Coquitlam by yourself? You do have a car?"

"Trevor has a car. I don't know the city well, though, just the area around here. I'll have to let you know."

In the end, Trevor agreed to drive her to the dinner party, but said he had other plans for himself. He was going to pick up Pierre at his home in New Westminster and maybe go to the gym or a movie or something. Nora didn't argue or try to coax him.

When they finally located the address on Regan Avenue, the driveway was so sloped that it appeared to go straight up. "Maybe you should let me out here and I'll just walk up," she offered, but Trevor just gunned the motor and lurched to a stop outside the door.

"I don't know how long I'll be here. Do you think you can find this place in the dark?"

Trevor just gave her one of his 'I'm a big boy now, stop mothering me' looks, backed out and sped off.

When Nora turned, it was to find a man standing in the open doorway. He was wearing light khaki pants and a beige golf shirt, stood about six feet tall and had dark wavy hair, slightly gray at the temples.

He extended his hand. "I'm Ron. Expect you're the Nora I've been hearing about. Come on in and join the happy throng." And he ushered her upstairs to the main part of the house.

Colleen was in the kitchen preparing the salad. Good roast chicken smells filled the air. She looked up from the sink, "Hi, there. No Trevor?"

"No," Nora said, giving no explanation. It seemed none was needed. "But he'll pick me up later. I didn't know what time to tell him."

"That doesn't matter. Whenever he arrives is fine."

Ron smiled. "As long as it's after we've eaten."

Jocelyn sauntered by just then—apparently, on a mission to some other part of the house. She gave Nora only a brief nod in passing.

It was slightly disconcerting, this obvious slight on the part of the guest of honor, and for a moment, Nora was uncertain as to her welcome. When she looked at Colleen for reassurance, Colleen rolled her eyes heavenward and shrugged. "It's one of those days. The universe is not unfolding as it should and I'm a rotten, interfering mother. You've had those kind of days yourself, I take it?"

Nora smiled. "Oh, no. Trevor is just the reverse. Uncomplaining, sweet-tempered, adores both his parents and is ever so polite. You saw the way he dumped me at your door. Like he had just picked up a felon and was driving the getaway car. Oh, no. Come to think of it, you didn't meet me, Ron did."

At mention of his name, Ron cleared his throat, smiled down at her and said, "No problem. We all have our trials. What would you like to drink?"

"Maybe just a little ginger ale with a chaser of arsenic, strychnine, whatever you have in the medicine chest."

"Sorry, we're fresh out. I must look into absinthe. They tell me it's coming back into fashion. But, for now, how about a glass of white wine poured over a finger or two of ground glass?"

"That should about do it, thanks."

Colleen flung off her apron. "One for me, too, please. Maybe several. I think it might be a good night to get drunk. And, Nora, you can put that very large gift— I presume it's a gift—over on the buffet along with the other things for little Miss Mary Fucking Sunshine."

Nora, who was tense, anyway, broke into laughter so contagious that Ron and Colleen joined her. The women were almost hysterical when Jocelyn waltzed in and asked, "Who died?"—which only served to increase the merriment and Jocelyn's scowl.

Finally, Ron put his arm around his niece and said, "Not you, my dear. Not even close. How about you forget that macabre attitude and join the world?"

She tried to jerk away from him, but he held her fast. "How about some wine to celebrate your coming-of-age?"

"My last earthly birthday, you mean."

"You'll have plenty of other birthdays. I'll be six feet under long before you will. Here, I'll get you some wine."

"Can't have any. My medication, as you well know."

"I checked it out with your doctor, you can have one glass."

"Oh well, all right. But it's on your head if it makes me sicker."

"I'll take full responsibility. How about a smile?"

"I'm not six years old. Don't treat me like I was."

Nora, who was completely involved in the conversation, almost blurted out, "Well, then, don't act like it," but caught herself in time. Instead, she went to the buffet, picked up the package she'd brought for Jocelyn and handed it to her with, "I hope you like it."

Like a six-year old, Jocelyn was distracted from her snit and immediately tore off the wrapping to reveal a beautiful white afghan. She gasped, "It's beautiful! Look, Mom, a beautiful afghan." She rubbed it against her cheek. "So soft! It'll be perfect on my hospital bed."

"A friend of mine made it. Her name is Maggie and she'll be pleased to know that you liked her work."

"Thank you. Thank her, too, please."

"I will."

In fact, Maggie had mailed the afghan to Nora when she complained, in one of her lonesome calls home, about the uncompromising stiffness of Aunt Annie's bedspread. Nora wept when she unwrapped it. It was so pristine and so perfect. That night, when she phoned Maggie to thank her, she discovered that Maggie had actually made it for Nora and Walter's twenty-fifth anniversary in late August.

"It was as close to silver as I could get," Maggie said. "Can't buy actual silver afghan wool. Didn't think you needed any more fancy pickle dishes in your house. Anyways, I started it a long time ago. Before... Well, before, you know—before..."

"Before Walter absconded?"

There was a puzzled silence for a moment before Maggie replied, "No, not that, I don't think. I meant, before he left us. I mean, *you.*"

At that news, Nora carefully re-wrapped the afghan, stood on a chair and stashed it on the already precarious pile of articles on top of Aunt Annie's bedroom bureau. She couldn't use it. After all, it was half Walter's. She wondered, briefly, how he would react if she cut it in two and mailed his share on to him. With love from Maggie.

She also wondered if he'd remember their anniversary and if he might try to get in touch with her. Then, realized it to be a remote possibility, indeed. He'd seldom remembered it before, even when they were presumed to be a happily married couple. Of all the impossible things she'd imagined, the likelihood of his acknowledging their twenty-five years together, was the most absurd.

But the parcel, looming large in the bedroom bothered her, so for a week or more, she moved it from place to place. Finally, when Colleen issued the invitation to Jocelyn's birthday dinner, Nora knew exactly what to do with the afghan.

She accepted Jocelyn's thanks and promised to pass along Jocelyn's appreciation to Maggie as well. A thing she wouldn't do in a thousand years. Maggie might be insulted. Or maybe not. It was hard to tell with Maggie. Not worth the risk.

Jocelyn's Uncle Ron presented her with a delicate gold bracelet, to which she responded with, "Just the thing. I can wear it alongside my ID. You know, the one I'll have to wear after the transplant. The one that says, 'irradiated blood only' in case I live long enough to get into a bad car accident."

Ron's face whitened, with rage or shock, Nora couldn't tell. Then he decided to turn it into a joke.

"Sorry, they were all sold out of winding cloths and oak caskets."

She looked at him, "What's a winding cloth, anyway?"

Colleen laughed and jumped in with, "It just a long cloth they give to mothers to stuff in the mouths of lippy kids. The kind that don't appreciate good gold when they see it."

Before Jocelyn could digest the import of that remark, Nora came to the rescue. "Aren't you going to open your mother's gift? It looks pretty important to me."

Colleen had chosen a small, but obviously expensive, video camera for her daughter. This time, there was a more agreeable reaction. Jocelyn smiled uncertainly at her mother and said, "How did you know...?"

"Oh, you know. You've only mentioned the lack of one eight or ten thousand times. I catch on quick."

Luckily, Ron knew how to work the camera—in fact, had purchased it—and the dinner turned into a rousing success when it was put on film. They took turns shooting the proceedings and caught Jocelyn making a gruesome face while chewing on a chicken bone, Colleen mopping frantically at a red wine stain on the gleaming white tablecloth and Ron gazing quizzically into Nora's eyes. Something she'd said, apparently. Then, of course, the blowing out of the candles. All on video tape.

Even Trevor, when he came to pick Nora up, was surprised at the door by Ron with the camera. "Hi, I'm Ron the Camera Man and you are Trevor, I presume." They shook hands. "Come into our humble abode and have some cake and coffee or a liqueur if you'd rather."

Trevor entered hesitantly saying. "Maybe some cake, but no coffee or liqueur. My medications," he added by way of explanation.

Jocelyn, who was already cutting the cake, rolled her eyes. "Meds! A pain in the ass, aren't they?"

"Jocelyn...!" Colleen warned.

She looked at her mother. "Why? You say worse things than that. You've even been known to call your daughter a pain in the ass."

Colleen laughed. "Not always, dear. Sometimes I call you 'a pain in the neck'. Then there are times like this when I call you my very own dear, grown-up daughter," she said, hugging Jocelyn close.

Nora could see the suspicious brightness in her friend's eyes and felt close to tears herself, but they all had to smile when Jocelyn said, "Mother, don't go all mushy on me or I may have to barf. And we do have guests, you know—one of whom is about to get fed a piece of my birthday cake."

Trevor ate two pieces of birthday cake and was far more at ease than Nora had expected. Jocelyn showed him her camera whose workings Ron explained in some detail, but they didn't stay late. Trevor seemed tired.

AFTER THE PARTY

"So, you had a pretty good time?" Trevor asked as they were driving home.

"Pretty good, yes. Really, very good. It was nice to get out. What did you do?"

"Not a lot. Went for a walk along the waterfront, worked out some games on Pierre's computer. Like that."

"You should have come to the dinner party. It was very nice."

"Yeah. Well, I wasn't in the mood. And they had meat. I could smell it."

"Just chicken, for heaven's sake. Colleen had lots of vegetables, you could have filled up on them. Besides, a bit of chicken wouldn't kill you."

"I suppose not. But it might be a mercy if it did. Quicker than cancer. Not as drawn out. Not as painful."

"I wish you wouldn't talk like that."

"Sorry," he said grudgingly. And in a moment, continued in the angry voice Nora was beginning to recognize as the prelude to a rant. "Mother, you just have no idea what it's like."

"I realize that, but I'm trying."

Trevor went on as though his mother hadn't spoken. "No matter what happens, my life is over."

"You've said that before and it's not true."

"It is true, damn it. Haven't you given it any thought at all?"

Nora tried to tell him that she hadn't thought about anything else for weeks, but he was not in a listening mood.

"No more university, no more tennis, no more being outside in the sunshine for any reason. Which also means I couldn't farm. Not that Dad would care one way or another."

"I'm sure your father cares for you. He would be very upset to know that you have..."

"And don't you dare tell the old bastard! I don't want him feeling sorry for me. Hanging over my bed telling me what a good boy I am. I don't want him anywhere near me."

"You may feel differently later on. No use burning any bridges."

"How can you be so damn cool about everything. Leukemia. Dad running off. It's like it all runs off you like water off a duck's back."

Nora could scarcely believe her ears. So that's how she appeared to her son. To others, too, perhaps—cold and uncaring. She swallowed the lump in her throat and bit her lip to stem tears, but she couldn't stem her own anger.

"Trevor, I'm not cool. Not at all cool. I have never been cool." Her voice rose. "It has taken years of practice to act cool in the face of terrible things. Things that hurt me so much I couldn't explain it to you if I tried. My father's dislike of me. It was dislike, no other way to explain it. The way my mother died. The way so many things were withheld from me. Love, for example. The way your grandmother has treated me. Like I was a no more than a piece of garbage. I guess I'm no more than that to Walter, too." That was where she stopped—when the tears started.

Trevor seemed truly shocked, but drove on in silence until they got to the wasteland that was East Hastings street. "I'm sorry," he said, "Grandmama isn't fit to clean your shoes."

Nora, over the worst of her crying fit, blew her nose before answering. "I know that now. I think I've known it for a long time. Maybe I've always known it."

"Dad, either."

Nora thought about that. "I don't think he can be tarred with the same brush as his mother. Before now—before Angela made her entrance—he treated me well."

"You don't have to apologize for him. I know what you've been through."

"A minute ago, you said you thought I didn't feel anything." She was close to tears again. "Cool, you said. As in cold?"

"I know. I'm sorry. Selfish of me."

"No, Dear Heart. One thing you are is unselfish. Always have been. And, believe it or not, I do understand what you are going through. What you don't understand, is that I am going through it with you, and I only wish the dreaded C disease had come to me. I wish it with all my heart."

Trevor was aghast. "Don't say that, Mother. Don't ever say that. That's the one thing I couldn't have stood—you with cancer. I'm younger. I can get through this. I'll come through it. Just watch me."

Nora knew her son was close to tears. "We'll get through it together. All of us. You, Sandra and me."

Trevor pulled into a vacant onstreet parking spot and turned off the ignition, but before he clamped the club on the steering wheel to make the car at least a little bit thief-proof, he turned to her and said, "There's just one other thing I want you to know. I'm not afraid to die. If it happens, it happens. It'll be a disappointment, but what the hell, I guess we all have disappointments."

"You'll live," Nora replied. "I'll see to that."

They were back in the apartment, sitting at the counter drinking some of Trevor's juiced fruit drink (the only kind Nora would consume) when he looked at her quizzically and asked, "Who is that Ron guy, anyway?"

"Colleen's brother. Jocelyn's uncle."

"I wondered. Didn't think he would be her dad."

"Why?"

"Because of the way he looked at you. Didn't figure Colleen's dad would look at you *that* way. Not in front of his daughter and his wife, anyway."

"And what way was that?"

"I don't know. Like he really liked you or something."

"I think you're imagining things."

But Nora *had* noticed. Had been taken with Ron's liquid brown eyes, which she felt were frequently sizing her up. They were eyes a woman was not likely to forget. She wondered how many pregnant ones had fallen in love with him. Well, she wasn't pregnant and certainly not about to fall in love with anybody's obstetrician. Still, it was flattering.

"I had another letter from Audrey today," she said, to change the subject.

"I know. I read it. I gather you've told her. About the leukemia?"

"Of course. Silly to keep such a thing from my own sister. And, if Sandra doesn't match, some of your first cousins might."

"They're all dorks. Except for the little Texan. I kind of admired his spunk. Anyway, I have pretty well decided against a transplant."

Nora sighed. "Jocelyn is just waiting for a match from an unrelated donor."

"She's kind of an odd ball. What did you think of her idea to put the whole deal on tape when the time comes. I mean, how droll can you get?"

Nora felt the need to defend Jocelyn. "It'll give her something to do to take her mind off it. She's going through a hard patch right now."

Trevor sighed. "I guess we all are."

✒

Nora called Martin the next morning. Conversations with him were brief and to the point. They were getting along just fine, no need to worry. The crops were coming off pretty good. He had a man in to help now and again. Some guy who didn't bust the machinery all to hell, he said—an oblique reference to the costly Floyd and Dorinda period. If everything went according to his calculations, she shouldn't have to worry about money. No mention was made of what he would require for all his labors, though. He reported that Inga was being a really good help and she and Maggie hit it off real well, although Inga could stand a lesson or two in cooking. Sam was fine and missed her. No, he hadn't heard a word from Walter.

Maggie's conversations took on more of a complaining tone at times. She missed Nora, she said, and when were the doctors going to get their acts the hell together and do Trevor's 'operation'?

There was some local news as well and, in disgust, Maggie relayed the story of her recent invitation. "Fran and Ruby come to my door one day. Yup. They actually come to my door. Asked me if I wanted to go walking with them. Silly bitches! I'm in the middle of baking bread and doing the laundry. Gotta work that in sometimes, you know, in between times when Martin needs me on the tractor. 'Go walking, for Pete's sake,' I tell them. 'What I really need is to go lay down for a spell.' Fran said she just thought that since you and I had such a good repertoire, I must miss you. And where were you? And when were you coming home? And what in hell is a repertoire, I'd like to know? I didn't know you and me had one."

In spite of Nora's anger at the women's presumption and their attempts to extract whatever information they could from Maggie, she almost laughed. "Rapport, I think they might have meant. Rapport. It means.... Well, it means, sort of a good feeling between people."

"Well I'm certainly never going to repertoire with them. Ever. I told them that, too."

"I think that's a good idea, Maggie. And what about Inga? Does she walk with them?"

"Nah, she's too busy, too. Some of us gotta work, you know."

"I know, Maggie, and I'm so sorry you have to work so hard on my account."

"Oh, Nora, I didn't mean it that way! You'd rather be here doing your own work. I know that. I'm sorry if I made you feel...."

"Not at all. Don't worry, I know what you meant. Anyway, how are you and Inga getting along?"

"Oh, good. We get along like a horse on fire. Most of the time. I think she yaks away to Martin more than she needs to, though. I don't always know what's going on like. Like one day—a real hot day—they sneaked into town and went to the Dairy Queen without me! I tell you, I coulda used an ice cream cone right about then."

Nora tried to sound sympathetic. "That's too bad. Why didn't they ask you, I wonder?"

"Martin said they only made a quick trip so Inga

could pick up the half-ton at the garage. I've always done stuff like that. I was on the swather that afternoon. The truck coulda waited another day. Until I was finished that field."

Then there were questions about Trevor such as, "Were him and his friend, whatshisname, still drinking that yukky juice?" She didn't ask about Colleen or Jocelyn or Ron, simply because Nora had never mentioned them—although she wasn't sure why she held back, since she saw all three fairly often. She didn't want Maggie to think other people were becoming too important in her life. Didn't want her to know that they were, in fact, becoming very important fixtures in her life. Maggie might feel slighted in some way, not understanding Nora's current need.

The conversations usually ended with the wistful questions. What was it like in Vancouver? Did Nora still go for long walks? If Maggie came out in the winter to visit, would there still be roses blooming in Stanley Park? Had Nora contacted Walter or vice versa?

Usually Nora felt better after the Kroeger phone calls and, always, after she'd spoken with Inga who, like Martin, was always upbeat and reassuring. It was the calls from Audrey and Sandra that got her down. Both questioned Nora's judgement in keeping Walter and his mother in the dark about Trevor's illness. Audrey would have flown right up to Vancouver to be with Nora in her 'time of need' except that their Western Wear store was so busy, and help so difficult to acquire and to keep, that she'd been obliged to start clerking herself. Nora offered up a silent prayer of thanks for that bit of news. She loved her sister, but the thought of having to entertain Audrey for days on end was inconceivable. In any case, Nora knew that her real 'time of need' had not yet come, but was looming up in her future. The near future, she hoped. When the transplant would take place.

Sandra threatened, "I think I'll just go ahead and get in touch with Dad. There's no way he shouldn't be told that his only son is in such a precarious state of health."

Nora bit her tongue to avoid spilling the information that Trevor wasn't Walter's only son and would only say that when, and if, she deemed it necessary, she would let Walter know. Sandra was to stay out of it.

Sandra accused her mother of being hard-hearted. Apparently neither of her children dreamed that she might have a nerve or a soft spot in her body. They had no idea how many antacid preparations Nora's stomach demanded—nor how terrified she really was. She would not admit to that, was trying to spare them, of course, and had adopted a superficial coolness. It was the only way she could manage to keep going. 'If I harden my heart, I'll lessen my chances of going crazy.' But she didn't say that. Only, "I'm sorry you don't agree with my choices. Mine and Trevor's, I might add, but they are ours and we're trusting you to do as we ask."

Sandra reluctantly agreed. During every phone call, it seemed, they went over the same territory with the same result. Her questions regarding the state of Trevor's health were always hesitant and, sometimes, she spoke only to him. They had evidently come to a mutual understanding, or at least a truce of some sort, since Trevor's voice carried no hint of animosity—either while he was speaking with her, or when he was speaking *of* her. That much was a relief. Nora was more relaxed when she spoke to her daughter.

"Tell me about school, Sandra. How is it going?"

"I think OK. A bit early to tell. One thing, though, I've been asked to teach biology to the Grade Tens. I took it in university, of course, but I've never taught it. Kind of an unpleasant surprise."

"I'm sure it was. But you'll do fine, dear, you're a good teacher."

"You really think so?"

"Of course, I do."

"I'm going to have to work like mad to keep ahead of my students."

"You can do it. How about Nick?"

"He's in a different school, but so far, he thinks it's going to work out OK. We're really busy."

"I'll bet you are. Try to get enough rest. Give Nick my love."

Yes, conversations with Sandra were definitely getting easier.

✍

Then came the call from one of the doctors involved with the transplant team. The good news—Sandra was a match. Trevor took the call and relayed the news without emotion. Nora was so relieved and happy she didn't try to keep it from showing, but Trevor just frowned at her and said, "I don't want the goddam transplant. How often to I have to tell you?" Then he left for the day without saying where, precisely, he was going.

Nora thought he would be going to the hematologist, to see Pierre, or to put in a few hours at the Cop Shop. She never would have guessed that he was going to see a psychologist, which was, in fact, what he was doing and had been doing for several weeks. This startling news came from Pierre when he brought another flat of wheat grass to the apartment to be turned into the vile green fluid, which both men continued to drink.

When he discovered that Trevor wasn't home, he

said, "Oh, I forgot. This is his morning with Rachel." Then quickly covered his mouth. "Oh damn! I let that slip out. For some crazy reason he didn't want you to know."

Nora had long wished that Trevor had a girlfriend—to share the heat, so to speak—so she cocked her head, smiled and asked, "Rachel?"

She was disappointed to learn who Rachel really was, but happy and astonished that Trevor actually realized he needed some help. He was going to a psychologist.

"Trying to deal with his anger," Pierre told her. "But I can't figure out why he has to be so secretive about everything."

"Me, neither," Nora said and, clearing her throat, asked, "did he tell you about his father?"

"Yes, eventually. He's really pissed off about that."

"That's part of the anger, I suppose." Nora admitted.

"And the other part?"

"He hasn't told you?"

"What? Told me what?"

"About his illness. His real illness."

Pierre was alarmed. "*Real* illness?"

"It's not allergies, you know."

"I was beginning to think it wasn't. What *is* it?"

So Nora found herself, once again uttering that awful word. "Leukemia."

"I figured it wasn't allergies he had, but I never thought of cancer. I wonder why he wouldn't tell me. I thought we were pretty good friends."

For an hour or so, over numerous cups of coffee, Nora and Pierre discussed the situation, offering possible explanations for Trevor's behavior and his reluctance to undergo, what the doctors considered to be the only solution. The transplant.

"The one good thing in all of this," Nora told Pierre, is that we just learned this morning that Sandra is a match. A doctor from the transplant team called. Sandra's his sister. Has he mentioned her to you?"

"Yes, he told me he has a sister."

"The match is really good news. The best. There was no guarantee that she'd be a suitable donor. This makes his chances better. Very much better."

"I'm real happy to hear that, Mrs. Fields."

"You can call me Nora."

"OK. I'm real happy to hear that, Nora," he said with a grin.

And, indeed, Nora was happier than anyone could know. The twenty-five percent factor had kicked in. No need, then, to involve Mario whose chances of matching were obscure to her. Not twenty-five per- cent, but certainly more than twelve and a half, given the relationship of his parents. Possibly twelve and a half plus six and one quarter. Nora had tried fruit- lessly to figure the odds. She was quite prepared, though, to have asked Mario to be tested, if Sandra's results weren't good. She wasn't above blowing the whistle where Trevor's chances were at stake.

She wondered, for about the thousandth time, what Walter's reaction would have been if she dropped that little bombshell, and she'd mentioned the possibility to Martin during one telephone conversation when Maggie was out of the house.

His reply was swift. "Of course. Listen, it's Trevor's life we're talking about here." (As if she didn't know.) "I've been thinking all along that Mario should be tested. You never know, and to hell with what any- body would think. Who cares about Walter and Angela's feelings, anyway?"

"I wasn't thinking of their feelings."

"I know. But if worst comes to worst...."

Luckily, the worst hadn't come to the worst. Not in that regard, at least, but Nora was under no illusion that the 'worst' was over by any means.

Meantime, Pierre was uneasy. "I wonder, should we tell Trevor we talked?"

Nora's reply was an immediate, "Yes. It's time."

"OK. I think that's a good idea. Just don't tell him I was drinking coffee."

Nora laughed. "Your secret is safe with me."

"Fine. I think I'll stay until he comes home, if it's OK with you. It's time we got a few things ironed out. Like why he thinks he has to hide stuff. Anyway, I can use the time to juice up this wheat stuff."

Nora sat on a stool and watched as Pierre got out the necessary equipment. He was amazingly neat and proficient at his work. She had to yell in his ear to be heard over the machine. "Do you guys really think it will help?"

He pressed the stop button, turned to Nora and shrugged. "Couldn't hurt. Won't cure leukemia, though. At least, I doubt it. But maybe it'll help us both feel better. I think it's helping me. Who knows?" he said giving another shrug before getting back to the business of extracting the unappetizing green stuff.

Despite all his efforts and the ensuing racket, very small amounts of liquid emerged from the sinewy wheat grass. Pierre finished the operation, retrieved a glass with about two ounces of green juice and, grinning, leaned over the counter and offered it to Nora. She shook her head. "I'd just about as soon eat dirt."

"That's what I figured. Oh well, I'll save it for Trevor."

"There's something I've been wondering about, Pierre. Maybe you could tell me."

"Sure, if I can."

"What I've been wondering is, does Trevor have a girl friend? I mean, he always had lots of girlfriends, but I haven't heard him mention any names at all. Kind of unusual for a guy who used to fall in love at least once every season."

He thought a moment. "None on the scene right now. At least, not that I know of. But he has talked a little about somebody called Mickey. At first I thought it was a guy. Then I found out it wasn't."

"Much? Did he talk about her much?"

"Not a lot. No. All of a sudden, one day, he pulled a picture out of his wallet. That's when I found out Mickey was definitely of the female persuasion." He laughed. "Definitely not a guy."

"What did he say about her?"

"He said they broke up last summer. Said they were getting too serious and he was in no position to get married. Or get into that kind of a relationship." Pierre was thoughtful. "You know, now that I think of it, I got the impression that he was pretty much in love with her. Maybe he still is. Or maybe not. Who knows? Anyway, he hasn't talked about her at all since."

"I'm sorry to hear that. I mean, sorry he hasn't got someone he really cares about right now."

"He cares about you."

Nora smiled. "Not quite the same thing, though, is it?"

"I suppose not," Pierre said, going about his clean-up operation. Before they could have any further discussion about his love life—or lack of same— Trevor came home.

Nora and Pierre exchanged glances when they heard him come in, hang up his jacket in the small foyer and shout, "Hi, anybody home?"

In the family's time-honored tradition, Nora replied, "Ain't nobody here but us chickens."

Trevor entered smiling. "Good. I ain't seen a good lookin' chick in a long while. And I see the mother hen has got some cure-all chick excelsior ready and waiting. Didn't expect to see you here, Pierre. What gives?"

"I forgot you wouldn't be here, but I'm glad I came when I did. Had a chance to talk with your mother."

Trevor's light-hearted banter turned to suspicion. "And what did you two find to talk about?" He looked from Nora to Pierre and back to Nora. "Me, I presume?"

Just as Nora said, "I told him about your leukemia," Pierre blurted, "I told her about Rachel."

Surprisingly, Trevor said nothing, but walked over to the window and stood gazing out for what seemed an eternity. Meantime, Pierre stood in the galley kitchen with a wet dishcloth dangling from his hand and Nora maintained a near-crouching position on her stool beside the counter.

Finally, when Trevor moved to a chair in the living room, sighs of relief were audible. "You two..." he began and then stopped.

Pierre threw the cloth into the sink and came into the room. "We two, have been talking about you, buddy. Don't blame your mother. I gave it away about Rachel. Didn't mean to. But it happened."

Nora swung around on the stool. "And I thought it was high time he knew about your illness."

"What are friends for, anyway? Couldn't you trust me, or what? And why were you being so secretive about it. Not a crime that I know of. No disgrace."

"We seem to be the ones on deck. The ones here to help you. Pierre and I need to know all there is to know," Nora said as she rose and went to Trevor's side. She touched his shoulder and continued, "By the way, I'm very glad to hear about Rachel. It's good to be getting some help in that way." She stood for a moment, undecided, then went on, "Pierre also mentioned that you had a friend called Mickey. Do you still see her?"

Trevor didn't reply, but sat staring at his hands, which were lying loosely on his lap.

The silence grew until Pierre turned to go back to the kitchen. "I brought some wheat grass over like I said I would. Juiced it. It's ready."

Trevor stirred and rose. "I'm tired. Have to lie down. Need to be by myself for a while."

"Drink the juice."

"Pierre, I don't want the damned juice right now."

But Pierre wasn't about to have his work go to waste, brought the glass to Trevor and handed it to him. "Gotta be drunk when it's fresh."

"Oh, all right, for chrissakes," he said and drank it as though it was a neat shot of whiskey, before banging the empty glass down on the counter, going to his bedroom and slamming the door.

After a moment, Pierre looked at Nora questioningly. "What do you think?"

"I think it went better than I expected it would."

THE CALL

W HEN THE CALL CAME, TREVOR WAS KEEPING AN appointment with Rachel. Nora was pleased with the progress her son seemed to be making, since he was no longer as surly and his nervousness had abated somewhat. He also opened up considerably and it was possible to have a conversation from time to time. He seemed to have come to an acceptance of his condition, although still adamant about not having a transplant.

Nora and Colleen had developed the habit of meeting in downtown Vancouver once a week for lunch and, occasionally, Nora visited Colleen for dinner at her brother's house. Twice, Trevor accompanied her to the dinners but seemed wary of becoming too friendly with either Jocelyn or Ron. He was clearly more comfortable with Colleen. Nora wished she had Colleen's more direct way with people. Her friend had no compunction about calling a spade a spade, although her remarks were always tempered with sympathy. Perhaps empathy would have been a better word.

These social occasions were important to Nora and she felt a closeness to the little family that surprised her. "Of course," as she said to Colleen one day over lunch at The Hotel Vancouver, "our similar circumstances would naturally draw us together, but it's more than that. I feel as if I've known you all my life."

"I feel the same way. Funny. Maybe we knew one another in a former life. Did you ever think of that?"

"I never thought of that. Never had much of a mystical turn of mind."

"Me neither. I don't know what Ron believes, but I have heard him say nothing happens without a reason."

"That surprises me in a way. I wouldn't have thought a man of his... well, his abilities and profession would think that way."

Colleen smiled. "Hard to know what Ron is thinking. One thing, though, he likes you."

Nora could feel the heat on her cheeks. "I'm kind of a lost cause these days. I can't imagine what there is for him to like."

Colleen looked at her friend with a puzzled expression. "Nora, why are you always putting yourself down?"

"Do I really do that?"

"A lot of the time you do, yes. If it's because of being left in the lurch—it happens all the time. Just ask me! Anyway, from what you've told me, it's no reflection on you. One swallow doesn't make a season—or whatever the saying is."

Nora laughed. "Boy! What my friend Maggie could make of that. She'd probably say 'one turd doesn't make a shovelful'. Or something."

"She must be quite a card."

"She is. Only Maggie would never equate Walter with a turd. She's too fond of him. She figures he'll come back—he's just temporarily off his rocket, as she puts it."

"The rocket that sent him to Florida, maybe?!" Colleen said, reducing them both to helpless laughter.

Nora blew her nose. "One of the things I like most about you, Colleen, is that you can make me laugh. Maggie could always make me laugh, whether she intended to or not."

"You miss her, don't you?"

"Almost as much as I miss Walter. But I know he won't be back. Not back to me, at any rate."

"Maybe back to Manitoba if Angela throws him out?"

"I suppose that *could* happen, but I wouldn't be there to welcome him with open arms. I seem to have passed that 'I'll take him back on any terms' phase. No, I won't have him back. Not now, not ever. I've had to cross too many mountains alone since he left. Anyway, I've come to realize that a one-sided love isn't worth wasting my life on."

"You figure you're worth more than that?"

"I guess you could call it that."

"Congratulations! I take back what I said a minute ago—about always putting yourself down."

"Thank you." Nora raised her coffee cup. "Let's drink to that"

Both women laughed when their coffee toasting resulted in the hot liquid being spilled over the table-top and into Nora's special of the day—hamburger and fries.

"I take it that, if you don't intend to go back to Walter, even if you had the chance...."

"Even if I had the chance." Nora repeated as though taking a vow.

"You would not be going back to Manitoba?" Colleen continued.

Nora hesitated. "Hard to say at this point. I seem to have this love/hate relationship with that province.

Something like you have with Saskatchewan."

"Well, we could always split the difference and go live in Alberta."

"Been there, done that."

"And you don't want a repeat?"

"The fates haven't spared me much so far, but I hope they never find it necessary to bring me to that unhappy pass. Again."

Colleen astonished nearby customers with her full-volume laugh before teasing Nora with, "You could always start a political party—that would keep you busy. And God knows, there always seems to be room for one more."

Nora fell in with it. "Speaking of God, there would be problems with Her, I'm afraid. I am not, and have never been, 'born again', whatever that means. I have no direct line to Her throne so I haven't been blessed with the authority to tell people what they must believe in order to be true-blue Canadians. Thanks for the suggestion, but I don't think it would work."

Colleen laughed, then sobered. "I guess not. You're not the baby-kissing, hand-shaking, bull-shitting, sanctimonious type."

"Thank you."

"Want to drink to that?"

"Lord, no! My sweater sleeve is still wet from the last time."

They accepted fresh coffee from the waitress and sat in silence for some time. Companionable silence. Eventually, they began to speak at the same time.

"You first," Colleen said.

"OK. What I'm wondering is what will happen after this leukemia thing is taken care of. Have you any plans?"

"Nothing other than just to see the kid through it."

"Me, too.

"You don't intend to go back to your farm once

this... once this thing with Trevor, is over?"

"I suppose a person can never say 'never'. But, at this point, I doubt it. I had thought for a while that Trevor and I should go back and have them do the transplant in Winnipeg. It would be more convenient in a way. Closer for Sandra, for one thing. She has to be there."

"I know. And you'd have the support of old friends back home."

"Old friends can be highly over-rated. Except for Maggie, I have no really close ties with 'back home'. I got to be friends with Inga, too, in the short time I had to get to know her. And, as I've found out, new friends can be supportive. Very supportive. Anyway, going back to Manitoba doesn't seem to be an option."

"And Trevor isn't in favor of the move?"

"Trevor is not even in favor of the transplant, as you know. But, in spite of all his talk, I think he's afraid to leave Vancouver. He knows the doctors— they know him. No. Apparently he feels no special ties with Manitoba, either."

"It sounds as though you'll end up making Vancouver your home."

"Probably, although personally, I wouldn't make any predictions about my future. Long term or im- mediate. What about you? Back to Saskatchewan when you can?"

"I'm in about the same situation as you are. What- ever Jocelyn wants, I suppose. I can't see us staying with Ron indefinitely. But my recent memories of Saskatchewan aren't exactly calling me back, either." Colleen was silent a moment before suggesting, "Maybe you and I could get a place together. We could raise cats, or something!"

Nora just smiled. "And Trevor and Jocelyn?"

"Aye," Colleen said sadly, "there's the rub."

When Nora got back to the apartment, Trevor was home from his appointment with Rachel and was sitting on a chair by the phone.

"You been back long?" his mother asked.

"About ten minutes."

"What's wrong? You look awful."

"There was a message on the machine."

Nora's heart sank. Whatever the message was, it was not good news. She sat heavily on a kitchen stool. "What is it?"

"I can check in at the hospital on Monday. And to call Dr. Webb."

"Have you called him?"

"No."

"Why?"

Trevor jumped to his feet and began pacing. "I'm not ready."

"And Sandra's not here," Nora said, thoughtfully.

"That part wouldn't matter for a couple of weeks. First a week of heavy-duty chemo and then a week off for some reason."

"Yes, to rest. I remember now. Then she'd have to be here."

"Right, without her marrow the goddam poison would kill me totally. I don't want to do it." He walked to the window and stood, gazing out. At nothing, Nora suspected.

Nora sighed. "Have you discussed this with Rachel?"

"About a million times."

"What does she say?"

"My decision."

"Could you talk with her again?"

"I've already seen her once today, remember?"

"Maybe you could see her again."

He turned then, walked over to Nora and looked

237

directly into her eyes. "Mother, please tell me why you're so sold on the idea of a transplant when you know right well all that has to happen. All the negative stuff. I keep trying to figure it out."

"Because I believe what the doctors say. That it's your best chance. You know as well as I do that the drug you're on can only be used for a limited time. And God knows what it's doing to your kidneys right now."

Trevor went to the fridge and poured himself a glass of juice. "But, at least, I feel pretty good right now. After a transplant—well, I've seen some of those people over at the Day Care place where I get some of my tests—hardly any life left in them at all. Shambling wrecks hoping to hell they don't catch pneumonia or a thousand other things that'll kill them deader than doornails. Maybe right now is all I've got."

"That's what I'm afraid of. I understand your reluctance to go through it, but Sandra's a really good match. That's what the doctors said, remember?"

"A seventy-five percent chance of coming through a transplant OK, instead of a fifty percent chance! Big deal!"

"Better than a zero percent chance, which is what you have right now."

Evidently the juice mixture was not to his liking, for he poured it down the sink and carefully rinsed the glass before saying, "But they'll come up with something soon. They're working on it all the time. The big insurance companies in the States are putting pressure on. They're not fussy about paying the costs of transplants. I've heard that there's work being done in Houston. A guy there thinks he's pretty much got it figured out. The gene thing. I know it wouldn't be ready for me to use just yet, goddam it to hell. But there'll be something else soon. Maybe within four or five years." He studied his mother's face for her reaction.

"You haven't got four or five years."

"Or sooner. They'll maybe have it sooner. In a few months."

"After which, whatever they come up with will have to be tested and go through all sorts of hoops before they'd ever put it into general use."

He came and stood at the counter across from her. "What if it doesn't work? The transplant."

"You die. We both know that. But you *will* make it. Don't even think about dying. Not for years and years and years."

"I'll have to give it more thought. I'm not ready."

"That's fine, dear. I understand." She leaned over and kissed his forehead. "I'm going to have myself a little lie down."

As Nora lay rigid on Aunt Annie's bed, she thought she could hear Trevor talking to someone, but unbelievably, she fell asleep without knowing who, if anyone, was in the apartment.

It was after five when she wakened and heard the familiar sound of the juicer swinging into action. So, Pierre was there. Thank God for that.

MAGGIE VISITS

It was late September by the time Trevor accepted the transplant procedure as inevitable and another date had been set for the following month—late October. Fall work on the farm was completed, Maggie's presence back home was no longer crucial and Nora asked her to come to Vancouver to be with her. Actually, she broached the idea privately to Martin first.

"I was wondering if you might like to have some company, and we can manage fine without her." Martin said. The 'we', Nora knew, referred to himself and Inga. "But Nora, it's time, you know. Time to tell Walter and his mother."

"Sandra's already done that." She sighed. "Without my permission, of course. Much less Trevor's."

"Will he come?"

"I don't know. He didn't tell Sandra and he certainly hasn't contacted me. How about you? Has he phoned you?"

"No, and I sure wish he would. There's money coming to him. You, too, of course. But we've already discussed that. Not only the money thing, but should I fertilize? What should be sowed next year? Things like that."

"I guess you'll have to use your own judgement about the land. I suppose just treat it as though it were your own and you'd be farming it next year."

"I'd sure like confirmation on that."

"I understand. Very well. I'll confirm it."

"You're not coming back, then?"

"I don't think so. Not to live, anyway. Probably to do whatever with the house, though. I'll see. I can't seem to think any further than next month."

"The date's set, I gather."

"I'm afraid so."

𝒪

Maggie's reaction to the invitation was undisguised joy. Not only would she see Nora and Trevor, she'd get to have her first ride on a plane and visit Vancouver.

"You really want me, Nora?!"

"Of course, I really want you. So does Trevor. He can hardly wait."

Although that was stretching things a bit, Trevor *was* looking forward to having Maggie around. "She can provide the comic relief. A little of that wouldn't hurt."

Three days before he was to enter hospital, Trevor and Nora picked Maggie up at the airport and went through the long performance of retrieving her luggage from the carousel while Maggie gaped at the crowds thronging the area. About all she could say was, "Jeez, I never saw so many people. Not even in Winnipeg. I never saw so many people wearing costumes like that. Jeez!"

"Not costumes, Maggie," Trevor corrected. "That's

what they wear all the time."

"Those funny things on their heads and like that?"

"Yup."

"I'll be darned. Only ever saw that on TV before."

On the drive to the apartment, Maggie was full of her flying experience. "They give us nice little trays of dinner," she said, fishing in her big tote bag. "See, I kept the cutlery—plastic, but you might could use them." She dug further. "These little pepper and salt things, the sugar package, the dinner roll and this piece of cake. I had to take it out of the dish to wrap it, so it's got a bit broken." She offered it to her hosts. "Air Canada don't give out very big serviettes."

"No thanks," Nora said. "I had a big breakfast and I've got our lunch all ready at the apartment."

"I have to concentrate on the driving," Trevor said. "How did you enjoy the flying part?"

"After I got over being so scared—you know, when you take off and you're going so fast. I tell you, my life flashed in front of me. I didn't realize it at the time, but I grabbed the little boy's hand—the one that was sitting beside me. Between me and his mother. Or somebody like that. And he didn't push me away. He only said, 'It'll be OK, lady, it's always like this.' I thought he was a pretty good kid explaining what would happen next and all that. Bad mouth, though."

Maggie was temporarily distracted by the scenery. "Wow! This is a big bridge—what's it called? What's this water we're going over? Is there always this much traffic?" She didn't wait for answers, though, before going on with her little boy story.

"Anyway, this kid helped me quite a bit. He told me that the big bump sound was just the wheels going up. 'Reacting' I think he said. He's flown a lot. Parents divorced. Mother in Vancouver, father in Winnipeg. Can you imagine?! A little kid like that—

242

maybe nine years old. I was surprised that sometimes the ride was real rough. I thought it would be
smooth sailing in the air. He said it was pretty smooth
compared to some. A good take-off, he claimed, even
though I was afraid we'd crash, for sure. He said it
was a good ride, so far, 'if only the pilot, didn't fuck
up the landing in Vancouver.'"

"Excuse me," she apologized to Nora and Trevor,
"but that's what he said. The mother, or whoever she
was, wasn't paying any attention. Turned out the
kid didn't care for the landing any more than I did.
All that screeching, and I'd seen the water when we
circled—knew the ocean wasn't far away—like maybe
we'd go ripping right into it. We held hands then,
too." She finally ended the monologue and sighed.
"Oh well, I'm here now. Say, this is a long drive. How
much farther?"

While Nora was getting Maggie installed in the
apartment, Trevor set sandwiches and muffins on
the table and plugged in the electric kettle for tea.

"Don't Trevor have a room-mate?" she whispered
to Nora.

"Well, he did, but he's gone to live with his girlfriend. Permanently, I guess. Or as permanent as
these things are."

"What happens if they break up—he comes back?"

"We'll deal with that if and when it should happen.
Don't worry. For now, you and I will share the big
bedroom and when Trevor goes to the hospital, you
can use his."

"When is that again? When does he have to go?"

Trevor overheard the question and answered. "Too
soon. Sooner than I wish it was."

Maggie went over and gave him a hug. Never one to
beat about the bush, she looked directly into his eyes
and asked, "Are you scared?"

"Shitless."

"Oh. Sorry to hear that."

"Thank you. Come, sit down, let's eat."

*

Although, a week or so before, Trevor had taken his mother on a dry run to the hospital, he wanted to take a taxi when it was time to check in. Nora, however, insisted on driving. She needed the practice. Maggie sat in the back of the car while Trevor fidgeted in the passenger seat ready to give his mother further instructions—or snatch the wheel if that seemed more appropriate. "If you could loosen that death grip you have on the wheel, it would be a bit more relaxing."

"This is the Burrard Bridge," Maggie intoned, as though reciting a lesson. "And the Molson's clock. We can see it when we go for our walks along the sea wall, can't we, Nora? Hey, that's gotta be Granville Island over there! What's that big building on the left? Isn't that a funny place for a car dealership? Does that store over there only sell crystal stuff, or what? Hey, this sign says, 'Broadway'; are we getting close? You said it wasn't far from the apartment. This is getting far."

Trevor had had enough by the time they reached the stop light at Oak Street and Twelfth Avenue. "Cool it, Maggie, just cool it, OK?"

"Sorry."

"It's just that I have to concentrate on the driving, so I don't need any distractions," Nora apologized.

Horns were honking behind them. "Turn, Mother! Turn, for God's sake!"

"On an amber?"

"That's the only way you can make a left at this intersection."

"That's insane. Look at the traffic."

244

"I'm looking. Turn before the light goes red."

"Oh, oh, it's turned red." Maggie informed them.

Nora was shaking. "Damn and blast"

Trevor patted her hand. "It's OK. Turn on the next amber."

They made it through and Trevor relaxed a bit. "Good. You just have to get used to it."

"I may never get used to it."

"Right lane now as soon as that van gets out of the way."

"Why is he travelling in that lane?"

"You'll find that, out here, vehicles travel in whichever lane they want. We have no control. Ours not to reason why. Now it's safe to get over. Quick! There's the entrance to the parking lot. On the right."

Nora found that her legs were barely able to carry her from the parking lot to the admissions desk in the hospital. Trevor carried his bag in one hand. It was heavy, transporting as it did, his radio, tape player, several videos, books, writing materials and Jocelyn's video camera. She had insisted that he record the transplant procedure for her benefit and, although his initial reaction was to refuse on the grounds that it was a gory thing to do, he reluctantly agreed. They had become slightly better friends over the past weeks, although he told Nora that Jocelyn was the 'loopiest cat' he knew. He also had pajamas, slippers, a robe and a couple of changes of clothing. Nora clung to his other arm and Maggie trotted along behind.

Inside, the wait felt interminable and none of the three was up to much conversation. Maggie seemed suddenly overcome by the seriousness of Trevor's situation and sat, silently, with her hands clenched tightly together. Trevor slouched in a chair with his eyes closed and Nora just sat, trying to empty her head of worries. She had to keep swallowing. When

Trevor's name was finally called, he turned to her and said, "This is it. Why don't you gals just go home, now? I'll have a phone. I'll call you later and give you the number."

Although she had assumed they would stay until Trevor was assigned a room and then accompany him to it, Nora didn't object to leaving. She just nodded, rose and left the hospital without even a goodbye or a hug. She was not up to either. Maggie trotted along behind.

They found the car easily enough, and after a lap or two around the lot, discovered an exit. "Now, since we made a right turn to get in here, we'll have to make a left to get out. Right, Maggie?"

"Right. Left, I mean. You're right."

Nora drove for a long distance—it seemed like miles and, perhaps it was—before she said to Maggie, "Shouldn't we soon be at that Twelfth Street and Oak intersection? I thought we would have been there quite a while ago."

Maggie looked around. "According to that sign, we're still on Twelfth Street. Is that good, or what? How far does it go, anyway?"

"I have no idea. Maybe we're going the wrong way."

"How could we? We turned left like you said."

"I think we should be going west. Do you think we might be going west?"

"Hard to tell. With all this rain, who can see where the sun is? One thing, though, I don't remember seeing any of this stuff on the way to the hospital."

"Me, neither. I'll have to find a place to turn around. We've done something wrong."

"Is this what they call the five o'clock traffic?"

Nora had wheeled into a service station and was desperately trying to make a left-hand turn so she could reverse directions. She was also crying.

"Back the car up about a car length and then stop,"

Maggie demanded.

"Why?"

"Because we're going to have to change places and we need a safe place to do it."

"You're going to drive?!"

"You're bloody right, I'm going to drive. Before you get us both killed."

⌐

Maggie got them safely back to the apartment and Nora went straight to bed. Maggie made an omelette and a cup of tea and took them to her on a tray. "You know what we did, don't you? We took a different ramp when we left than the one when we went in. That's how come we got going the wrong way. I finally figured it out."

"I know. I figured it out, too. And if you tell Trevor, I'll wring your neck."

"I kinda thought you might feel that way."

They were into the long haul at last with routines becoming more-or-less established. Trevor phoned the apartment the next day to report that he'd been hooked up to a Hickman Line. This conveyor line which went into his chest would carry all the chemicals, bone marrow, blood, blood components and a myriad of other mysterious compounds to enter his body without using needles. The line would remain in place throughout treatment and beyond. "It wasn't that bad, really. Then they did some kind of a heart test using dyes. Other kind of nasty things, too, but the bone marrow test was the pits—as usual. Excruciating, if you really want to know. Anyway, I think you'd better wait until tomorrow to come see me."

Nora and Maggie both went to the hospital the next day, but only Nora went in. Maggie stayed with the car in the parking lot. "I'll just listen to the radio.

Give Trevor my love."

Someone directed Nora to the leukemia unit on the sixth floor where a nurse took her to the large sinks and described the hand and arm-scrubbing procedure before leading her to the pressurized room in which Trevor was incarcerated. Or, at least, that's how he described it. On one wall was a large chart with a stupifying list of items—some checked off, some not. Once Nora learned how to read it, the chart would become the barometer by which she determined how her son was faring.

He was glad to see her and smiled wanly. "Welcome to my cell. I've been started on chemo. They say I'm lucky that Sandra's match is so good, I won't have to have radiation. Just chemo. Lucky?!"

Nora leaned over the bed to kiss him.

"No, no. Mustn't touch. Doctor's orders."

So she sat on the chair beside his bed and looked around the room. Obviously, he'd been busy before the treatment was started. Everything was neat and tidy and, in spite of cramped quarters, he'd found places for all his possessions. Books lined the corner shelving beside his radio, camcorder, VCR and writing materials. A small television set, supplied by the hospital, also shared shelf space. His clothing was hung neatly in a tiny closet beside a chest of drawers. An easy chair sat in one corner.

He grinned at her. "Home sweet home. Do you think I'll be able to stand it for the next few weeks?" Then, looking at his mother closely, added, "Do you think *you'll* be able to stand it?"

"Of course, I'm a big brave girl. Besides, I can leave any time I want to." Although Nora had tried for a light touch, she knew immediately that it was the wrong thing to say. "Absolutely insane," she told Colleen later.

Trevor only said, "Well, lucky you," and bit his lip.

Before she could apologize or make any kind of amends, a nurse popped in with a wheel chair and said, "Sorry, Trevor, more tests. You'll have to come with me."

"A wheel chair?" Nora asked in some alarm, "Can't he walk?"

"Not with all these tubes and things. I'm on a pretty short leash. It only stretches as far as the bathroom." Trevor said. "I'm completely at their mercy otherwise."

"Sorry," the nurse said to Nora. "I presume you are his sister?"

Both she and Trevor laughed. "This young lady happens to be my mother," he said—with some pride, Nora thought.

The nurse smiled and said, "My name is Terry, pleased to meet you Mrs. Field. Sorry to interrupt. I don't know how long this will take. Maybe you should come back tomorrow."

So ended the first visit.

As Nora approached the car, she saw that Maggie was sitting in the driver's seat with her head bent over the steering wheel. She sat up quickly when Nora opened the passenger door. "So how is he doing?" Maggie asked, not meeting her eyes.

Nora couldn't answer for a moment. She got in the car, gathered up the damp, crumpled Kleenex from the seat between them and stashed them in the small plastic garbage bag.

"Sorry, I'm messy."

Nora reached over and put her arm around her friend. "It's OK, Maggie, but crying isn't going to help."

"I know that. I won't do it again."

Nora sighed. "It's going to be hard. I only stayed a few minutes before they hauled him away for more tests. The nurses seem very nice, though. Terry, especially." She laughed shakily. "She thought I was his sister."

Maggie blew her nose and eyed Nora doubtfully. "I suppose she *could* make a mistake like that."

"Maybe she was just being diplomatic—trying to make me feel good about myself. Oh, well. Home James and don't spare the horses."

"I kinda figured I better drive."

"That's what I meant."

"Oh. I'm never sure what you mean."

Maggie was good at maneuvering through the city traffic, although she did a lot of muttering under her breath. Nora figured the skill must be inborn since Maggie had not had much prior experience with city driving. She quickly learned how to give other drivers the finger at, what she figured, were appropriate times. It was a bit unnerving.

"You'd better be a bit more careful. That guy that just cut us off looked like he might be a Mafia type. Maybe carrying a gun. Maybe shoot you."

"Just let the stupid bugger try."

"Actually, I'd rather he didn't."

"He won't. Just got a big head, is all. Nothing in it, either. I know the type—all hat and no cattle."

Nora was relieved, though, to have Maggie take over the driving and dreaded the time when it would become her own responsibility, since Maggie would surely have to go home at some point. Nothing was said about it, however, and aside from worrying about Trevor, Maggie was delighted with the sights and sounds of Vancouver. She liked to walk and much of their free time was spent outdoors, even though the walking was often up and down very steep terrain.

The daily visits to Trevor were difficult for both women, though. Maggie always drove and usually accompanied Nora into the hospital room, but she was so overcome with the surrounding paraphernalia involved in the treatment that she hardly said a word. Trevor's chemo treatments which were designed to kill off all his own bone marrow and make way for the new transplant from Sandra were unpleasant. He was sick and, in order to avoid the dreaded sores in his mouth, sucked almost continually on chipped ice. His main complaint was the food.

"It's not fit for a dog, Mom. I keep thinking about food, but I can hardly stand the thought of actually eating it. And when they bring in those hospital trays and lift up the lids, the smell makes me vomit."

This upset Maggie—the fan of good nourishment—and she welcomed the chance to do something productive for her beloved boy. "What kinda stuff would you like? I can make you up a big mess of baked beans."

Trevor laughed. "That's nice of you, but the gas would probably kill me before this goddam cancer does."

Tears filled Maggie's eyes. "What then? What can I do?"

"I wish I knew what to tell you. Maybe some grapes or something. Darned if I know."

But nothing Nora and Maggie brought from Granville Market did the trick. Not even the superhuge cookies Trevor requested one day between slurps on his ice chips. He considered the possibilities of various kinds of food, but when it was offered, couldn't manage to eat it. That was when the necessity of providing home-cooked meals became apparent to Nora.

Rest for him was difficult because of the many trips to his tiny bathroom to vomit or pee. These frequent visits had to be accomplished amid a veritable jungle of tubes from which he could not be unhooked. When, after a week, the chemo treatments were over, there was a week of respite before the bone marrow transplant was to take place. By this time, Sandra was well settled in to her new Ontario school. Trevor fretted. "I hate having to ask her to take the time off and fly away out here."

"She doesn't mind. She's prepared to do that. More than happy to do it."

"And I'll die if she doesn't. Right?"

"Right," Nora answered. She was becoming more accustomed to the subject of death; had adjusted by never letting it actually reach the place in her head where possibilities became probabilities, where percentages were factored and taken into consideration.

"At least, the Red Cross will foot her airfare tab. It won't cost her anything. I'd hate for it to cost a lot of money. And you stuck with the bill..."

"Lucky all around, I suppose," Nora said. "Saves your mother from a life of crime."

"Crime?"

"Yes. If we had to pay for Sandra's airfare—and if Canada's medical system wasn't paying for the transplant, I'd have to rob a bank. Several banks."

Trevor laughed. "With Maggie driving the getaway car!"

"She's sitting in it now, waiting for me. I think I'd better let her drive to the airport tomorrow, too. To pick up Sandra. She's a better driver than I am. Just ask her!"

"I know. She already told me. And listen, you'll be busy tomorrow, so don't bother coming in until evening—after Sandra gets here."

Nora hesitated, wondering how to bring up the subject.

"What is it Mom? You got something to tell me?"

"No. To ask you."

Trevor looked at her for a long moment before averting his gaze. "OK, I'm ready. Fire away."

"It's about Walt... Your father. Should we ask him to come?"

The rant Nora half expected never came. Instead,

Trevor, with his head still turned to the window, just murmured, "Whatever."

She rose, patted his arm and said, "I'll phone you in the morning, See you tomorrow night." He didn't answer so she quietly left the room.

"How am I going to go about this?" Nora asked Maggie when they got home.

"I mean, I don't speak to Walter on the phone, and there's no doubt in my mind that Trevor wants him notified."

"Maybe Sandra could phone him? She's already told him Trevor's sick. Maybe she should be the one to tell Walter that he wants him to come."

"It needs to be soon."

"Do you think Trevor's afraid?"

Nora's eyes filled with tears. "Of course, he is. But he can't be any more afraid than I am."

Maggie came and put her arm around Nora. "I'll call Sandra right now. You go lie down."

*

When Maggie came into Nora's room a half hour or so later, she said, "I couldn't get an answer at Sandra's. So I found your address book and phoned Walter myself. He came right to the phone. No problem."

"What did he say?"

"He'll come."

"Anything else?"

"I told him what I could. I also gave him Trevor's phone number so he can call him at the hospital."

"How did he seem?"

"Hard to tell. I think he was crying at the end. Didn't say goodbye, anyway."

"Thanks, Maggie. I'm such a coward. I should have called him myself."

"It's OK. I understand."

And Nora believed that Maggie really did understand that she had only so much strength left in her body and no surplus to deal with her husband.

"I also called your friend, Colleen."

Nora was alarmed. "What did you tell her? I don't want to worry her. After all, she's still going to have to deal with Jocelyn. And dealing with Jocelyn now is quite a trial."

"Oh, I don't think I worried her. Just told her you could use some company."

"That was nice of you. But *you're* company."

"I know. It's not the same, though. I know that."

Maggie was full of surprises—learning to truly empathize with others. Maggie has grown up, Nora thought, but such a hard way to have to do it.

"I told Colleen we weren't going to the hospital tonight and she said she'd send Ron over to take you out to dinner."

"My God! A rescue effort. How embarrassing."

"It's not like that at all. She said she'd been wondering why you hadn't phoned and she hadn't called you because she didn't want to butt in. She also said that Ron has been worrying about you and wants to see you."

"What else *could* she say? Anyway, what time is my date going to pick me up? I must look a fright!"

"About six-thirty, and you look pretty good. Considering."

Nora found that somehow, in spite of the ever-present ache in her chest, she could still find Maggie's left-handed compliments amusing. She laughed. "Maybe after a shower and shampoo. Lordy! Do I have time for a shampoo?"

"If you hurry. And wear that blue denim dress. It makes your eyes look pretty. Maybe some high heels if you've got some."

"Don't have any."

"We should go shopping some day. You need better clothes."

Nora laughed again. "I need a whole new life."

"That's what I mean. I think."

While Nora was still in the bathroom, Maggie knocked on the door. "I'm just going for a walk along the sea wall. I'll maybe eat something at the Sylvia." So she was alone when Ron arrived.

Nora was shaking when she opened the door. He didn't speak, but looked for a long moment into her eyes before taking her into his arms and holding her as though she were the most precious thing in the world. This was away past the hug she was used to; it was a lover's embrace.

When Ron finally released her, he asked, "How are you?"

She laughed nervously. "Quite a bit better now."

"Me, too."

"You've been sick or something?"

"Not sick, exactly. Just worried. About you."

Nora could feel tears starting.

SANDRA ARRIVES

When Nora got back from her 'date' it was after eleven. Maggie was still up watching television, but came to the door to meet Ron and extended her hand. "I've heard lots about you," she said.

"Only good things, I hope."

Maggie looked puzzled. "Of course. What else could there be?"

Ron grinned at her. "And you're exactly the way Nora described you."

"My God! What did she tell you?"

At this, he laughed out loud and patted her shoulder. "Only that you're the best friend she has in the world." Then he looked at her seriously. "And thank you for that—for looking after her."

Maggie was flustered by the pat, unexpected thanks and the 'best friend' label. "Oh, we're practically related. I don't deserve any thanks. Nora's the one who looks after everybody. Not me. I just hang around, drive the car. Like that."

"Nevertheless, I'm really glad you're here. And so

is Nora."

Maggie bit her lip. "I only wisht there was more I could do."

"We all do what we can."

"I know," Maggie said and disappeared tactfully into the living room to resume her television watching.

Although Nora had been listening intently to the exchange between Ron and Maggie, she hadn't spoken. When they were alone in the hallway, Ron said, "You're quiet. What are you thinking?"

"Just that it was nice the way you two seemed to hit it off. The way you managed to make Maggie feel important."

"Nothing to it. Just telling the truth helps sometimes." He took her in his arms and whispered, "Other truths come to mind right now, but I think it's too early to express them." Then he kissed her quickly on the lips said, "I'll call you tomorrow," and was gone.

Nora walked into the living room more-or-less in a trance.

"So how was it?" Maggie asked. "Your dinner, I mean."

"The dinner was fine. We just took the ferry across to Bridges. Got the last ferry back."

"What did you have to eat?"

"I can't remember."

"Can't remember? Jeez! It wasn't that long ago."

"Something fishy, I think. Maybe salmon."

Maggie turned off the television. "He's a nice guy. You like him quite a bit, I think."

"Yes. Quite a bit."

"Did he kiss you?"

"Hmmm."

"A lot of times?"

"Not a lot," Nora said and wandered into the kitchen for a glass of water.

Maggie started for the bedroom, stopped midway and said, "I wonder what Walter would think."

Although it hadn't been said in a mean-spirited way, the idea still brought Nora up short for she hadn't given Walter a passing thought during the entire evening. Curious to know if Maggie might be upset by Ron's appearance in her life, she asked, "What do *you* think Walter might think?"

"I dunno. Apple sauce for the goose is whatever for the gander I guess. Anyways, I asked you first."

"Maggie, I have no idea what he may or may not think about anything I do. I can't imagine that he would care one way or another."

"What about Trevor, then?"

"Trevor is an entirely different matter."

"I won't tell him."

"He already knows Ron pretty well, and knows I like him. He likes him, too, I think. But I'm not sure what he'd make of his mother kicking over the traces, so to speak."

"Like I said, I won't tell him. He has enough to worry about as it is. Anyways, I like Ron. I guess him and Colleen have both been good friends to you. And that kid, whatshername."

"Jocelyn. They have, indeed, but not as good as you." She gave Maggie a hug. "It's past bedtime. We need to rest up for tomorrow."

Before Maggie went into the bedroom, she turned. "Like I said, I think Ron's an OK kinda guy, but I don't think you should figure on marrying him any time soon."

Nora laughed. "Not any time soon. Probably never. He'd have to ask me first in any case."

"He's gonna ask you sometime. I can feel it in my bones. What would you say then?"

"Lord, Maggie, we've got enough on our minds without a wedding looming up in the future. Forget it.

Good night."

Nora sighed with relief when Maggie went to bed. She'd had a long, confusing day and needed time and solitude to think. Her head was spinning and not entirely from the two glasses of wine she'd consumed at dinner. The delicious feeling of being in Ron's arms and the memory of his cool lips threatened to overshadow worries of the crucial days ahead and made her feel somewhat ashamed. Still, her attraction to Ron—a mutual attraction, she knew—was a comfort she would never have dreamed of when she'd made the anxious trip to Vancouver short months ago.

True, she'd been aware for some time that theirs was a changing relationship. His soft touches on her shoulder whenever he was near and their frequent lingering eye contact spoke of more than just a casual fondness. She was greatly attracted to Ron's eyes. They were dark—brown, obviously, but sometimes, like tonight, she detected tawny golden streaks.

Nora admitted to herself that on her many visits— ostensibly to visit Colleen and Jocelyn—her main interest was in seeing Ron. After Trevor dropped her off—for it was always Trevor who provided the transportation to Coquitlam—she would feel a sense of disappointment if Ron happened to be at the gym or the hospital.

In the weeks before Maggie's arrival, the visits were often weekly events. Trevor would, occasionally, stay for a short time, but usually had some excuse to go elsewhere.

The times that he did elect to stay for a meal or a cup of coffee, she and Colleen were both pleased to note that Trevor and Jocelyn were reaching a certain level of friendship. An improvement on the mutual toleration that had marked their first meetings. They were not buddy-buddy by any means, but had a rather wary 'we're both in the same boat and we may as well make the best of it' kind of under-standing. One that was marked often by the gallows humor both employed, whether out of nervousness or silly ploys to shock their elders, Nora could never figure out.

On a night that Trevor was staying for dinner, he took off his jacket and, grinning, turned to show off his tee shirt. Nora had never seen the shirt before and was not amused by the message printed on the back: "Life's a bitch, and then you die." Jocelyn, how-ever, thought it was hilarious and asked, "Hey, where did you get that? I want one just like it."

"Actually, it's an old one, probably the only one left in captivity. Got it at a Goodwill store on Hastings. I go there sometimes with Pierre."

It was Colleen's turn to be shocked. "You shop on Hastings? My God! You want to be robbed or knifed or something?"

"Oh well, we only go there in the daylight. Lots of interesting stuff."

Jocelyn was fascinated. "Would you take me some-time? I could use some new tee shirts."

But before Trevor could answer, Colleen glared at her daughter and said, "Over my dead body," which sent both Trevor and Jocelyn into gales of laughter. Dead bodies, apparently being the black humor of the day. "Anyway, you've got more tee shirts now than you'll ever wear."

"You've mentioned that before, Mother, and you're probably right." Then Jocelyn turned to Trevor. "You know, I heard Mother telling Uncle Ron that after I'm gone she's going to sell all my tee shirts and go on a cruise."

"Mine will probably sell all my juicing equipment and buy a one-way ticket home."

Nora was furious, but speechless. Colleen was also

furious, but never speechless. "OK, enough! Knock it off." Then in a more amiable tone, "Jocelyn, why don't you show Trevor the new computer Ron bought. Maybe he can figure out the e-mail mysteries."

It got the two young people out of the room and Colleen sighed. "Did they upset you—those two nut cases?"

"No more than usual, I guess. How does it go when we're not around?"

"About the same. Everybody's edgy, but Ron does his best to help when he's home—keep things on an even keel, pretend we're just a normal household. But I get really tired. I mean, I eat, sleep and dream leukemia. What a life!"

"I know what you mean."

"There's one thing, though, that I haven't told you. It just came up this week. There's a possibility—just a faint possibility mind you—that they might try a new drug on Jocelyn instead of a bone marrow transplant. It's called Gleevec. It's being used in Seattle, I understand. Ron has been making inquiries. We haven't told her yet, but the doctors have agreed to do a bunch more tests to see if she might be a reasonable candidate."

Nora was astonished. "It's never even been mentioned to us."

"That's because Trevor has a matched donor. Jocelyn doesn't. Apparently they like to go the transplant route when they can. But time is fleeting and so far, no match for Jocelyn."

"What happens now?"

"Tomorrow we have some appointments. Maybe we'll find out something then."

"Why haven't you mentioned it to Jocelyn before now?"

"Too risky, given her state of mind. And she's past listening to anything I have to say or suggest. She needs a doctor to explain the ins and outs—the percentages..."

"Those damned percentages. Wish I'd never heard of percentages!"

"Me, too. However, she has to know. Also, possible side effects. All that."

The evening progressed on a happier note when Ron came home and joined Trevor and Jocelyn at the computer. Trevor had lots of experience and was able to provide Jocelyn with a good deal of information. The machine had come with a complicated book of instructions and he was able to translate them into a language she could understand. Ron, too, was still in a learning mode so the mealtime conversation was conducted mainly in computerese.

"She's a quick learner," Trevor said on the drive home.

"Of course, she is. Jocelyn is no dummy."

"I know, but she's always seemed so... I don't know...."

"Unstable?"

"I'm not exactly sure. Maybe immature, is all. For sure, scared as hell."

Nora thought of telling Trevor about the possibility of Jocelyn having an alternate treatment with the drug, but decided against it. It wasn't a sure thing, in any case or in any way. They all needed to learn more about it.

The evening visit had ended, as usual, with Ron managing to send meaningful glances her way, before giving her the warm embrace that had lately marked their good byes. He'd also whispered in her ear, "See you soon, dear heart. Keep your chin up."

It was difficult to keep those memories at a distance—the feeling of being in his arms, the way he looked at her, his soft words...

✍

Nora scarcely slept after her 'date' with Ron—the night before Sandra was to arrive. She hadn't heard from Trevor, didn't know if Walter had phoned him at the hospital or not. When she got out of bed to find herself alone in the apartment it was nearly noon, but a note from Maggie informed her that she'd taken some soup to the hospital for Trevor's lunch, gone shopping, and was on her way to the airport. Apparently, Trevor had requested some meat loaf and a baked potato and they needed ground beef. During the two weeks he'd been in the hospital, she and Maggie had been cooking various treats in order to provide something that Trevor might actually be able to eat—and keep down. This was something new. Meat. Unusual for him, but nourishing if it worked.

They had gone the route of omelettes, salmon loaf, rice pudding, vegetable chili, borscht, spaghetti with tomato sauce, even Kraft Dinner. No sandwiches since bread was out of the question—it turned to metal in his mouth, or so he said. Although he always tasted everything and sometimes ate small portions of their offerings, nothing was really satisfactory. He did manage to consume small cans of fruit, though, drinks called Snapple and boiled eggs. The discovery of the acceptable boiled egg was a blessing since the hospital then provided him with one for every breakfast, thus requiring Nora and Maggie to make only two food-runs a day to the hospital instead of three.

The preparation of the various test-meals was always a painful procedure since Nora was convinced that everything had to be absolutely sterile. With no immune system left, Trevor had little chance of beating off any bacteria that might accidentally come his way. Therefore, all his utensils were boiled and often Nora or Maggie's hands, as well. The food was cooked thoroughly, covered immediately and then quickly placed in the insulated blue Labatt Lite zippered bag they'd found in the apartment. Then, off they sped with the bag.

Sometimes Pierre was there ahead of them, in which case either Maggie or Nora remained in the waiting room, since Trevor's tiny room was crowded with even two extra people and there was always a parade of nurses or doctors just popping in. Pierre came three or four times a week, always bearing books, newspapers, magazines or video tapes. Together they'd watched innumerable Black Adder episodes designed to create laughter and promote healing—or so Pierre contended.

Nora, too, believed that laughter was a huge asset and always tried to find something amusing to relate. Not always easy, especially as D Day, as they called it, drew near. Maggie was always able to elicit a laugh, or at least a smile from him, just by being herself. And the day that she informed Trevor that the lasagna they'd brought was made entirely of 'orgasmic' vegetables, Nora was afraid he'd roll off the bed laughing.

⌒

She hoped that Sandra would be able to keep a happy face on things, too, and not be too overt in her anxiety, but she felt doubtful when Sandra and Maggie arrived from the airport later that afternoon. Sandra was jet-lagged, hungry and fearful—not an auspicious beginning to the days ahead. After the mother and daughter reunion, tearful though it was, Maggie and Nora soon had Sandra fed and put to bed.

"My God, she's thin," Nora said.

"Hasn't been eating, she told me. Worried. I tried

to tell her everything would be OK. Trevor's a big, strong boy and she's a big, strong girl."

"Not all that strong, I don't think. Either of them."

Maggie sighed and plopped on the sofa. "You and I have to be, that's for sure. Have you talked to Trevor, started his supper? I left the meat and stuff in the fridge before I went to the airport. You were still sleeping."

"I know. I was awake until about four-thirty and then I guess I just conked out. Thanks for the shopping trip. Everything's underway. And yes, I talked to Trevor earlier."

"Did he say if Walter had called him?"

"Yes, he called. Late last night, but Trevor didn't say much about what was said other than that Walter would come if he wanted him to."

"Does he want him to?"

"He didn't say. I don't think he knows for sure. Anyway, we'll find out more tonight when we take his supper. Maybe. We'll let Sandra sleep for a couple of hours and then we'll all go."

Maggie stayed in the waiting room. Nora led Sandra to the washing up area and, together they scrubbed their hands and arms the requisite number of times with the strong hospital soap. "Good God, it's a wonder you've got any skin left," Sandra said, before they went together to Trevor's room.

Sandra was nervous as a cat and when they entered, the whoosh of the air-pressured door startled her quite visibly. But both women were startled, indeed, by what they saw.

Trevor thought their shock was humorous. "Didn't expect to see me without a damned hair on my head, did you?"

Nora gasped, "When did it fall out?"

Sandra's reaction was to cover her mouth and whimper.

"It didn't fall out—it was shaved off *before* it could fall out. Saves a mess."

Trevor was sitting in his big chair and Sandra went to his side bending over to kiss him. "Uh uh, sister dear. No can touch. Doctor's orders. No contact."

"Oh. I didn't know. How are you?"

"Fine. How are you?'

It seemed at first as though there was nothing to say, but soon the two were chatting away, Sandra telling of her and Nicks's school experiences and their apartment, Trevor regaling his sister with stories of the various nurses and doctors. Everything, it seemed, was being discussed except for the next day's procedure.

THE TRANSPLANT

Nora tossed and turned until about four in the morning and then fell into a deep sleep. She awoke a couple of hours later, panic stricken to find herself alone in the apartment. But the note Maggie left explained that she had driven Sandra to the Cancer Agency Building for her six-thirty appointment. They didn't want to wake her.

Nora was furious. "Didn't want to wake me! Jesus Murphy!" she yelled at the walls. "On the most important day of my life—our lives! She started to weep, then checked herself. "I have to be calm. I have to be patient. Please, Lord, let me do all the right things."

She had showered, dressed and was shakily applying lipstick by the time Maggie returned about seven. She had also cooled down enough to resist telling Maggie that *she* had wanted to be the one to accompany her daughter to the bone marrow extraction procedure.

Maggie evidently guessed at Nora's mood. "Don't be mad at me," she called through the bathroom door.

"It was Sandra's idea not to wake you up. You couldn't have gone into the operating room with her, anyways. They wouldn't let me go in."

Nora counted to ten before she felt secure enough to face Maggie, who was standing white-faced in the hall. "You should have wakened me."

"I wanted to, honest. It was Sandra..." She was practically wringing her hands. "I knew you'd be mad. Besides, you were sleeping like a hog."

It was Maggie's last statement that broke the tension. "Like a log, Maggie, I've told you before—people sleep like logs. Not hogs."

"Not you. I've been around lots of hogs, and you were sleeping like one. For sure."

"Well, that conjures up a pretty picture, I must say."

"Not as pretty as you might think."

"Never mind. Let's go. Where to, first?"

"I'll drop you off to see how they're doing with Sandra and then I'll go over to see Trevor. Then we can change off. It's not far to walk if you take the short cut."

And that's the way it went all morning—visiting first one, then the other.

Sandra came out of the anesthetic feeling drowsy and sore. "I think a truck just hit me," she mumbled. "I just wanna sleep." But, as a day patient, she was not to be allowed that luxury. "Upsadaisy," a nurse said, trying to get her to her feet. Then Sandra fainted.

"I guess it'll take a while longer. But she'll be OK. They had to take 750 units instead of the usual 500. Your son must be quite a bit bigger than she is."

Nora felt a bit faint herself.

"You'd better leave now. Get yourself a cup of coffee or something. Your daughter will be fine. We'll let her sleep. Come back in an hour or so."

Once outside the door, Nora could see the hospital, but it looked to be miles away and she doubted that she had the strength to make the trip. There was a path between the buildings and she came upon a small garden, which earlier in the year would have been filled with blooming plants. In mid November, though, it looked as tired and worn out as she felt. The plot was enclosed with a stone wall. A place to sit while she practiced the deep-breathing exercises she remembered from prenatal classes. Today's trauma was rather like a birth, she thought. Or a re-birth. Only this time, Sandra was giving Trevor life. A second chance at life. Please, God.

When the shakiness subsided somewhat and Nora continued to the hospital lobby, she smelled coffee from the tiny food concession and remembered that she'd had no breakfast. She ordered a cup of Espresso and a sugar doughnut. "If this doesn't kill me, nothing will," she said to the young man on duty.

He grinned. "We don't aim to kill our customers, Ma'am. We actually aim to keep 'em alive!"

"Maybe a good sugar/caffeine rush will do the trick, then."

"I sure hope so. Have a good one. And, oh yes, have a good day!"

It was a spirit-lifting exchange, and by the time she had finished her breakfast and got on the elevator to the sixth floor, Nora's heart had pretty much resumed its normal rate.

She met Maggie emerging from the leukemia ward. Just as she said, "How is he?" Maggie asked, "How is she?" They both laughed nervously and exchanged such news as there was.

"Well, I'm off to see Sandra now. I wanna make sure she drinks that chicken soup I left her in the thermos. I'll tell her you were asking for her."

"For Pete's sake! I just came from there. I'll go and see Trevor now."

She found her son looking tired, but cheerful.

"Damn fluids they keep pushing into me with the IV, have me going to the bathroom every ten minutes or so. Because of the strong chemo, I'm told. I never peed so much in my life. Can't rest, of course."

Even though the bathroom was close by, the relentless process of getting out of bed and arranging all the tubes so he could access the toilet, was an awkward one. And tiring. No wonder he was weary.

"How's Sandra?"

"She'll be fine. A little sore, but she'll be fine."

"Will she come over for... for the actual transplant?"

"Probably not. She may have to rest. We'll see. She'll come to see you as soon as she can. I brought that silk shirt you asked for."

"The one with the short sleeves?"

"No, the other one."

"Damn. I get hot. Never mind, I'll get 'em cut off."

And the next nurse to appear in the room cheerfully made the alteration. "Snip, snip," she said, as portions of the sleeves fell to the floor. "There. Gone, but not forgotten."

"Like my hair?"

"Don't worry. Your hair will grow back. Unlike these," she said tossing the blue silk remains into the waste basket. "Try to get some rest." Looking at Nora, she added, "You, too."

So they dozed off and on. Trevor between visits to the toilet and Nora between bouts of anxiety.

Later in the morning, when Trevor said he thought he could eat some stewed apricots, she opened a can and left to go back to see Sandra. She found Maggie sitting on the same stone wall she had rested on earlier. "She was awake when I left, but they're in no hurry to let her go. Keeps on fainting. The doctor said, maybe about five or so, she could go."

"Trevor's still the same. God, I'll be glad when this is over!"

Maggie stood and hugged Nora. "Me, too. Me, too. Everything's gonna be OK, though, just wait and see. It'll be OK."

Two or three more times the women exchanged patients. Nora had lost count by the time the nurse came into Trevor's room bearing the bone marrow in a plastic bag. She was holding it like a trophy. "This is the elixir. This is the magic potion that will make you better," she said.

Nora looked closely at the bag's contents. It was not at all what she expected bone marrow to look like, although if anyone had asked her what she had expected, she could not have told them. It was a watery looking fluid, orange/red in color. Innocuous in appearance, life-saving in potential.

As the nurse prepared to hook up the 'elixir' to the tree, Trevor suddenly remembered. "Hey, the video camera. Mom, turn the camera on, OK? It's all set up, ready to go."

And so the procedure, undramatic as it turned out to be, was video taped. When the marrow bag was in place and hooked into the line leading into his chest, Trevor, looked into the camera and said, "Well, here goes. Kill or cure."

At that, the nurse leaned over and said, "It's *cure, honey, don't forget that!"

After those initial remarks, there seemed little else to say and, in a half-hour, the fluid in the bag had disappeared into Trevor's body. He looked at his mother and grinned. "Wasn't that exciting? I hope Jocelyn enjoys the picture show. Like watching paint dry!"

Nevertheless, Nora was exhausted and judging by Trevor's pallor, knew he felt the same. She had just lived through the most harrowing half-hour of her life and was preparing to leave for the walk back to the Cancer Building when Trevor's phone rang. It was Maggie. Sandra had been released and they were on their way over to see Trevor.

Sandra was white-faced and shaky when she came into Trevor's room. Nora hugged her and whispered, "Don't stay long," and left to join Maggie in the waiting room.

"I thought they needed time together. Just the two of them."

"I don't think she'll stay long," Maggie said. "She's pretty well pooped. Needs a couple of good night's sleep before she goes back to Guelph. I'm dead on my feet, myself. How about you?"

Too tired to talk, or even think. Both women fell asleep in their chairs.

Sandra wakened them with, "Well, do I have to walk home, or what?" She was being overly cheerful, but Nora knew she'd been crying. "He says not to bother coming back tonight. Not to bother with supper. He'll phone later, he says."

Maggie was disappointed. "And I had that chicken soup ready to heat up for him, too!"

"He says if he gets hungry he'll eat another can of apricots. Or get somebody to boil him an egg. Let's go, I need to lie down again."

⚬

There were two messages on the machine when they got back to the apartment. The first, from Walter, asking if Sandra would call him back to tell him how the day had gone. The second, from Colleen, said, "Phone me the minute you get back. We love you."

Nora left Sandra alone to phone her father and went directly to the refuge of her bedroom. Tired as she was, the need to talk to her friends was overwhelming, and she returned Colleen's call as soon as she knew the line was clear. Ron answered.

"Dear Heart, how are you?"

Nora could only manage a "Just fine," before the weeping started.

"How is Trevor?"

"Just fine," Nora sobbed.

"You're back at the apartment?"

"Mmhmm."

"I'll be there as soon as I can."

He came alone, bearing a large box from Colleen. "A care package, in case you're all about to starve to death." He looked around, "Do I get to meet your daughter?"

"Later, maybe. Right now she's sleeping. Pretty much done in."

"And Maggie?"

"Likewise. On the couch in the living room."

"We won't disturb them, then. I don't suppose you have the energy for the seawall tonight. We'll just go for a car ride, instead."

But they never left the parking lot. In the privacy of Ron's car and in the comfort and safety of his arms, Nora fell asleep. She woke later in a panic when she realized it had been nearly two hours since they'd left the apartment. When they got out of the car to go back inside, Ron almost fell. "It's OK. Leg's just asleep."

"My God! I've crippled you!"

They were laughing when Nora unlocked the apartment door, but stopped abruptly when she sensed that no one was there. A note on the kitchen counter read, "Trevor's been phoning and phoning. Must be hallucinating or something. We went to him. Where the hell have you been?"

Without a word, the two returned to the car and made the hasty trip to the hospital.

"I'll wait for you," Ron said.

"No, thanks, but no. I'm in enough trouble as it is."

And she hurried inside to go through the waiting-for-the-elevator, washing-up routines.

Sandra was sitting by Trevor's bed and they both seemed cheerful enough. "Trevor's been worrying that I've been taking birth control pills and they've somehow got into his body. I told him I quit weeks ago. Now he thinks maybe he's pregnant."

Trevor laughed weakly. "Just some bad dreams. I can't even explain them. Scary, though. Sorry to have brought you all running."

Sandra looked at her mother. "Well, *some* of us came running."

The unspoken accusation, left hanging in the air, demanded some sort of an explanation, but what could she say? I just stepped out for a breath of air? I went for a car ride with a friend and ended up sleeping with him? But it's not like you think...

All she could say was, "I needed to get out for a while."

"Colleen?" Trevor asked.

"Ron."

"I thought it might be." But there was no condemnation in his voice.

"Somebody left a big box of goodies," Sandra said.

"That would be Colleen," Trevor answered. "If there's anything you think I could eat, Mom, save it for me. Anyway, I think I'm OK now and the night nurses are good; they're trying to control the fever. Why don't you all go home now and come back in the morning?"

They woke Maggie who was sleeping noisily in the waiting room and almost nothing was said on the drive home. Even Maggie was quiet.

"Trevor told me the doctors have now raised his chances of a successful engraftment to sixty percent," Sandra told her mother the next morning.

"Damn the percentages. They make me crazy. I wish

they'd just shut up about them. It's going to be a hundred percent."

Sandra gave her mother a brief hug. "I know. That's what I told him. I think I'll spend as much time with him as I can. I'll be gone soon enough. When I'm ready, I'll phone you and we can change shifts. You look as though you could use the break."

Watching her daughter limp awkwardly out of the room, Nora's heart ached knowing that it was she who needed rest. No one had told them what a painful operation the donor had to undergo—especially people like her children, with hard bones, difficult to penetrate without injury. Just as well not to know in advance, she supposed.

✐

The next morning Nora asked Maggie what she knew about Sandra and Walter's exchange on the telephone. "Did he say anything about coming?"

"I think he's leaving it up to Trevor. When he wants to see him. Or something. She didn't exactly tell me. Just what I overheard. I think she said, maybe when Trevor is feeling better or something like that."

"You'd think he might like to see his son when he's *not* feeling better, wouldn't you?"

"Hard to say."

"Maggie, what do you *really* think?"

"I think he's a son-of-a-bitch. That's what I think. That's also what I told Sandra. Not to come to your only son when he's at death's door. That's a son-of-a-bitch." Strong words for Maggie, particularly when they were aimed at Walter. After a beat, in a quieter tone, Maggie continued, "What will you do if he comes?"

"The same thing I'm doing now—the best I can. He'll have to figure out what to do with *himself.* I already know what *I* have to do."

There was no further conversation on the topic of Walter, and Maggie continued crocheting squares for another afghan while Nora picked up a partly used crossword puzzle book.

Later, Nora went with Maggie to pick Sandra up at the hospital and they sat waiting in the lounge.

In about half an hour, Sandra came into the room and plunked down on one of the leather sofas. She looked even more drained than before, but all she said was, "I wonder what misanthrope designed this ugly furniture."

"Miss who?" Maggie wanted to know. "Ann somebody? You figure it was a woman built that awful couch?"

Sandra finally smiled. "I wouldn't be surprised."

"How did he seem to you?" Nora asked.

"Pretty good, believe it or not. Better than I am by a long shot."

Nora moved to sit beside her daughter. "It'll work out OK, you'll see. We just have to have faith and patience."

"I know."

Maggie couldn't wait. "What did Trevor say about Walt...? Your dad?"

"He'll come when Trevor tells him it's a good time. Not right away. He says he doesn't really want him around until he's feeling stronger—until my bone marrow kicks in."

Nora bit her lip. "I have to admit I'm relieved. I mean, I'm relieved he offered to come, but that it won't be right away."

"Right. Trevor and I agreed on that."

Maggie packed up her bundle of wool. "Anybody for supper? I'm starved, myself."

Nora got to her feet. "I'll just go look in on him again for a minute. I'll pick up the bag and his dishes.

By the way, did he eat any of that meat loaf we left?"

"A little. About three forks full. Do you two do this every day? I mean, hauling food down here?"

"Twice a day, so far." Maggie dug out the car keys "It's no problem and there's plenty left at home. We'll go as soon as your mother gets back. We'll have a good supper and you can get a good night's sleep. Morning will come early."

✐

Maggie drove them to the airport the next morning and Nora went through the second hardest day of her life. She said goodbye to Sandra. The girl was still not well, limping and very pale. She looked like she should be getting medical attention, herself. "I'll go see a doctor when I get back to Guelph. Maybe they'll give me a shot or something. Something to get my energy level back up and my blood count up to normal."

"Chicken soup," Maggie said. "Get Nick to make you some."

The apartment was empty and depressing after Sandra left, but both women tried to keep their spirits up for the frequent hospital visits. Pierre was a help. He visited Trevor as much as he could, telephoned often and sometimes just popped in to the apartment of an evening.

Every time Nora went into Trevor's hospital room, the first thing that met her eyes was the huge chart on the wall. This indicator of his progress showed what his platelet level was, among other things. She tried never to examine it too closely before greeting her son, for she dreaded interpreting the numbers— the daily disappointments. The good changes were very slow in coming.

"They told me about four weeks or so until

engraftment could be expected," he explained, sensing her unease. "We have to be patient."

"I know. I'm not worried." But she was. Worried sick. Then the fevers started and this time they seemed unrelenting. The horrible shaking fevers that left him chilled and weak, and kept her and Maggie as well as the nurses running with hot blankets when his teeth were chattering with the cold.

At one point, when Nora ran into a nurse in the hall and inquired about the frightening situation, she explained patiently, "This is a normal reaction; it happens to them all. His may be worse since his blood type, which used to be B, is in the process of changing to his sister's O."

"I didn't know that," Nora said. "Lots of things we didn't know."

The woman smiled kindly and touched her hand. "It's just one of the things they all seem to have to go through. Don't worry about it. He'll be fine." But Trevor looked shrunken and very ill.

Although that particular problem did improve, the following days showed little progress towards engraftment, but Trevor remained cheerful, at least in Nora and Maggie's presence, and spent many hours watching television and video tapes that Pierre kept him supplied with. One day, while they were visiting, Pierre came along with a fresh supply and the women decided to leave the two men to visit and go tend to some errands.

They went to a London Drugs and, with their purchase of speakers for Trevor's radio, a telephone extension cord, a footstool and some canned drinks, they were given a complimentary hockey stick. Nora wanted to refuse the hockey stick, but Maggie, never one to turn down a free item, insisted they take it. Together they struggled their purchases back to the hospital—each of them holding an end of the stick

with the packages hanging, strung out along its sur-
face like washing on the line.

It was an awkward trip, and in spite of the wintry
drizzle, they were hot and sweaty by the time they
managed to trundle their loot into Trevor's room. He
and Pierre were watching an old John Candy movie
and were already into gales of laughter, but the sight
of the two frazzled women bearing their burden was
too much. When Trevor could catch his breath, he
said, "My God! A hockey stick!"

Maggie tried to explain about the 'bonus', but when
Pierre asked, "Where are the shoulder pads and hel-
met?" she got into a huff.

"Maybe we'll get 'em next week," she said, tossing
her head. "I'll be in the waiting room."

"Do you think Maggie is mad?" Pierre asked.

Trevor wiped his eyes. "She'll get over it. She always does." Then, "Why don't you sit down, Mom?
You look beat."

"I am, but you will notice, there's no place for me
to sit until I stash this stuff. Where do I put the hockey
stick?"

When neither man could give her a sane answer,
Nora said. "I guess I'll just have to take it home, then."

"Good idea, Mom. See you tonight."

Before Nora had got halfway down the hall, Pierre
poked his head out Trevor's door and shouted, "I hope
your team makes it to the playoffs, Ma'am. Good luck!"

✍

It was an amusing tidbit to offer Colleen when they
met downtown at the Pacific Mall for lunch several
days later. Maggie had insisted that Nora take the
afternoon off while she went to visit Trevor and take
his meal. Nora had resisted at first, then thought of
the long invigorating hike uptown to visit her friend

and relented.

"You look tired," Colleen said as they hugged.

"I walked. Uphill all the way!"

"I know. Why didn't you take a cab, or even a bus, for heaven's sake?"

"I needed the exercise and the fresh air. Or as fresh as it gets here."

"Dare I ask how things are with Trevor?"

"About as usual. It's getting to be a long haul. Thank God for Maggie. She does yeoman service and gets along swimmingly with the staff now. It took a while, but now she's right at home in that little cell of a room. She says it's because she has established a good repertoire with the nurses."

Colleen laughed. "Well, I'll bet they enjoy hers! And, speaking of rapport—at least, I guess that's what we were speaking of—Ron is upset that you haven't wanted to see him lately."

"Not so much, haven't wanted to. Just not sure what to do."

"Trevor?

"Not exactly, although I'm sure he wouldn't object. It's just that... Well, my life is rather chaotic right now and I'm not always able to look on the bright side. If you know what I mean."

"Of course I know what you mean. But, don't you see, that's exactly why you *should* see Ron. At least now and again."

"I don't want to drag him down with me. I know how that works and it's a terrible thing to do to some-one you... Well, you know, someone you respect."

"Or someone you love?"

Nora nodded, avoiding Colleen's eyes as she stirred a second full packet of Sweet and Low into her coffee.

"My God, that stuff will kill you. Anyway, we're on the town today, Nora. Use real sugar," and she called the waiter over to bring Nora a fresh cup.

"It's sort of Walter. He'll come to see Trevor some-time. Maybe soon, I'm not sure and I don't know how I'm going to handle it."

"Do you still love him?"

"No. Of that I *am* sure. There's a lot of history be-tween us, though, and until I can get past that, I don't know what to do about Ron."

Colleen leaned across the table and took Nora's hand. "I can tell you what to do about Ron. Just let him into your life. Let him love you. Love him back. That's all he wants."

"You really think so?"

"Positive."

"I'll think about it. Anyway, tell me what's happen-ing with Jocelyn. The new treatment?"

Colleen cleared her throat. "It seems to be going well so far."

Nora felt that her friend was being evasive, holding back the good news that the new leukemia treatment was working for her daughter when it was not even an option for Trevor. "Look, I really want to know. Trevor really wants to know. We're both happy that she'll be spared this goddam transplant business."

"OK. First of all, no side effects. Not yet. The Inter-feron wasn't working and *was* causing side-effects we could all have lived without. The depression, for one thing, as if the kid wasn't depressed enough. And the injections and fever and stuff. Now, with the Gleevec, it's just a pill. A simple pill. Can you believe it?"

"The miracle cure."

"That's what we hope."

"And her outlook is better?"

"Much. Although you know Jocelyn, she'll never give up that macabre sense of humor. Or what passes for humor. And we are all so sorry this new treatment isn't something Trevor could have had."

Nora's eyes filled with tears. "I know," she said.

GOING HOME

AND THEN THE UNEXPECTED HAPPENED. ALTHOUGH TREVOR had been going through the usual ups and downs, he seemed to be doing well. Engraftment had finally taken place and his spirits were good. Maggie stayed on in Vancouver with Nora and they continued their daily routine of visits and food runs to the hospital. But all was not well.

About three-thirty one morning, Trevor phoned. "Sorry to bother you,' he wheezed. "Something's wrong. Trouble breathing. On oxygen. Still in my room now. Might move to ICU. Might not be in my room in the morning. Don't worry. Love you."

Nora's knees went weak. Without waking Maggie, she managed to get herself dressed and to the hospital. Trevor was still in his room, but his lips were blue. Speech was difficult for him, because he had to lift the oxygen mask to talk. Still he tried to reassure her. "I'll be OK. Tired, though. Can't rest. Every time I go to sleep, stop breathing. A respirator, soon I hope."

It was an infection—whether from the gut or from the site of the Hickman line was never determined, but Trevor was transferred to ICU and put on a respirator. The procedure required giving him a drug to produce paralysis so that his body wouldn't involuntarily try to do the breathing that machinery was put in place to do. He was also kept anaesthetized and lay, loosely strapped down, in a rocking bed to keep his body fluids moving.

This was the situation Walter walked into four days later—a son who lay incommunicado and a wife who was barely able to speak to anyone but her son. Nora had made a practice of talking or reading to Trevor and had also set up a radio on a windowsill near his bedside. It played quietly day and night. When Walter appeared she was reading to Trevor—a passage from *The Englishman's Boy*—but stopped at the sight of her husband. She could think of nothing to say to this man who seemed almost a stranger. Greyer and thinner than she remembered, he was trembling almost uncontrollably.

"I got here as soon as I could after I got the phone call. Airplanes... Taxi cabs..."

Nora just nodded, but in a moment said, unnecessarily, "He's unconscious."

"How long?"

"How long, what? How long since he's been like this or how long has he got?"

"Both, I guess."

"He's been in here four days. As to how long... We hope he'll get better. Obviously."

"Does he ever come to? Regain consciousness, I mean."

"No. He's not supposed to. At least, not yet. Not until he's better."

"My God! I want to talk to him," Walter wailed.

"What did you want to say?" Nora asked.

"I don't know."

"Tell him whatever's on your mind. He might be able to hear."

But it was some time before Walter could get himself together enough to murmur, "I just got in. Sorry I've been so long." Then he stopped.

"Go on," Nora urged.

"I'm sorry. Sorry for everything," he finally managed, looking at Nora as he said it—including her in the apology. Then, unable to say more, he left the room weeping.

Nora took over then, and spoke reassuringly to Trevor. "Everything is all right, dear. You just rest and get well. Your dad is here now." Then she picked up the Vancouver Sun and began quietly reading aloud news from the front page.

*

In ten days, when the doctors asked permission to discontinue life-support, they were all there for Trevor's last hiccuping breath—Nora, Walter, Maggie, Pierre and Colleen.

Nora remembered little about those terrible last days. Others had stood watch while she was periodically sent home to rest, but she went reluctantly and rested little. She didn't really remember having called Walter, but she must have, and somebody—possibly Walter—phoned Sandra sometime during the last couple of days when hope had dwindled. Sandra was told not to make the trip to Vancouver; there was nothing she could do.

Nora did remember clearly the last words she spoke to Trevor when the life-support machinery had been removed. "You will be all right my precious son. Remember, we love you. You will be safe. There will be no more pain, no more disappointments. You are free

284

to go." She'd repeated the last sentence until the lines on his monitor were flat.

✑

Walter had booked in at a nearby motel and, other than a few distracted, but necessary exchanges of information, there had been little conversation between him and Nora in the days that followed his arrival. That he was heartbroken was clear. After Trevor was gone, he took her in his arms and, weeping bitterly, sobbed, "I'm sorry, I'm so sorry. If I hadn't left.... I'm so sorry."

"I know," she said. "We're all sorry. But there was nothing you could have done. This is not your fault." Then, business-like, added briskly, "Phone Sandra, then come over to the apartment. Maggie will bring you. Oh, and you'd better call your mother. Maggie will get in touch with Martin when we get back."

Colleen led her out of the room and to the car where Ron was waiting. He took Nora in his arms and whispered only, "I'm here."

Back at the apartment, they were greeted by the aroma of fresh tea and coffee. The dining room table, spread with sandwiches and cake, was presided over by a strange woman who, it evolved, was Pierre's mother. His father was there, too. A kindly, but taciturn man—Trevor's former boss. Pierre, himself, had got there ahead of everyone and, although red-eyed and shaken, was on hand to delegate seating and make such conversation as he was able.

"Pierre came home late last night and made the sandwiches. He seemed to know what was going to.... Anyway, I made the cake. He called me from the hospital to bring the food over late this afternoon after they unhooked.... I mean, when they decided.... They were good friends, Pierre and Trevor," his mother said tearfully, and then gave both Nora and Walter hugs.

The little wake must have been torture for Walter, but strangely, all Nora felt was a sense of relief. It was all over. Trevor was at peace. She was overcome with an indescribable exhaustion that masked her sorrow—too tired to weep.

Walter, though, was obviously overwhelmed with grief, regret and anger. Inconsolable. Nora sincerely regretted that she could find no words of comfort for him. Maggie, however worn out herself, did what she could for her one-time hero and tried to talk him out of his anger. She led him out to the balcony where they remained for some time. When they returned, Maggie was speaking to him. "It's no use to carry on like this, Walter. You finally did the right thing by coming. He maybe knew that. Sandra gave him his chance to live, and let me tell you, it hurt her. She was a sick girl, but she did it anyways. Nora and I did all we could. The best food we could make. Chicken soup and everything. It was no use. You couldn't have done anything more. Like the saying goes, 'The universe is folding up as it should'."

It was exactly the right thing to say. Walter smiled wanly, exchanged glances with Nora and sat down. "You're right, Maggie. It seems to be folding up at a God awful pace."

If Nora had no words of comfort, neither did she have words of reproach. And later, when Walter came to her and asked, "Do you want me to come home to Manitoba? To stay?" she knew that was not really an option that either of them wanted, or that would work, even if she had wanted it.

She only shook her head and said, "No. That time has passed." And then, repeating the words she had so recently spoken to her son, added softly, "You are free to go."

Although Ron stayed close by all that evening, he

was careful to retreat to the sidelines whenever it seemed Walter wished to speak with his wife. His frequent eye contact with Nora plainly said, 'I am here for you. I love you.' Although their relationship must have been apparent, Walter seemed too distracted to notice.

Plans had to be made and Walter agreed to see to the cremation arrangements and have the ashes shipped to the funeral home in McClung. Possibly a summer interment when Sandra and Nick could be there. Nothing beyond that was discussed. Presently, Walter took his leave after saying hesitantly to Nora, "I'll go back to Florida when I've finished here, then?" A question, really. He seemed to need her permission.

"I think that would be best, yes," Nora said.

Then he scribbled a phone number on a piece of paper, and handed it to her. "Here's how you can reach me at the motel. Call if you need anything." Then he was gone. The others, except for Maggie, left the apartment soon after.

✏

Nora and Maggie spent the pre-Christmas season packing up and making final arrangements with Aunt Annie's nephew to vacate the apartment. Bruce, Trevor's former room-mate, had moved in permanently with his girlfriend, but paid a visit to Harrow Street to extend his condolences and to collect the few possessions he'd left earlier.

The place required more cleaning than Nora would have thought since, except for cooking, nothing much had been done in the way of housekeeping for weeks. Colleen came to help. "Jocelyn wanted to come, too. I wouldn't let her. She's also mad at me for not letting Ron bring here over her the night of... You know, the night we all gathered here. She's doing fine so far on the Gleevec treatment, but she's very nervous. Still, I should have let her come. I think I was wrong about that."

"Maybe you should tell her, then. Explain."

"I've already done that. Apologized. Sort of. She feels terrible about Trevor. Guilty, or something. I can't figure it out. The grief, yes. The guilt, no. I think, in the end, she had a mighty big crush on him. Even after all their silly squabbling talk."

Nora wandered over to the window and gazed out. "I wonder how it would have worked out," she murmured. Then, turning abruptly and going over to the piano, she dusted off Aunt Annie's picture and said, "I'm going to miss you, too, Old Girl."

The women worked on quietly, packing up the many articles Nora and Maggie had accumulated. Trevor's clothing had been carefully laundered and Nora, working in his bedroom, went about grimly sorting it into various piles—one for Goodwill, one for Pierre and one containing garments she would take home. Not willing to give any of it away, but knowing it had to be done. She kept only a few things—some of his favorite silk shirts and several sweaters and tee shirts as well as the baseball cap he had worn after his hair was gone. She wasn't ready to part with everything. She might never be ready.

Boxes and suitcases were piled high as Maggie and Colleen went about their cleaning duties in silence. Finally, Maggie, from her crouching position under the kitchen sink, spoke to Colleen, "Be nice to have the radio on, but those Christmas carols were driving us batty. Had to turn it off."

Nora, white-faced, appeared from the bedroom carrying her pile of keepsakes and trying to appear cheerful. "Hey, guys, how about I play a few tapes or CDs or something? Might make us all feel a bit better."

Colleen went and took Nora in her arms. "Look, I

know how hard this is. Music isn't going to help."

For the first time since Trevor's death, Nora gave in to tears. "I don't think anything is ever going to help," she sobbed. But regaining control in a few moments, she backed away from her friend and dried her eyes. "Just look at me! Crying will get you nowhere, as my father used to say. On with the show!"

"You know, you are *allowed* to cry. To feel grief. In fact, you should. Not good for you to keep holding everything back. Isn't that right, Maggie?" But Maggie had disappeared into the bathroom, presumably to deal in private with her own sorrow.

By mid afternoon, most of the work had been accomplished. With some difficulty, the women had managed to get all of the cartons and suitcases packed into the trunk and back seat of Trevor's car. The plan was that Nora and Maggie would spend their last two nights with Colleen and Ron. Colleen went ahead with Nora and Maggie following in the loaded car. It was Christmas Eve.

Somehow, Ron and Jocelyn had managed to prepare a good hot meal and had laid out the dining room table attractively with a Christmas arrangement of flowers gracing the center. "Aah, comfort food," Nora exclaimed as Ron pulled out her chair. "Nothing better than tuna casserole and a Caesar salad on a chilly damp night."

"With some good white wine?" Ron suggested.

Maggie pulled a face. "No wine for me. I might get drunk or sick or something. One time I drank most of a bottle all by myself. I snuck it up to my room. It was Martin's, but he wouldn't give me any. Said I was too young to drink. Tasted pretty good, too. On the way down, that is. Coming back up was different. I had a headache for a week. Never touched a drop since." So began an evening of Maggie's nervous chatter that lasted until they'd finished eating.

Then, Ron rose and said, "OK. Everybody into the TV room. Nora and I will do the washing up."

"Do you think the Simpson's might be on tonight? Maggie asked hopefully.

"Wouldn't be surprised," he said ushering them out.

"Alone at last," Ron took Nora in his arms and kissed her cheek. "Looks like we're not going to have much alone time before you go. I really wish you'd change your mind. What's the hurry?"

"Oh, Ron," she wailed, pulling away. "Part of me wants to stay, but the sensible part says I have to get home—get on with things."

"But driving through the mountains in the winter doesn't seem all that sensible to me. I mean, the mountain passes and all...."

"We'll go home on the Yellowhead; the passes aren't so high on that route. Maggie's a good driver and I'm fairly competent, myself."

"I know that, but I'd feel easier if you waited until spring?"

"I can't wait, Ron. There'll be so many things to do."

"Aside from warming up a cold, empty house, what do you have to do?"

Nora felt tears starting, but bent to her task of rinsing out the coffee cups in the sink. In a moment she gained control of her voice. "For starters, I'll have to make a trip to Guelph to see Sandra. And Nick, of course. Sandra is taking this pretty hard and she needs to see me. We need to see each other."

"I know. I can understand that."

"Then there's my sister, Audrey. She's pushing me to come to Texas for part of the winter. Warmer there, she says. I think I'll do that. I want to see her, too. Maybe some distance will help me get a new perspective on what's happened with my life. With Trevor, with Walter. With you. When I'm far away from here—

from the scene of the crime, so to speak."

"You can fly to Ontario or Texas from Vancouver, you know. Planes leaving every day."

"They also leave from Winnipeg. I'm flattered by your persistence, but I really have to get home. So many things seem to be hanging fire. And Maggie... Well, I think she's had enough of Vancouver for the moment. The place has lost a certain luster in her eyes since... I don't want her making the trip alone. And making some hard decisions without me."

They worked on in silence for a time before Ron asked. "What about Walter? He coming back?"

"Probably for the interment next summer. Not to stay, in any case."

"Did he ask to come back?"

"Yes, but his heart wasn't in it."

"And yours?"

"Not mine, either."

"A divorce, then?"

"As soon as humanly possible. For everybody's sake. There are other things that have to be worked out, too. Such as who will run the farm. I don't intend to, and obviously, Walter doesn't." Nora sighed. "Then, as I said, there's Maggie..."

"Maggie again."

"Yes. Martin and Inga are living together now in the Kroegar house. Maggie won't want to live with them. That leaves either Inga's place or mine. She's going to feel left out no matter what happens. And I can't keep her with me forever. She wouldn't expect that, anyway. But I just don't know right now what will happen. Maybe if I sell or rent my house, Maggie would be happy in Inga's place. It's small and cozy."

"Why don't you just come right out and ask her?"

"I've been putting it off. I guess we'll have to talk about it on the way home. She likes Inga all right, I think, but Maggie was put out of her own home once before and it was a very bad situation."

"Sorry to hear that. Guess there's lots of things I don't know."

"And some you're better off not knowing. Anyway, there's something else, too, besides the farm and house business. It's that I need to make peace with my mother-in-law."

Ron looked surprised. "I didn't even know you *had* a mother-in-law. Another thing I didn't know."

"She hasn't been on my mind very much lately. She's getting old and... Well, we haven't been on very good terms. In fact, the terms have always been pretty bad."

"Sorry about that. I *liked* my mother-in-law. It was my wife I couldn't stand!"

Nora gave a short laugh. "Lucky you. About the mother-in-law, I mean. Anyway, I've given it a lot of thought and realize that I have to go back if only to tie up some loose ends before I can get on with a new kind of life."

He turned to her. "I hope your new life will include me."

She touched his arm gently. "My precious friend, my life from now on will always include you. God willing,"

Jocelyn meandered into the kitchen at the moment Ron and Nora were sharing a warm embrace. "You two! Mushy, mushy! No wonder you wanted the rest of us out of the way. Have you decided, Aunt Nora?"

So now she was Aunt Nora.

Ron answered for her. "She has to go home now, but she'll be back real soon." Then, looking into Nora's eyes, asked, "Won't you?"

"Just as soon as I can get things worked through." Then, to Jocelyn, "Maggie and I will leave on Boxing Day."

"The day after Christmas?! Poop. I was hoping you'd just stay on. Run interference for me with my mother.

You know, all that kind of stuff."

"You're well enough to handle your mother by yourself now."

"Always was well enough for that."

"That's for sure," Ron said as Jocelyn disappeared into the living room.

She popped back in. "I heard that crack, Uncle Ron." Then she turned soberly to Nora. "I didn't get a chance to tell you how sorry I am about Trevor. Mom wouldn't hear of me going over to your place that night. And I wanted to."

"I know. I'm sorry about that. And she's sorry, too."

"I don't know why she treats me like an infant."

"It's only because she worries about you all the time."

"Well, I wish she'd stop."

"I hope she will now that she knows you're on the mend."

Jocelyn broke down, sobbing. "Trevor was just about my best friend. At least, my best friend out here. We talked on the phone almost every night. He was scared, you know. Did he tell you that?"

Nora's mind flashed back, and she was silent for a long moment before saying, "He told me once that he wasn't afraid to die."

"He *lied*. And I should have been there to hold his hand."

"Your mother thought it would have been too hard on you."

"I wish, just once, that she'd stop trying to run my life. I just wanted to hold his hand. Say goodbye."

"I understand," Nora said. "Believe me, I understand. And I do plan to have a talk with her about it before I leave."

"Me, too," Ron promised. "I'm sorry you thought I was making a crack about your ability to handle your mother. What I meant—if I'd given it more thought—

is that you'll have to find another way. Not just sass her back like a little kid. Take a different approach. Reason with her like an adult instead. And Colleen.... Well, she's over the top sometimes with worry. She's got to let go and stop being so damned bossy. I've been meaning to speak to her about it and I will. I promise to do what I can. But, in the end, you two will have to work it out for yourselves."

"I know." She was about to leave the room, but stopped and turned back. "Aunt Nora, I keep thinking you probably wish it had been me instead of him. He had a lot more going for him than I do."

Nora was aghast. She took the shaking girl in her arms. "Never, never, never think a thing like that, Jocelyn. I would *never* wish you dead. You are just as important as Trevor was. Everybody is important. Bad things just seem to happen... Well, randomly."

"You mean, life is just one big crap shoot?"

"It would seem that way. But promise me you'll just get on with your life. We're all grieving over Trevor, but he wouldn't want you thinking a thing like that. I'm just so glad that *you're* getting a chance to get better. Truly better. Trevor was, too."

"Really? He was *really* glad that I fit into the drug program even though he didn't?"

"Of course, he was. He was very fond of you, you know."

"Really? He was *really* fond of me?"

"Why wouldn't he be?"

"Because sometimes I'm a little shit. At least, that's what Mom says."

Ron burst into laughter.

Jocelyn turned on her uncle. "What's so funny?"

Ron put his arm around her. "*You* are. Very funny. And you've often been a little shit, but we know that's going to change. Isn't it?"

The atmosphere lightened, Jocelyn smiled faintly

and wiped her eyes. "Well, I'm going to start working on my personality now, too. I'll be such a strong, healthy, proper Miss Manners that you won't be able to stand it."

"We'll see if we can handle the pressure. Now, off with you. Nora and I are going for a long Christmas Eve sight-seeing trip after she's finished shining up the last wine glass."

Nora looked at him questioningly. "Well, a walk or a drive or something," he coaxed. "Anything to get away for a while. Have you to myself."

They drove to Stanley Park where he parked over-looking the water and where they sat for a very long time, sometimes talking quietly, and sometimes just taking comfort in the warmth and nearness of one another.

🖋

Christmas Day was a far different one than any of them had ever experienced. In spite of their best efforts, sadness hung in the air, mingling with the good turkey and mince pie aromas coming from the kitchen. It was as though each of them had made the difficult decision to remain cheerful in spite of the grim circumstances. The gift opening, however, did provide some lighter moments.

Jocelyn gave Nora, Maggie and her mother each a bottle of expensive French perfume. Colleen had made up a box of her special Christmas pastries for them to eat on their trip back to Manitoba and Ron gave Maggie a miniature totem pole. "A souvenir from Beautiful British Columbia. In case you forget us."

"As if I could ever forget B.C.," Maggie said, eyes brimming. "I'm kinda fed up with your province right now. No offence intended."

"None taken," Ron said, putting his arm around

her. "We understand. A perfectly natural reaction. But, hey, look! Here's another present for you."

And when Maggie tried on the lovely hand-knit sweater that was Colleen's gift, she was overwhelmed and said, through her tears, "Don't suppose I ever looked so fancy or smelled so good!"

Then Ron turned to Nora and handed her a tiny box containing an emerald ring. "So you won't forget me." Their eyes locked for a moment. "A pinkie ring. Until I can put one on your proper ring finger—left hand."

"This is...?"

Jocelyn fairly shouted, "An engagement ring, Aunt Nora!"

Nora scarcely knew what to say. "I feel like such a klutz. I didn't do any Christmas shopping at all. Nothing. I simply forgot, I guess."

But nobody minded—hadn't expected her to. But Maggie hadn't forgotten about Christmas—had, apparently, been working at her gifts off and on for weeks. She bestowed her beautifully finished afghan on Colleen. "I figured it would go with your rug," she said, modestly, forgetting entirely that it was really Ron's rug, his house.

For Ron she had a birdhouse. "Got it at that big seed and plant place. Figured you might could use some birds around to keep you company. Once we've left, that is."

To Jocelyn, she gave an electronic note pad. "Got it at Radio Shack for Trevor, actually. A few weeks ago. He never got to use it. Thought you might like to have it."

Then Maggie shyly handed Ron another package. It contained a handsome silk tie. "Man at the store said it was the latest thing. Figured if you ever get really gussied up. Like, for a wedding or something..." She looked at Nora and grinned. "I thought of it after I'd boughten the bird house."

Ron hugged her. "Exactly what I would have chosen. I'll keep it for exactly the right occasion."

After the rest of the gifts had been distributed and admired, Ron and Jocelyn took Maggie sightseeing. "She's never even seen the Capillano Bridge for God's sake," Jocelyn said. "Not to mention the Queen Elizabeth Gardens and all kinds of other stuff. We'll be back by five for dinner."

Colleen and Nora worked in the kitchen. Nora was glad to be alone with her friend for she felt emotionally spent and knew Colleen would understand her mood and occasional tears. Not that the others wouldn't. It was just that she needed time to steel herself for their final dinner together.

Colleen, hesitantly brought up the subject as the two were laying out silver on the white linen tablecloth. "So. Am I going to get a new sister-in-law, or what?"

Nora, caught off guard, felt her face redden. "Probably. As soon as I'm free. As soon as I get my life in some kind of order." She paused and then made the decision to continue. "Ron wanted me to.... I mean, we could have, you know... slept together last night."

"I was surprised that you didn't."

Nora laughed shortly. "Me, too. I wanted to. Or, at least, part of me wanted to. The other part of me isn't ready yet. I think he understands."

"You have lots of baggage to sort out, I know."

"Yes. And I don't want to rush into another marriage until I'm sure."

"May I say, I hope it won't be that long. For myself—and selfishly—I need a sister and Jocelyn could sure use an aunt like you. This, of course, all aside from what Ron needs. And what you need, too, if I may be so bold as to suggest."

"Be as bold as you like. I can handle it!" And both women laughed.

⚘

Nora could swear she caught the scent of West Coast salt sea air and pine when the three sightseers returned and opened the door. Everyone seemed in a more festive mood. Maggie enjoyed the outing, but remarked, "That was fun. Real educational. But I have to tell you, I won't mind not seeing another mountain for a while. I have a hankering for some wide open fields and that. Where I can clap my eyes on the horizon and it stays put."

"But you'll come back?" Jocelyn asked.

"Sure. If you want me to. I'll come back. Not for Easter, though. Maybe Nora will come for Easter, but I'll have seedlings to plant and look after by then. Somebody's gotta take hold of things back home and I doubt if Inga's gonna want to. Then there'll be the harvesting. She doesn't know one end of a tractor from the other. And Inga's not a very good cook, either. Couldn't fry shit for a hobo. She'd rather look after dogs. I might be free by Thanksgiving, though, if you'd like to put me up then."

When she could stop laughing, Colleen assured her, "We'd be absolutely delighted to put you up any time."

Then Maggie looked at Nora. "You figuring to plant a garden this year?"

Without a moment's hesitation and without giving it a thought, Nora replied with a firm, "No."

"Because you won't be in Manitoba to harvest it?"

"Probably not."

Then the five sat holding hands around the table while Ron asked the blessing, gave thanks for friendship and love and prayed for safe journeys for all of them.